PUMPKIN PIES &
POTIONS

A MELTING POT CAFÉ PARANORMAL COZY MYSTERY #1

POLLY HOLMES

Western Australia

Copyright

From the Author

Hi! Welcome to the mysteriously wonderful new world of Saltwater Cove. My imagination went wild creating this new series, and if you love anything paranormal and witchy, then you'll love the Melting Pot Cozy Mystery Series.

Pumpkin Pies & Potions is the first book in this collection, and with many more to follow, make sure you sign up for my newsletter to get notifications of when the next book is due for release.

You can sign up for my newsletter here:

https://www.pollyholmesmysteries.com/

That's enough from me for now. Turn the page and dive into the magical world of Saltwater Cove.

Polly

xxxooo

Also by Polly Holmes

The Cupcake Capers

Cupcakes and Cyanide

Cupcakes and Curses

Cupcakes and Corpses

Murder and Mistletoe

Dead Velvet Cupcakes

Publishers Stocking

Polly Holmes Books

Amazon

Gumnut Press

Novella Distribution

CHAPTER ONE

"Oh, my goodness, breakfast smells divine," I said, bounding down the stairs two at a time toward the lip-smacking scent streaming from the kitchen. Rubbing my grumbling stomach, I peeked over Aunt Edie's shoulder at the green gooey concoction boiling on the stove. I've been living with my aunt for the past eleven years since my parents died, and not once have I questioned her cooking abilities. Until now. I folded my arms and leant against the kitchen bench. "I know it smells amazing but are you sure it's edible because it sure as heck doesn't look like it."

Aunt Edie frowned and her eyebrows pulled together. Her classic pondering expression. She snapped her fingers and looked straight at me with her golden honey-brown eyes glowing like she'd just solved the world's climate crisis.

"Popcorn. I forgot the popcorn. Evelyn, honey be a dear and grab me the popcorn from the second shelf in the pantry. The caramel packet, not the plain."

Caramel popcorn for breakfast? That's a new one.

I shrugged. "Sure." Walking into Aunt Edie's pantry was like walking into the potions classroom at Hogwarts. Every witch's dream pantry. Normal food on the left-hand side and on the right, every potion ingredient a witch could possibly need, clearly labelled in its allocated spot. Aunt Edie would always say: a place for everything and everything in its place.

"I can't believe Halloween is only three days away," I called, swiping the caramel popcorn bag off the shelf. Heading back out, the hunger monster growing in my stomach grumbled, clearly protesting the fact I still hadn't satisfied its demand for food.

Aunt Edie's cheeks glowed at the mention of the annual holiday. "I know. It's my most favourite day of the year, aside from Christmas, that is."

"Of course." I handed her the bag of popcorn and made a beeline for the coffee machine. My blood begged to be infused with caffeine. Within minutes, I held a steaming cup of heaven in my hands. As I sipped, the hot liquid danced down my throat in euphoric bliss.

"I love how Saltwater Cove goes all out for Halloween. Best place to live if you ask me."

She paused stirring and glanced my way.

"I'm so glad you're back this year. *The Melting Pot* hasn't been the same without you. *I* haven't been the same without you."

The pang of sadness in her voice gripped my heart tight.

The Melting Pot is Aunt Edie's witch themed café. Her pride and joy. We'd spend hours cooking up new delicious recipes to sell to her customers. Her cooking is to die for, I guess that's where I get my passion from. My dream was always to stay in Saltwater Cove and run the business together, but she insisted I travel and experience the world. Done and dusted.

I glanced around the kitchen, my gaze landing on the empty cat bed in the corner. "Where is my mischievous familiar this morning? Doesn't she usually keep you company when you're cooking?"

Miss Saffron had been my saving grace after my parents died. She'd found me when my soul had been ripped out, when I had nothing more to live for. Thanks to her friendship, I rekindled my will to live, and love.

It isn't uncommon for a witch to have a familiar. It's kind of the norm in the witch world, but

7

none as special as Miss Saffron. My diva familiar, of the spoilt kind. Her exotic appearance with high cheekbones and shimmering black silver-tipped coat still dazzles me. They say the Chausie breed is a distant cousin of the miniature cougar. She certainly has some fight nestled in her bones. But Miss Saffron's best features are her glamourous eyes. More oval than almond-shaped with a golden glow to rival a morning sunrise.

"Oh, I'm sure she's around somewhere. She's probably found some unexplored territory to investigate. I'm sure she'll turn up when it's time to eat or you get into mischief."

Although not completely wrong, I ignored the mischief comment. "Speaking of eating, what is that?" I asked, leaning in closer, my mouth drooling at the sweet caramel aroma. A cheeky grin spread across Aunt Edie's face.

Oh no, do I want to know?

"Well, Halloween's not for everyone and some of the kids were complaining last year certain townspeople were grumpy when they went trick or treating so it got me thinking. I thought I'd spice things up a bit this year with a happy spell."

My eyebrows went up. "A happy spell?"

She nodded and scooped a little spoonful into a pumpkin shaped candy mould. "When I'm done, we'll have cheerful candy to hand out for all the grouchy Halloween spoilers out there. Within ten seconds of popping one of these little darlings in their mouth, their frown will turn upside down and they'll be spreading the happy vibes to all. I'm going to make sure this year is as wonderful as it can be."

"Aunt Edie, you can't." My stomach dropped and I gripped the edge of the kitchen bench with one hand. The disastrous implications of her words sent shivers running down my spine. "You know it's against the law to use magic to change the essence of a person. You could be sanctioned or worse, have your powers stripped."

"Relax, sweetie," she said, pausing, her smile serene and calm. "This falls under the Halloween Amendment of 1632."

"What are you talking about...The Halloween Amendment of 1632? I've never heard of it."

A subtle puff of air escaped her lips. "Halloween wasn't exactly your favourite holiday growing up, especially after your parents died, and then you missed the last two or so travelling."

"But I was back by last Christmas."

She smiled. "Yes indeed. And it was the best Christmas ever. But Halloween was always a reminder you were different."

"Yeah, a witch."

"Yes."

She placed her hand on mine. A sigh left my lips at the warmth of her reassuring touch.

"A day when young girls dressed up as witches. Where their fantasy was your daily reality."

Aunt Edie's words were like a slap in the face with a wet dishcloth. "Was I really that self-absorbed? I'm so sorry to have dumped it all on you. I guess I was pretty hard to live with at times."

"Hard? Never," she said, her jaw gaping in mock horror. "Challenging, now that's a definite possibility."

She burst into laughter and my heart overflowed with warmth as the sweet sound filled the room.

I threw my arms around her and squeezed. "I love you, Aunt Edie."

"I love you too, sweetheart."

I pulled back and drilled my eyes into hers, wanting answers. "Now, what is this Halloween Amendment of 1632?"

Her eyes sparkled like gemstones and she resumed filling candy moulds with green slimy goo. "The amendment is only active for five days leading up to Halloween and finishes at the stroke of midnight October thirty-first. It allows any graduate or fully qualified witch to enhance the holiday using magic as long as it is temporary, no harm or foul comes to the object of the spell or intentionally alters the future."

"Are you serious? That means me. I'm a graduate witch," I said. My inner child was doing jumping jacks.

Aunt Edie tutted. "True. A graduate witch who is still learning the ropes and until you receive your full qualification at twenty-five, even then, you must always strive to be the best witch you can be. We can't afford another mishap like graduation."

If it wasn't for my three besties, Harriet, Jordi, Tyler and, Aunt Edie's guidance and training, I may never have made it to graduation. My mind skipped back to the disastrous end to the graduation party. It wasn't exactly my fault the party ended in rack and ruin. Who knew having a shapeshifter for a best friend could cause so much havoc?

I caught the upturned lip of Aunt Edie and chuckled. "Oh, come on, even you thought it was funny when Jordi shifted into a raven and chased that cow, Prudence McAvoy around the ballroom. She's had it in for Jordi ever since I moved to Saltwater Cove. I guess she pushed one too many times, I mean, no-one taunts Jordi and gets away with it." I giggled, the blood-red face of Prudence covered in banoffee pie was the best graduation present, ever.

"Besides, my involvement came down to wrong place, wrong time. Prudence eventually owned up, it was all on her. But I get the message. Be a good witch."

"That's my girl." Aunt Edie huffed, dropping the spoon back in the empty pan. She wiped her sweaty brow with the back of her hand and smeared the remains of the gooey green substance on her hands down her apron. "There all done. Time to let them set."

"How do you know the spell works? I mean, will they work on everyone?" I asked.

Aunt Edie crossed her arms and pinched her lips together, her cheeks glowing a cute rosy pink. "Of course, they'll work on everyone, even those beings of the paranormal kind. Since when *hasn't* one of my spells worked, young lady?"

True. You don't earn the title of master witch by doing terrible spells that fail.

She rubbed her chin and continued. "But I wouldn't say no to testing them before Halloween rolls around."

"Have you got a guinea pig in mind?" I paused at her sly grin. "All I can say is, it better not be me."

Daily life was made a whole lot easier since The Melting Pot joined Aunt Edie's house. Walking next door to work suited me just fine. Kind of like an extension of her kitchen. She loved to share her passion for cooking delicious food with the rest of the world. A passion we both shared.

I twisted my wavy blue-streaked chestnut hair into a messy bun on top of my head and shoved it under my witch's hat. Glancing at my reflection, I saw it screamed modern classy-chic witch in an understated way. My dainty black satin skirt fell just above my knees showing off my trendy black and orange horizontal strip stockings. A slick black short sleeve button-up blouse fit perfectly covered in an orange vest, the words The Melting Pot embroidered above the right breast pocket in white. To add the finishing touch, I slipped my size seven feet into a pair of black lace up Doc Martin ankle boots and tied the black and silver glitter laces in elegant bows. I surveyed my reflection one last time in the mirror and grinned. I mean, who else gets to dress up every day as a witch to go to work. "Me, that's who."

An electric buzz filled my blood as I pushed open the door and stepped into The Melting Pot, closing it swiftly behind me. A clever tactic on Aunt Edie's part to design her café like a witch's cave. Everywhere I looked shouted witch heaven. Cauldrons of various sizes and candelabras standing high on their perches framed the seating area.

Pumpkins scattered among the witches' brooms and replica spell books. Potions and brews strategically placed high on display shelves gave off the perfect image of a witch's cave. Best not tell anyone they're real. Aunt Edie insisted on an element of authenticity. Every child's Halloween dream all year round. I squeezed my hands together in front of my heart. "Gosh, I love my job."

A purr echoed from the floor to my right and glancing down, I saw my four-legged feline slinking elegantly in a figure eight between my legs. "You love it here too, don't you, Miss Saffron?" She stretched and catapulted up onto the counter, her agility and poise qualities to admire. Her big yellow eyes stared at me and she purred. "I swear you know exactly what I'm saying."

Aunt Edie's merry voice trailed into the main serving area from the kitchen. "I've got a wooden spoon here dripping with the last of my famous chocolate-strawberry sauce. Unless someone comes to claim it in the next ten seconds, I'll have to wash it down the sink."

"Shotgun," I whispered in Miss Saffron's direction then took off dodging tables and chairs in record time to make it to the kitchen. "Don't you dare. You know it's my favourite."

Miss Saffron sat tall on the counter, her beady eyes keeping a firm gaze on the chocolate covered spoon in my hand. My insides salivated as I licked it clean. "Oh my God. A-MA-ZING." The best part of my childhood was beating mum to the spoon and bowl when Aunt Edie was cooking up a storm. My gut clenched. I missed my mum and dad so much some days the hurt was unbearable.

The cowbell above the main entry door jingled and I jumped, startled by the unexpected intrusion. I glanced at the antique wall clock. Eight fifteen. We weren't even open yet.

"Anybody here?" Barked a familiar grouchy pompous voice.

Great. Why does today have to start with a visit from the Queen of Complaints?

"Evelyn Grayson. Stop scowling right this instant," said Aunt Edie. "You look like you're sucking a lemon. It may be fifteen minutes before we open, but you know my policy, every customer deserves a warm witch welcome."

My chest hollowed out as Aunt Edie's words curbed my inner snob. "Of course, you're right. I'm sorry," I said, dropping the spoon in the sink and wiping the chocolate sauce from my face.

"But…" Aunt Edie paused and handed me a plate. The cheeky twinkle in her eyes confused me. "It wouldn't hurt Saltwater Cove's town grouch to be happy once in a while."

I looked down at the plate and a gasped in jubilation.

Green happy candy.

"Why Aunt Edie, you are positively sinful. I love it. But I'm not even sure a happy spell will work on Camille."

"Worth a try. After all what better guinea pig could we ask for?"

I nodded and grabbed the plate. Plastering on a smile I headed out ready to see if one happy candy can soften the most bad-tempered creature I've ever had the pleasure of meeting.

"It's about time. What does a woman have to do to get service around here?" Camille Stenson snapped. "What sort of business are you running, making customers wait so long?"

I bit my tongue and held back the cynical comment chomping at the bit to get out. "I'm terribly sorry to have kept you waiting, Miss Stenson. What can I do for you?"

Her jaw dropped and a fiery shade of red washed over her pale complexion. I pursed my lips tight together to stop the laugh growing in my belly from escaping.

"It's Wednesday or have you forgotten?" She asked, her eyebrows raised, showing the stark whites of her eyes.

A shudder bolted through my body.

Scary. Yes, I know, Mr Bain's dinner, of course.

Why he can't come in and get it himself is beyond me. She's supposed to be the loan's officer at the bank, not his wife. The sarcastic tone fuelled my inner desire to squash her like a petulant fly.

Perfect guinea pig.

I eased the plate of yummy caramel scented candy in front of Camille's nose. "My sincere apologies. Please accept one of Aunt Edie's treats as a peace offering. She made them especially for the Halloween season."

"Pfft, Halloween is a waste of time if you ask me." Camille leaned in to examine the plate and frowned. Her brows crinkled together in an unattractive monobrow. "Mmm, you're not trying to poison me, are you?"

Poison? No. Cheer you up so you can stop making everyone else miserable? Yes.

"How could you say such a thing?" I said, feigning hurt. "You know Aunt Edie's food is the best for miles around. That's why people keep coming back."

17

"Fine." She rolled her hazel eyes to the roof, huffed, and popped a candy in her mouth.

I stood frozen, waiting, my pulse pulverising my temples as if I was standing on the edge of a cliff ready to jump. One...two...three...four. Camille stared at me, her hazel eyes clouding over. Five...six...seven. Nothing, absolutely nothing. Eight...nine. My eye caught Aunt Edie peeking in from the kitchen and she shrugged. I guess it doesn't work on people whose core being is made up of such deep-set crankiness. Ten.

"Evelyn, my dear precious Evelyn." Camille's tone shot three octaves higher. A smile flashed across her face as electric as a neon sign in the dead of night. "You look positively radiant as always. I never seem to tell you enough how beautiful you are. Just like your mother. God rest her soul."

My mother? How did she know my mother?

I swear I'd been transported into an alternate universe. "Um, thank you. That is kind of you to say. But how..."

"Pfft, nonsense," she interrupted with a sashaying movement of her hand. "It so great to have you back in Saltwater Cove. I bet your aunt is pleased you're home?"

Did she mention my mother? Maybe I imagined it. I made a mental note to follow up

Camille's comment about my mother with Aunt Edie.

"I…." Stunned by Camille's reaction to the spell, my words caught in the back of my throat.

"That I am," Aunt Edie said, threading an arm around my waist. With her head turned from Camille's view, she gave me a cheeky wink.

She handed a paper bag to Camille and smiled. "Here you go, Mr Bain's dinner. His usual, just how he likes it."

"Perfect. He doesn't know how good he has it eating your wonderful meals four nights a week. He's off to some big Banking Symposium at Dawnbury Heights this afternoon but insisted I still pick up his dinner so he can take it with him. He can't stand hotel food, mind you, who can? Makes him all bloated." Camille said, placing the food inside a bigger tapestry carpet bag.

It kind of reminded me of Mary Poppins' bottomless bag. She turned toward the exit and waved.

"Ta-ta now. You ladies have a wonderful day, and may it be filled with all the magical wonders of the world."

The cow bell rattled as she left. My jaw dropped, and I stared at the closed door in silence. I looked at Aunt Edie and within seconds we were both into hysterical fits of laughter.

"Well I'd say…that spell…is a winner, wouldn't you?" I said, barely able to speak between giggles.

She nodded and cleared her throat wiping a tear from her eye. "I hope she stays that way for the next hour and a half. But who knows, it all depends on the individual person."

I laughed so much a stitch stabbed my side. "Aw," I said, pressing against the pain. "Okay, I give up, why do we want it to last an hour and a half?"

"Because Vivienne has an appointment with Camille in about thirty minutes regarding her loan application. If all goes well, she'll be able to expand her business just like she's always planned."

Vivienne Delany and Aunt Edie have been best friends since primary school. Aunt Edie ran The Melting Pot and Vivienne was the proud owner of *Perfect Pumpkin Home-Made Treats* where she made every kind of dish out of pumpkins one could dare to conjure up. And even though they both ran food business; they'd die before letting harm come to the other. That's what best friends do for each other.

"Let hope your spell does the trick." The cow bell jiggled over the door, signalling the beginning of the morning rush. "I guess we'll have to wait and see."

CHAPTER TWO

The day passed in a blur and by closing time my muscles screamed for a long hot steamy shower. Tonight is Harriet's birthday surprise get-together at our regular hangout, *The Four Brothers Bar and Grill* and if you knew Harriet, you'd know how hard it was keeping anything from her. She may not be a witch like me or a shapeshifter like Jordi, but she had a knack for uncovering a secret before the rest of the world even knew it existed.

I showered and dressed in record time checking each meticulous detail of my outfit. Faded denim three-quarter jeans and an off the shoulder knitted black top accentuated with a shimmering rainbow fluorite drop pendant. Perfect.

I tucked Harriet's present into the side pocket of my bag, bid farewell to Aunt Edie and headed to The Four Brothers, the popular bar and eatery down on the Esplanade complete with stunning views of the harbour. It was a hive of activity for a Wednesday evening which wasn't unexpected considering Halloween was only three days away.

The magnificent Halloween decorated interior was something else. Aunt Edie was right, Saltwater Cove embraced the annual holiday whole-heartedly. The image only superseded by the tantalising aromas wafting from the kitchen.

Halloween was alive and kicking in Saltwater Cove.

I sat impatiently with my gaze glued to the entrance, every nerve ending twitched waiting for Harriett to arrive. I held tight to the pink and silver wrapped jewellery box. There was no way she could know Jordi and I had a surprise cake out back.

"Can I get you something from the bar, Evelyn?"

The soft voice of Nerissa nabbed my attention. The petite woman flicked a mass of lengthy brunette ringlets over her shoulder with her inch-long, blingy acrylic nails, then opened her order pad.

"You look in desperate need of a refreshment," she said. Her cheeky grin matched the mischievous twinkle in her eye.

"You know me so well," I said, bursting into laughter. "Thanks, but Jordi has already taken care of it. She should be back from the bar any minute now."

Nerissa smiled. "No problem." She paused and bit her bottom lip. Her expression clearly had unfinished business written all over it.

"Was there something else?" I asked, unsure if I wanted to know the answer.

"Well," she said, sliding into the bench seat opposite. "Have you seen the new busker? You know, the one who's taken up residence on the pavement opposite The Melting Pot outside the grocery store."

"Seen?" I pried, then nodded.

Sort of. I've heard his sweet tunes lulling me in like a modern-day Pied Piper.

I shrugged a shoulder, the memory of his voice ignited sparks inside my belly. "I've only seen him through The Melting Pot window, so I didn't get a good look. I believe he's quite good though. A great singing voice, apparently."

"Oh my God, that's not all he's got going for him. He's totally *to-die-for*. Finally, some new male blood in Saltwater Cove."

"Are you sure you're fully over Nicolas?" I asked. Her eyes widened and she glared a thousand daggers at me. "I mean, I'm just concerned about you. I know you and he were a solid couple up until about a month ago—"

24

"When he dumped me and started dating Prudence McAvoy," she said, finishing my sentence. She shrugged. "I'm not gonna lie, Nicolas broke my heart, but that ship's sailed. I'm a free woman now. Besides they're off travelling the world together with Prudence's bestie, Tiffany and I'm here."

"And the new busker is here." I grinned.

"I hope he's single."

The twinkle in her eye had manifested to pure lust and I squeezed my lips tightly shut to prevent an inappropriate comment from escaping. Too late.

"Really? I suppose if you like the tall, lanky type." I blurted. *Please hurry up Jordi and get your backside back here and save me from any further conversation about Saltwater Cove's newest chick magnet.*

"Holy crap," Nerissa said, bolting upright in her seat, her eyes staring straight past my head.

My hand flew to my chest pressing against the knot forming. Heat shot up from the base of my neck and rode up to the top of my head like a tidal wave.

No, no, no. Please don't be standing right behind me.

"What's wrong? I asked. The need to know outweighed the potential for embarrassment.

"It's Mercer, and he doesn't look happy I'm sitting down socialising on the job." Nerissa stood, straightened her ruffled skirt and re-clipped her hair. Before leaving, she winked and smiled. "It's all good though. I've helped him out on more than once occasion so I can't see him firing me."

With that, she flounced away leaving me to squirm in my own humiliation.

Note to self. Do not talk about hot sexy newcomers…scratch that…do not talk about anyone without checking if they are standing behind me first.

"Here we go." Jordi placed a jug and three glasses on the table and she huffed, plonking herself down in Nerissa's vacated spot.

"What was that for?" I asked. I poured while glancing at the entrance every now and then. "And how come it took so long?"

Jordi gulped down a few mouthfuls. Her dead-straight raven locks slicked back into an elegant high ponytail glowed like satin, and her exquisite beauty was only superseded by her siren-like voice. "You know how Prudence was in line to be the manager of The Four Brothers Bed and Breakfast?"

I nodded and sipped. My interest piqued.

"I just heard from Mercer himself that he's bringing in a professional manager." The twist of her lip into a smirk spoke volumes.

"Don't look so happy about it. Prudence is going to be shattered. She'd graduated top of the class in her hospitality degree and had the hotel work experience under her belt. At least I thought so. She had her heart set on that job."

"Pfft," Jordi said.

She dismissed my comment with a simple swish of her hand.

"We all know Prudence gets what Prudence wants. The string of zeros in her trust fund help make sure of that. This time there's someone better for the job and I for one, am glad."

"Glad about what?" Harriet asked.

"Harriet," I said, startled by her sudden appearance. "Oh my God, you're here."

She frowned and her emerald eyes glanced from me to Jordi and back again.

"Of course, I'm here. You invited me for drinks, remember?"

"Yes, I know." I jumped up and threw my arms around my best friend. My heart overflowed with love. "Happy birthday."

"Thank you."

She smiled against my cheek and held on a moment longer.

Jordi crossed her arms and stuck her bottom lip out. It was the cutest picture of jealousy I'd ever seen. "Hey, no fair. My turn to hug the birthday girl."

Harriet giggled and finally let her arms slip. "The night's young and I have plenty of cuddles to go around."

Laughter and fits of giggles erupted around the table. Harriett was right, the night was young, and I had plans for an exceptional evening of drunken antics and celebrating with my best friends.

All, but one. Tyler Broderick.

The image of Tyler standing in the airport departure lounge would forever be branded in my mind. Travelling was in his blood. Through high school he always talked about seeing the world and he did, we both did, but when he returned, he was unsettled as though he was itching to leave again. It's been a year since he left Saltwater Cove the second time for greener pastures. A year since the fabulous four had been torn apart. Again. A year since my soul had been shattered.

"So, where's my rainbow cake?" Harriett asked. Sitting, she wound the strap around her miniature purse several times and placed it in the centre of the table.

Jordi glared at me. Her eyes thinned and her lips pursed tight together in a thin line.

"Hey, don't look at me like that," I said, holding my hands up in defence. "I didn't tell her."

"Well, I sure as hell didn't," Jordi snapped.

"Neither of you told me. You should know by now you can't keep a secret from me." Harriett giggled, play punching my shoulder. "But I promise I'll act surprised when it comes out."

Jordi frowned. "You better."

Soulful tunes emanated from the stage in the corner. A wash of serene calmness worked over my insides as the lyrical voice of Jazzamay sailed across the bar. As if hypnotised by her vocals, my gaze locked on to Talen, Jazzamay's brother, as his fingers moved like lightening, darting across the neck of his twelve-string acoustic guitar. A familiar shiver tip-toed up my spine.

"I just adore the sound of Jazzamay's voice, don't you?" Jordi asked with a contented sigh.

Harriet rolled her eyes and cleared her throat, obviously wanting the focus back on her. "Yes, we all know they are an amazing duo, but forget the music for one second, who wants some goss?"

My back straightened and my ears pricked. Jordi's head spun; her eyes glowing.

Goss? Hell yes.

"That's a silly question, Harriet." Jordi huffed, baiting her. "Come on, don't leave us in suspense."

The mischievous twinkle in Harriet's eye said it all. She shuffled in her seat and cleared her throat once more. "Okay, I was getting out of my car when I happened to hear Camille's voice half-way down the carpark. Truth be told, it was hard to miss, she was shouting, and it didn't exactly sound like a pleasant conversation."

"At whom?" I asked, my eagerness bubbling over.

Harriet shrugged and her emerald eyes widened, teasing me a little more. "I have no idea. I subtlety tried to look, but all I could see was the back of them."

"Man or woman?" Jordi asked, the tension in her voice mirroring my own.

"I couldn't tell. But they were tall and wore a long black hooded cloak, kind of all spooky and mysterious."

My stomach dropped and Jordi and I stared at each other. My blood ran cold. A spooky mysterious person in a black cloak can't be a good sign. Jordi's questioning eyes tightened my chest.

Harriet continued. "Anyway, Camille's threats were coming thick and fast and then they left leaving her standing there visibly shaking. The strangest thing happened though."

"What?" Jordi and I blurted. Jazzamay's vocals were doing zero to settle the knots brewing inside my gut.

"I'd paused and pretended to check my makeup in the rear-view mirror and whoever it was passed my car. As they did, the weirdest sensation came over me as if I'd been dropped into a raging volcano. My entire body was pinned against my seat. Unimaginable heat flooded me from head to toe and then I was falling, faster and faster and I couldn't stop myself. Images blurred around me and I tried to see through the haze, but it was useless. It was the scariest feeling ever. It took me a moment before my head stopped pounding and righted itself. It was only a few moments, but that has never happened to me before."

My jaw dropped and I tried to make sense of her words. It sounded like magic. *'My entire body was pinned against my seat. Unimaginable heat flooded me from head to toe.'* What on earth does it mean? *'Then I was falling, faster and faster and I couldn't stop myself.'* I bet Aunt Edie will know. I put it in on my to-do list to ask her first thing tomorrow.

A moment of unease fell over the table. Jordi piped up. "Then what happened?"

"She went to her car and I came in here."

The ribbon of Harriet's present tickled my thumb and my gaze dropped to the box in my lap. Relief soared through my veins. Now more than ever I knew my gift was just what Harriet needed. I held it out towards her and smiled. "Happy birthday, gorgeous."

Harriet's eyes watered and her hand flew to her gaping mouth, muffling a surprised gasp.

I smiled and placed it in front of her on the table. "It's nice to know you don't know *all* our secrets."

A smile spread across her face as she undid the pink bow, tearing the wrapping open like a child on Christmas morning.

She gasped. Her hand clutched her heart. "Oh my God, Evelyn, it's beautiful." Harriet held up the pink gemstone necklace encased in a dainty cage of gold, its stunning fuchsia pink stone shimmering under the lights. "This is the most gorgeous piece of jewellery I've ever seen."

Jordi eyed the stone. "I bet it's more than just a necklace."

"What do you mean?" Harriet asked, an inquisitive eyebrow raised at Jordi.

My heart filled with love for my best friend. "It's a Tourmaline stone. The October birthstone dating back to the fifteenth century. It also happens to be your favourite colour." Harriet nodded, smiling. "And as an added bonus, I put a protective spell on it so as long as you wear it, nothing can harm you, and judging by the story you just relayed, it's the perfect gift."

"Really?" she said, clipping the chain together at the back of her neck.

I nodded. "Yes, really. Promise me you'll wear it always."

"Promise."

She threw her arms around my neck almost knocking me off the chair winding me in the process.

"Whoa there." I grabbed the edge of the table preventing both of us from tumbling to the floor.

"Thank you so much. You guys are the best friends a girl could ever wish for." She righted herself linking hands with both of us.

Her gaze found mine and a knot formed in the back of my throat.

"I'm so lucky to have you as my best friend, Evelyn, a witch and you—" She switched her gaze to Jordi. "—my other best friend, a shapeshifter. I feel the safest human being in the whole wide world." Her smile fell.

"What's wrong?" I asked around the knot, a chill bled through my bones.

"I just wished *all* my best friends were here to celebrate my birthday. It's not the same without Tyler."

The mention of his name clawed at my heart once more. I missed him more than I cared to mention. He was in the remote parts of Nepal and has been for the past six or so months. Doing what, I have no idea. Maybe he finally decided to see what Mount Everest Base Camp looked like. I haven't spoken to him in forever.

Jordi skulled the remainder of her drink and poured another. "You won't have to wait too long, I hear he's coming home. Actually, he'll be back by Halloween."

What?

Heat rose from my neck and a burning flush warmed me from the inside out. The pounding in my ears dulled the celebrations around me. "No, that can't be right. He would have told me if he was coming back early," I muttered more to myself than the others.

After all, I'm his closest and dearest friend. At least that what he said just before he bordered the plane.

I clutched the glass in front of me, disguising just how much my hands were shaking on hearing Jordi's revelation.

"Okay, enough doom and gloom chat for this evening," Jordi said, snapping me back to the present. "Is this a birthday celebration or what?" She held up her glass. "To Harriet."

Tonight is Harriet's night. My stomach clenched, but I smiled at my best friends, suppressing my growing anger at Tyler's inconsideration. I'll get to the bottom of his early return one way or another. I gripped my glass and rose it high in the air. "To Harriet."

The high-pitch clink of our glasses was muted by the loud argument coming from the left- hand side of the bar. It wasn't as if it was a private conversation. It roared loud enough for everyone to hear. I opened my mouth to speak and Jordi and Harriet both gave me a look that clearly said: don't even think about it.

"I beg your pardon?" Camille snapped, slamming her half-drunken beer down on the counter, the frothy liquid sloshing over the rim. She shot off her stool and turned to face Vivienne.

"You have some nerve showing your face in public, Camille," Vivienne blurted. Her arms flew in all directions and her cheeks reddened as she continued her barrage of words targeting Camille. "You deliberately hung me out to dry today. You're determined to see me fail and I bet you think denying me my loan would be the end of my business. Well,

PUMPKIN PIES & POTIONS

I've got news for you. I'll get the money and I will make you eat your words, if it's the last thing I do."

My jaw just about hit the table. I had never seen such rage fuelling Vivienne before.

"Oh please, I don't have to help you fail," Camille said, thrusting her hands on her hips in a domineering Wonder Woman pose. "You're doing a great job of that all on your own."

"I can't believe Camille just said that. She has been on edge these past few weeks," Harriet whispered. "She can be tough, I should know. As her assistant at the bank I usually get the brunt of it, but I've never seen her be so obtrusively rude. Especially in public."

"I wonder if it has something to do with the mysterious cloaked man, she was with earlier," Jordi whispered loud enough for both of us to hear.

Maybe I should get Aunt Edie to work out how to make the happy spell last longer. It would definitely make Harriet's life much easier.

"Okay, that's enough you two," Mercer said, his gruff, demanding voice securing the attention of both women, and half the bar patrons. "If you don't calm down, I'm going to have to ask you both to leave. I will not have you destroy a busy evening with a bickering squabble."

Camille snatched her handbag off the bar. "No problem Mercer, I was just about to leave anyway. There's a rotten stench in here and I don't mean the pumpkin display." Camille spun on her heel and stomped toward to exit leaving a fuming Vivienne frozen to the spot.

"Great," Harriet said, slumping back in her chair. "Work is going to be a barrel of laughs tomorrow."

My guess is it won't take long before Aunt Edie will have the whole story from Vivienne. A little coaxing on my part should reveal all the nitty-gritty details, including the dirt on Camille.

"So," Jordi turned, her familiar smirk was a dead set give away she was about to discuss the male species. "Anyone check out the new busker? I hear he's easy on the eye."

You would hear that.

I pursed my lips and shook my head. "No, no, no. This is Harriet's night so there will be no more talk about men. The only words I want to hear are whose shout is it for the next round. Do I make myself clear?"

Jordi's back stiffened and she saluted, her voice three octaves lower. "Yes, Ma'am." Her sly gaze found Nerissa's and her arm shot high in the air.

"Ness, Alice in Wonderland shots all round and keep them coming."

Harriet clapped her hands together at her sternum. "Alice in Wonderland shots? My favourite."

"Well, you are the birthday girl."

Nausea welled in my gut at the memory of my last self-inflicted run in with Tequila. My memory vague of the events that followed, but it had something to do with caterpillars, a graveyard and skinny dipping. Not one of my proudest moments.

Do I really want to put myself through that again?

The glowing smile spread across Harriet's face was all the encouragement I needed. "Okay I'm in, but someone is going to have to pick up the pieces tomorrow."

"Don't be such a wuss," Jordi said, handing each of us a full shot glass from Nerissa's tray. "To Harriet."

"To Harriet," I said, knocking back the delectable drink in one gulp, the warm liquid igniting an inferno down my oesophagus.

Oh God, please don't let me do anything embarrassing tonight.

I rolled to the side of the bed and grabbed my throbbing head praying the blurry walls would stop floating six foot above the floor. A coppery furry taste hung in my mouth. An agonising moan seeped from my lips.

"Oh God, someone help me," I moaned, clutching my stomach to stifle the rising nausea tossing around deep in my gut.

When I get my hands on Jordi, she's a dead woman.

Squeezing my eyes shut, I sucked in a slow deep breath through my nose and slowly released it, my head whirling like a spinning top. I eased my legs over the side of the bed colliding with a solid object.

"Ouch."

I daren't look down to see for fear of hurling vomit all over the plush bedroom carpet.

"Aww."

Jordi's grouchy voice hit my ears. She rolled over, lifting herself up on one elbow.

"Watch where you shove those smelly feet of yours. I *was* asleep and Henry Cavill was about to throw me over his shoulder and run away with me to a deserted island where we were to live out our fantasies for the rest of eternity. That was until about two minutes ago when your hoofs shattered my love fest."

I bit my bottom lip. My head was about to explode, and it was all Jordi's fault. "Seriously? You're the reason I'm going to hurl any second. I'm surprised I even managed to get to sleep with the amount of alcohol I consumed last night."

Jordi giggled and I saw red. "You just need some coffee. I'm sure Aunt Edie will have some brewing downstairs. If not, I bet she has a great spell to cure a hangover." She rolled over in the pull-out bed and hiked the doona up to her chin snuggling back down to sleep.

Coffee...YES! Spell for a hangover...NO!

Wrapped up in my dressing gown, I moved slowly down the stairs one at a time as to not reignite the fading nausea in my belly. Aunt Edie insisted she was not given powers to help with self-inflicted party injuries. I can hear her taunting voice in my head.

If you consume the alcohol, you suffer the consequences.

The seductive scent of coffee hit my nostrils as I entered the kitchen and another wave of nausea flared up and I clung to the wall. My head spun like a merry-go-round in high speed, I sucked in a deep breath. "Woah. Easy stomach, keep it together."

"You look like you could use this," Aunt Edie said, holding out a cup of steaming frothy liquid.

I smiled and leant against the wall for support. "Thank you. Do I look as bad as I feel?"

"Worse," she said, raising an eyebrow. "But it's to be expected when you drink that much Tequila in one night."

She paused and frowned at me and I felt as small as Tinkerbell.

She sighed and shook her head. "I know I don't normally help out, but you do look worse for wear. Just this once I'm willing to relax my self-inflicted rule. Would you like a spell that will have you feeling better in a blink of an eye?"

"Thank you but no. All choices have consequences, and this is mine. Although, I'm not sure how much help I'll be at The Melting Pot today. That's if I can keep the nausea at bay long enough to get some food into me."

"No problem, we're all good. We have a new part-time employee," said Aunt Edie in a matter-of-fact tone. "It also frees me up to work on the menu for the Halloween dinner on Saturday night."

"What new employee?" I asked, jolting upright off the wall more sharply than my stomach would have liked. "I don't remember you mentioning a new employee. Who is it? Do I know them?" Aunt Edie fussed around with the dishwasher humming as she stacked one pan on top of the other on the bottom shelf.

What are you up to? I love you, but you can be sneaky when you want to be.

I looked over at the empty cat bed in the corner. "Where's Miss Saffron this morning?"

Aunt Edie shot up from the dishwasher, a chocolate covered plate held tight mid-air. Her honey-brown eyes twinkled as she glanced at Miss Saffron's bed. "Well, since I knew you'd obviously be under the weather when you woke, I have Miss Saffron next door keeping an eye on our new employee."

I opened my mouth to protest but the quirky voice of Tones and I singing Dance Monkey blared from my mobile on the kitchen bench. My hand flew to my thumping temple and I made a silent promise to myself.

No more Tequila in this lifetime…or the next.

"Hello," I said, easing into a chair at the kitchen table. Distraught female sobs pounded my eardrum and all else was instantly forgotten. My attention was now focussed on the obvious distress radiating from my best friend's voice.

"Eve…Eve…I didn't…It wasn't me…They think I did it."

"Harriet? Slow down. What happened? Are you all right?" My words coming out faster than my brain could process them.

"Oh God...it's awful, Evelyn and...and they think I did it, but I swear...I swear it wasn't me," Harriet said, through muffled sobbing gasps.

"Did what?" I asked.

"Kill Camille. They think she's been murdered."

CHAPTER THREE

"*Camille Stenson…murdered?*

The blood rushed from my body and it took a moment for Harriet's news to sink through the fogginess in my head. My gaze locked onto Aunt Edie's shocked expression and she mouthed, "What's going on?"

I covered the mouthpiece. "Camille Stenson is dead," I whispered around the lump in my throat. "They think she was murdered."

"How can Camille be dead?" I asked Harriett. Knots formed in my belly and it had nothing to do with Tequila. "We all saw her last night at the Four Brothers and she was perfectly fine."

Harriet sniffed. "That's what I told the police. But they're saying I'm a suspect because I found the body. What am I going to do?"

My chest tightened as a fresh bout of sobs echoed down the line. "Harriet, listen to me. Try to stay calm and I know that's going to be hard, but you must try. They need evidence before they can arrest you on murder and you and I both know you did not do this awful act so there won't *be* any evidence."

The sharp inflection in Harriet's tone sent shivers sprinting down my spine. "They said when they are finished here at the bank, they're going take me to the police station for questioning. Can they do that?"

"I'm afraid so, but the best thing you can do is be honest," I said, my body renewed with purpose. "I promise you will not face this alone. Jordi, Aunt Edie, and I will do all we can to help you. They can't convict you of a crime you didn't commit."

At least I hope they can't.

"Damn straight," Jordi said, taking up the seat next to me followed by a convincing nod and thumbs up from Aunt Edie. I hadn't even realised Jordi entered the kitchen.

"Jordi and I will head to the police station and wait for you, then you're coming back here. You can fill us in on everything. You're not alone in this."

A gruff male voice spoke loud enough it was clear as day on my end.

"I'm afraid that's long enough, Miss Oakley. Please end your phone call so we can continue with the investigation."

"I have to go now, Evelyn, but I'll see you soon?" she asked.

The desperate tone in Harriet's voice crushed my soul.

"You most certainly will. Be strong." The staccato click ending the phone call had the hairs on the back of my neck spiking.

"This is not good, not good at all," Aunt Edie said, stirring her tea aimlessly. "I had wondered why Camille hadn't arrived this morning to pick up Stanley's pre-made dinner. But never in a million eons had I imagined she'd been murdered."

"We don't know for sure if she has been murdered. It could've been an accident."

A stagnant silence fell over the table and an icy shiver shot through my body as if someone trampled across my newly dug grave.

"Aunt Edie?" Jordi said, slicing the growing tension. "Can I ask you something?"

"Of course, love," Aunt Edie said, her warm smile inched a fraction closer to thawing my insides.

Jordi continued. "Something strange happened to Harriet last night before she came into the bar and neither of us know what to make of it."

Of course, how could I forget?

"That's right," I said, a glimmer of hope threaded its way into my heart. "It was the weirdest thing. Before Harriet joined us, she spotted Camille outside in the carpark arguing with a person in a dark hooded cloak. She couldn't see who it was but when they walked past her car, she said it felt as though she'd been dropped into a raging volcano. Heat flooded her from head to toe, unimaginable paralysing heat. Whatever it was had her pinned against the car seat. She kept falling and wasn't sure she would stop, blurred images surrounded her. She tried to reach out to them but failed. I thought it was odd and she said it has never happened to her before. Do you have any idea what it means?"

A frown marred Aunt Edie's expression and she bit her bottom lip. "Yes. Yes, I'm afraid I do."

Oh no, please don't be bad news. Things are terrible enough for Harriet as it is.

"Harriet has always maintained she doesn't have any powers. But if what you're saying is true, I fear she is about to find out the exact opposite. In fact, she may have one of the most envied powers in Saltwater Cove."

Jordi and I stole a startled glance at each other. "But how can that be?" I asked.

"Oh love, magic can be unpredictable and can turn your world upside down in two shakes of a wand. How one comes into their powers is different for every witch, but what you are describing sounds awfully familiar. I suspect Harriet's bloodline contains witch blood, how far back I'm not sure." She turned and smiled at Jordi. "Do you ever remember not being able to shapeshift?"

Jordi's head tilted to the side and it was like watching the wheels inside her brain tick over one notch at a time. "No, I've always been able to shift just like my mum and dad and theirs before them," she said, shaking her head.

"Exactly. You grew up in a household of magic, so it was the norm, and you, my sweet."

Aunt Edie squeezed my hand, her warm touch inched up my arm.

"Even though you didn't find out you were a witch until after your parents' deaths and you came to live with me, I think deep down you always knew you had it inside you. Your mum and dad embraced normality. I watched you grow into a beautiful young lady and it became clear to me they wanted you to have a normal childhood. They wanted it to be your choice to use your powers and for that, they will always have my love and respect."

Heat soared through my chest burning its way up to my cheeks. I missed them so much the pain seared a hole clean through my heart. My gaze blurred as I fought back salty tears. "Please don't make me cry, Aunt Edie," I said, swiping the tea towel off the table and patting my wet cheeks dry. "This is about Harriet, not me."

Jordi shrugged and smiled. "Makes sense. Your powers surfaced as soon as you moved to Saltwater Cove and started hanging out with the rest of us weirdos."

Any more talk about my parents was going to turn me into a blubbering mess.

I cleared the frog in my throat and reverted the subject back to our present situation. "What about Harriet then? Her parents were human, weren't they?"

She nodded. "Yes, but that doesn't mean there isn't witch blood running through her veins from generations back."

"You said something about she may have the most envied power in Saltwater Cove. What exactly does that mean?"

"From what you're describing sounds like she's heading into *The Turn.*"

The Turn? Sounds like the name of a rock band or a horror movie.

Aunt Edie continued. "Up until now, Harriet has always believed she was human with friends who have magical powers. The intense heat you were describing indicated that she will come into her powers within the next twenty-four hours."

"And the cloaked man?" Jordi pried.

"Simply put, pure evil was present which explains the paralysing sensation she felt as they moved past her." She paused and her hands clenched together.

My voice came out hoarser than I expected. "What is it? What are you not telling us?"

"You know how it's hard to keep a secret from Harriet?"

Jordi and I nodded in unison. *Do I ever.*

"If I'm right, I believe she has the power to see the future, she just doesn't know it yet. Making her one powerful witch. But there's more."

"What?" I said, my breath hitching in the back of my throat. "You're joking, right?"

Of course, she's not joking. If anyone would know, it would be Aunt Edie.

"And she can see the future?" Jordi asked, shaking her head. "Just because intense heat ran through her body paralysing her?"

Aunt Edie nodded. "Yes, but not just because of the heat, but the endless falling with the images indicates she may be able to combine her visions with time travel."

"Whoa, whoa, whoa, hold up a second." I slapped my forehead. "I don't believe what I'm hearing. Harriet's a witch who can see the future and time travel?" I switched my gaze between the two of them. "I'm still asleep, aren't I? Or my hangover is way worse than I imagined. Now I'm hallucinating."

"Then, so am I," Jordi said under her breath. "The same hallucination."

"Oh girls, neither of you are hallucinating. As for the hangovers, I've no sympathy, that's your own fault. I've said it before, Tequila will get you every time." A familiar giggle filled the kitchen. "But you do have a lot to learn, hence why you are still graduate witches. My job is to guide you and it appears Harriet will also need my help. You both had family to help you understand you were different. Harriet's parents both live on the other side of the world. She's going to need our help to understand what's happening to her. On a positive note, she has been hanging around you two for quite some time and she's seen some weird happenings. Her own supernatural abilities shouldn't be too hard for her to believe."

Jordi shoved her hand out flat on the centre of the table and smiled. "Count me in. Harriet's like a sister I never had. I'm in this for the long haul. Who's with me?"

The conviction in her eyes and lightened tone eased the heaviness clamping my chest. I slapped my hand down on top of Jordi's. "I'm in, for as long as it takes to prove Harriet's innocence."

Aunt Edie joined in and placed both hands on top securing the bond between us. "Me too. I'll be there every step of the way. It's not going to be easy, but if we stick together there's nothing we can't face."

I stood from my chair, energised with a new focus. "Right, enough sitting around. I know I said we'd meet Harriet at the Police station, but I have an idea. Aunt Edie, did you say you still have Mr Bain's dinner?" She nodded. "Okay, Jordi and I will pop upstairs and get dressed, if you can get it, we'll use it as a reason to head over to the bank and see what we can suss out. And if they have already gone to the police station, we'll head straight there."

"Sounds like a plan," Aunt Edie said. "See you back here in ten minutes."

Ten minutes!

I turned and bolted up the stairs. "Shotgun the bathroom."

"Meet you downstairs, Jordi," I called over my shoulder shutting the bedroom door behind me. Looping stray tendrils of damp hair into a top knot, I scooped my jacket off the coat rack and hiked it downstairs.

The nausea that consumed my stomach was now replaced with a multitude of festering knots. Who knew Harriet was a witch? I certainly didn't pick it.

"Okay, Aunt Edie I'm ready. Have you got Mr Ba…" Turning the corner to the kitchen, I froze, my words vanishing as if being zapped away by a vanishing spell.

Oh my God, it's you. Why are you standing in my kitchen looking sexy as hell?

I fought to keep my libido in check as my internal thermometer crept higher. Spellbound by his cobalt blue eyes, I opened my mouth to enquire why this gorgeous busker was standing in Aunt Edie's kitchen holding a brown paper bag. Nothing, silence streamed from my lips. Failure.

"I'm sorry. I didn't mean to startle you," he said, sliding backwards widening the space between us. "My name's Eli. You must be Evelyn."

I nodded. "Eli?" His name oozing from his lips weakened my knees. "What are you doing in my aunt's kitchen?"

He shoved his free hand into his pants pocket. "Um, I thought Edie told you?"

"Told me what?" I asked, folding my arms in a protective barrier across my chest. Damn, racing pulse of mine.

"I'm the new part-time employee at The Melting Pot," he said, his back straightened, and his head shot up straight. "I'm new in town and your aunt was kind enough to give me some part-time work until I get on my feet."

"Oh." My stomach quivered and my mind raced to find words. "Well...um, welcome to Saltwater Cove, and The Melting Pot."

One night with my good pal Tequila and I'm replaced by the new guy in town. A sexy one at that. This is not over by a long shot, Aunt Edie.

He smiled and nodded. "Thanks. It sure looks like a nice quiet place to live."

Have I got news for you? I cocked one eyebrow at his initial description of Saltwater Cove. I'm not sure it can be described as quiet of late.

"It has its moments but on the whole it's a great place to live. I'm sure you'll love it."

"I know I will. It's already growing on me," he said, the enchanting glint in his eyes sent electric shivers through my extremities, tingling the tips of my fingers.

The awkward silence stretched between us as my gaze dropped to his sensual lips. I gasped and jumped clean off the floor as the door between the kitchen and The Melting Pot slammed shut with a resounding thud. "What the?"

"Oh, I'm sorry dear," Aunt Edie said smiling, her gaze shooting between the two of us. "Oh good, you've met Eli. We can always use an extra pair of hands, especially at this time of year."

"I'm more than happy to help," Eli said. He placed the brown paper bag on the counter and moved to grab the boxes from Edie's arms. "Between my busking and the work here, I should be able to find a reasonable place to rent."

"I guess that means you're planning on sticking around for a while?" I asked. The flippant tone in my voice was in total opposite to the raging butterflies dancing in my stomach. "I heard you singing the other day. You have a lovely voice."

His chest puffed out and a broad smile spread across his face. "Thanks. I never know how my voice will be accepted in a new town. I've been told I'm an acquired taste."

An acquired taste I'd like to get to know better.

Where the hell did that come from? My head jerked back and I cleared my throat. "I'm sure you'll do great here."

"Who'll do great here?" Jordi asked as she entered the kitchen fiddling with the collar of her black leather jacket. She stopped at the table and her hazel eyes widened. She tilted her gaze toward me. "What is the new busker doing standing in your kitchen? I thought you said you didn't know him."

"I don't." My hand clenched my jacket to my side.

"My fault I'm afraid, Jordi," Aunt Edie said as she scooted around the kitchen. "This is Eli, he'll be helping out at The Melting Point in between busking sessions so I hope you'll make him feel welcome."

"Of course, would I do anything else?" Jordi said, a cheeky laugh bubbled from her lips. "So glad you've joined our little town."

Eli's tone lightened. "Thank you. I look forward to getting to know everyone."

A familiar spark in Jordi's gaze had my eyes rolling. Look out Eli.

"Okay, enough with the introductions," Aunt Edie snapped. "I've updated Eli on the situation."

"The situation?" Heat surged up my arms tensing my entire body. "What situation is that exactly?" Surely, she wouldn't reveal to a total stranger we're witches.

As if sensing my alarm, Aunt Edie's expression softened. "The Harriet and Camille situation."

A wave of relief exploded from my chest. "Is that Mr Bain's dinner?" I asked, pointing to the brown paper bag on the kitchen bench.

"Sure is," he said, handing it over to me.

My hand skimmed his and he paused, his lips parting. "Thank you. I'll take it from here." The unusual reaction my body had to Eli baffled my mind. He was just another single guy passing through Saltwater Cove. At least I hoped he was.

Eli dipped his head toward my direction. "Nice meeting you, Evelyn...Jordi. I'll be heading back in now. Let me know if I can be any assistance."

Three pairs of eyes watched him as he sauntered back through the door to The Melting Pot. Jordi was the first to break the silence with her one-track mind.

"Oh, I'll definitely be needing assistance in the future. Count on it." Jordi's playful belly laugh lightened the mood.

"Come on you," I said, linking my arm through hers. "We have a best friend to save."

CHAPTER FOUR

I stood outside the Saltwater Cove Founders Bank, squinting through the murky glass bay window. One policeman snapped photos of every angle of Camille's office, while another bagged objects of all shapes and sizes into plastic evidence bags.

My gaze locked on Harriet quietly sobbing in the corner. It was clear by the distress in Harriet's glazed emerald eyes the nightmare was far from over. A stocky-built man leant against the edge of a desk with his back to me. His casual clothes and long trench coat clearly said detective. The man's commanding frame seemed familiar, but I just couldn't put my finger on it. Was he new in town? I locked on to the shimmering pink gemstone secured around Harriet's neck and my knees went all jelly-like and nearly buckled.

Thank God she's still wearing the amulet I gave her.

"What are you still doing out here?" Jordi asked, as she ended her phone call slotting it into her back pocket.

A heavy sigh blew out my mouth and my steamy breath fogged the glass. "I've been waiting for you to finish your phone call. I figured two would be better than one. Who was it anyway that it was so important it couldn't wait until after we rescued Harriet?"

"I'm sorry," Jordi said, biting her lower lip. "I didn't know you were going to wait for me. It was one of my suppliers having issues filling a fabric order. But I'm here now and I say we do whatever it takes to make sure Harriet is cleared of a crime we both know she didn't commit."

I nodded and my chest tightened. "Agreed. Let's do this."

Pushing through the stained-glass door I marched toward Harriet, Mr Bain's dinner tightly in my hands. Jordi matched my strides perfectly.

"Hold it right there, ladies," a loud burly voice called from Camille's office. "This is an active crime scene."

I stopped in the centre of the room and my pulse pounded my neck. "Crime scene? Oh my, really?" I said, feigning innocence. "We had no idea. We just came over to drop off Mr Bain's dinner.

Camille forgot to pick it up this morning. Isn't that right, Jordi?"

She nodded. "That's right," she said, blinking rapidly. "What crime has been committed?"

Before anyone could answer, the detective-looking man focused on Harriet, stood tall and turned. My breath caught in the back of my throat and Jordi's gasp confirmed my thoughts.

Detective Micah Huxton? The man who stole Aunt Edie's heart and then trampled it. What are you doing back in Saltwater Cove and why doesn't Aunt Edie know about it?

"Evelyn Grayson, nice to see you again," he said, as he tilted and nodded his head in acknowledgment of my presence. His stern gaze found Jordi's. "You too, Jordan Stone. I wish it was under better circumstances."

"Detective Huxton," I said, my voice sharp. "What brings you back to our little town?"

His eyebrow raised and with one word he sent chilling goose bumps scramming up my arms to the base of my neck. "Murder."

"Murder?" Jordi said, with an exaggerated gasp. "Who on earth has been murdered?"

His eyes squinted and his brow creased. "We all know it's hard to keep a secret in Saltwater Cove, but I'll play along. Camille Stenson's body was found by Harriet Oakley this morning under suspicious circumstances. Currently we're treating it as a homicide."

Harriet's strained voice rung out across the room. "I didn't do it, I swear. I found her that way when I came to work today. You have to believe me. I could never murder anyone."

My jaw locked as Harriet fell apart before my eyes. "Detective Huxton, surely you don't think my best friend had anything to do with this?"

He cleared his throat. "At this point we're ruling no-one out as a suspect. Now if you would kindly vacate the premises, I'd very much like to continue with the investigation."

"But…" I paused, sweat beading the palms of my hands. "The least you can do is let us have a quick word with Harriet. You can see she's extremely upset. Maybe a calming word from her best friends will make your investigation run smoother."

I knew my request had fallen on deaf ears. As far as I can remember Huxton had never been one to bend the rules.

His jaw loosened and he gave a half-hearted shrug. "I guess five minutes wouldn't hurt."

Woah, did I just hear correctly?

"I've already explained to Harriet everything we're doing here is routine and if she did, in fact kill Camille, I will find out, so she may as well come clean now to save us a lot of wasted time and if she didn't, I'll be the first one to apologise."

A hysterical gasp followed by a continuous stream of hiccupping sobs from Harriet ripped my heart out.

"Harriet did not commit this atrocity as sure as I'm standing here in front of you, but I understand you have protocols to follow." My body tensed and my lips thinned into a forced smile. "May we speak to her now?"

He stepped back and opened his arm paving a clear way for Jordi and I to walk.

Crouching down beside Harriet, Jordi at my side, I brushed tear-soaked wisp of hair from her damp cheek. Her head down and her shoulders hung low. "Harriet listen to me," I said, in a soft whisper. Her glazy emerald eyes darted from me to Jordi and back again. "I need you to stay strong. We all know this is one big misunderstanding and I'm sure it will be cleared up in no time."

"Do you really think so?" Harriet sobbed.

"Of course," Jordi said, holding a united front. "The evidence will prove you didn't do it and if the police can't find it, then Evelyn and I will, no matter what it takes."

I huffed. "Damn straight, girlfriend."

A tiny smile turned up the corner of Harriet's lips, and with a shaky influx of breath, she threw one arm around my neck and the other around Jordi and squeezed.

"Thank God, I have you two."

I held on to her tense body praying I could keep the promise I'd made. "Remember the amulet."

Harriet pulled back and her hand clutched the pink stone around her neck. "Yes."

I lowered my voice to keep prying police ears at bay. "Don't forget, as long as you wear it nothing can happen to you. The protective spell will see to it. Just promise me you'll never take it off."

"I promise," she said, squeezing the amulet to her chest.

The muffled scuffing of shoes along the wooden floorboards signalled an impending intrusion.

"Five minutes is up," Detective Huxton said, standing alongside another policeman. "Harriet, it's time to go. She'll be accompanying us to the station for further questioning."

Jordi stood and crossed her arms, her gaze drilling his. "And we'll be there to pick her up when she gets out."

Huxton nodded. My gut tightened and nausea turned my stomach as I watched my best friend escorted out the door toward the waiting police car like a common criminal.

"How is your aunt doing these days?" asked Huxton.

The nausea in my gut transformed into a hardened barrier. "Better than ever," I said over my shoulder. "If you don't mind, I'd like to head to the police station so I'm there for Harriet."

"Of course." He picked up his notebook from the desk and pocketed it in his coat. "Please say hello to Edith...I mean your aunt for me."

"Sure."

Jordi paced the foyer of the police station, "How long does it take? She's been in there for ages."

The foyer's homely décor was doing zilch to soothe my fuming insides. My phone conversation with Aunt Edie was on repeat in my mind. How could she be so calm hearing Micah Huxton is back in town. Leaving four years ago without so much as an explanation really did a number on her. Even I thought they were going to get married. There's only so much heartache one witch can endure. I wanted to murder him myself after he skipped out on her. A laugh bubbled in the back of my throat at the irony.

Maybe murder wasn't the right word especially since one has just been committed in our beautiful little town and my best friend is the number one suspect.

"I'll wait as long as it takes," I said, sliding into a chair easing the weight off my legs. With a sigh, I dropped my head back against the wall.

"Oh no, not again," Jordi said, her forehead creased like a crinkled chip packet.

I sat up. "What's wrong?"

Her eyes glued to her illuminated phone screen and then her pleading eyes sought mine. "I have to return this call real quick. I've cancelled it three times now. It looks like Harriet isn't getting out any time soon. I'll pop outside and deal with whatever crisis has developed, and I'll be back before you know it."

"It's cool." I smiled her way. "Go. I'll hold the fort down here until you return." Sucking in deep breaths, I watched Jordi exit through the glass doors, my thoughts interrupted by a familiar buzz vibrating my right buttock cheek.

"What the?" I shuffled uncomfortably in my chair as Tyler's text brought me crashing back to reality.

Hey, Evie girl. Surprise. Arriving back in Saltwater Cove this evening. Any chance of a pick up from the airport? We've lots to catch up on.'

"Lots to catch up on…That's the best you can do?" Jolting pain ran along my clamped jaw. He didn't have the decency to tell me himself he was coming home and now an impromptu request to pick him up from the airport. What's wrong with his parents picking him up? That's right, they are in Paris. My fingers moved double time over the keypad.

Hey stranger, we certainly do! Text me the details and I'll make sure I'm there.'

An incoming beep alluded to Tyler's response, but my attention was quickly diverted by a female voice that sounded a lot like Harriet, only harsher.

"I promise you I won't be going anywhere until this mess is sorted out." Harriet stood outside the open integration door, her arms folded across her chest, her cheeks flushed. "As I said you're wrong and when you find out I'm innocent, I'll be collecting on that apology you offered earlier."

I bolted off my seat, the sight of Harriet standing tall with her chest out tossing her bronzed hair over her shoulder took me more by surprise than I anticipated.

"Harriet? Are you all right?" I asked.

She threw me a momentary glare that gleamed new-found confidence.

"I certainly am. Good day, Detective Huxton," she said with a nod. A brash turn on her heel had her heading for the glass exit doors.

"Harriet, wait," I said, walking double time just to match her one stride. "What's going on? What happened to the blubbering mess of a woman who was sitting in the bank an hour ago?"

She stopped a metre from the exit and spun, the veins popping on the side of her head.

"That man is the most frustrating man on earth…no, the most frustrating man in the entire universe. Do you realise he was using every tactic in the book to get me to confess to a murder I didn't commit?"

My eyebrows shot up. "What?"

"You're right, I was a blubbering mess and then it hit me. What would Evelyn and Jordi do in a situation like this? They wouldn't fall apart, especially if they knew they were innocent. So, I didn't either. Oh, he tried, but once I decided he wasn't going to get to me and I started dishing out the questions, I think he realised he was fighting a losing battle."

I found my cheeks hurting from the enormous grin spread across my face. "I'm so proud of you."

Harriet's shoulders relaxed. "Thanks, but I'm not out of the woods yet. He said they think Camille was poisoned."

"Poisoned?" Jordi said. Her gasp alerting Harriet to her presence. "Sorry, I wasn't here when you came out. You said she was poisoned? How about you start from the beginning and tell me everything I missed."

Harriet shrugged. "I said they *think* she was poisoned. There isn't much more to tell. He kept asking questions and trying to force me to stumble over my words, but it didn't work because there was nothing I could say except the truth."

"And the truth is?" I asked, my heart racing.

"When I got to work, Camille's light was on in her office which was unusual as I'm usually in before her. Mr Bain, the manager is away for two days at the Banking Symposium, so he charged me with opening up this morning. I threw my bag in my desk drawer and went to check in and found her face down in one of Vivienne's pumpkin pies. I initially thought she had passed out, but then I took a few steps closer and what I saw sent my blood curdling. Even though her skin was cherry red like a bright red-brick house, she was frozen stiff with black gooey stuff around her lips. Her icy stare will haunt me for the rest of my life. After halting my gag reflex and almost throwing up my breakfast, I called the police and waited at my desk until they arrived and the rest you know."

I gripped my stomach, smothering the rolling waves of revulsion that surfaced thanks to Harriet's description of Camille's lifeless body. Jordi on the other hand, soaked up every ounce of drama.

Jordi frowned and rubbed the back of her neck. "I don't know, it sounds like they're hiding something to me."

"Well of course they're hiding something, they're the police," Harriet said, rolling her eyes. "It's part of their job description."

A giggle rumbled in the base of my belly. "Shhh, I wouldn't speak too loud, the walls have ears." Unable to hold it in, both Harriet and Jordi joined me, and laughter graced the foyer of the police station. "Okay, I think it's time to get out of here."

Jordi's focused gaze found mine and she nodded toward Harriet raising a questioning eyebrow. Harriet's reality came crashing through the brief moment of happiness.

Oh God, we still have to tell Harriet she's a witch. And if Aunt Edie is right, a powerful witch who will be the envy of all witches.

I bit my bottom lip. "Harriet, Aunt Edie and I were thinking and we would like you to stay with us for a few days. At least until this nightmare is sorted. I know you love living in your unit by yourself, but we feel you might need some company this week and if you do, one of us will be there for you."

"Thank you." A smile spread across her face and her eyes moistened. "You read my mind."

Jordi clapped her hands together. "Great, it's settled. You two head back to Evelyn's house and I'm going to do some discreet eavesdropping…incognito of course. I'll join you as soon as I have some information to share."

"I love how you have the power to shift into an animal," Harriet said, her bottom lip jutting out. "If only I could help in some way."

You can, you just don't know it yet.

"See you at your house," Jordi said, waving goodbye, a cheeky grin plastered on her face. As she exited the glass doors, an array of glittered sparkles rose from the ground up and shone bright like diamonds across an ocean. Jordi disappeared around the corner out of sight before either of us could see exactly what kind of animal she morphed into.

"Okay, let's go," I said linking my arm through Harriet's, my nerves raw and on edge picturing Harriet's shock reaction when Aunt Edie and I'll come clean about her powers.

I sat at the kitchen table with Miss Saffron lounging in my lap, her hind legs curled around my right thigh. The spread of her soft fur warmed my legs. A slow purr vibrated my skin. My fingers scratched her favourite spot behind her ear, the twitch in her whiskers a clear indication her pleasure buttons were being satisfied.

"You've been pretty quiet since you got home, love," Aunt Edie said, as she placed a mug of steaming chai latte in front of Harriet.

She shrugged, stirring the hot liquid. "It's been a pretty full on day and I guess reality is finally sinking in. If they don't find the evidence to clear my name, I could spend my next birthday, in fact, all my birthdays from now on behind bars."

"Oh, fiddle faddle," Aunt Edie said, with a flamboyant swish of her hand. "That is never going to happen, mark my words."

Harriet put on a half-hearted smile, but I could tell the confident woman I picked up from the police station was slowly slipping away before my eyes.

"Thanks for the vote of confidence." Harriet sipped from her mug, her shoulders slumped.

This is crazy. Harriet should know she's a witch. It's time to come clean. "Harriet you're one of my best friends and I think it's time you knew—"

She held her hand up shutting me down like a brick wall. "I know you're trying to help, but I just don't think I can deal with any more today. I'm exhausted. If you don't mind, I think I'll go and lay down for a while."

"Of course," Aunt Edie said, placing a reassuring hand on Harriet's shoulder. "I've made up the room next to Evelyn's. It's yours for as long as you need it. I may be Evelyn's blood aunt, but I look on both you and Jordi as my nieces and I love you just as much."

"Thanks Aunt Edie." Harriet's washed out pale complexion indicated her trying day. She glanced at the wall clock. "Can you wake me in time for lunch? If I'm staying, I'll need to pop home this afternoon and grab a change of clothes. I don't think I'll feel up to driving home. That reminds me, my car is still at the bank."

Aunt Edie tutted. "No problem, love. I'm sure Evelyn will take you home and either Jordi or I will pop down and drive your car home."

"Sure, I can take you home," I said, ignoring the warning niggle in the back of my neck. Miss Saffron's head shot up and we both watched Harriet drop her car keys on the table then trundle across the kitchen toward the staircase, her eyes unclear and in a daze, as if she was sleep walking.

I'm not sure how I am going to be in two places at once this afternoon, with Harriet, and *picking Tyler up from the airport.*

"Poor girl, she must be going through hell," Aunt Edie muttered, clearing the coffee cups away. "That is why we must wait to tell her she's a witch. You can see she was almost at her wits' end. Revealing our suspicions could push her over the edge. She'll be in a better frame of mind after she's had a rest. I say we move onto discussing Saturday in a little more detail."

I raised an eyebrow and Miss Saffron looked at me like I'd lost my mind. "Saturday?"

She huffed and shook her head making me feel like my brain was sixty years old instead of twenty-three. "Halloween, silly."

"I know another topic I'd rather discuss. One of the male species." I said, fidgeting with the pink

Gerbera flower decoration in the middle of the table. I waited for her to spin and take me to task for my off handed comment, but her focus stayed on the coffee cups in her hand.

Did she not hear me? There was no missing the rosy glow that crept up her neck to her cheeks. I blinked a few times as if I imagined it, her glowing complexion a clear indicator she knew exactly who I was talking about. And judging by the quickened pace of her movements, she did not want to talk about it.

"No problem." I stood, scooping Miss Saffron into my arms joining her at the kitchen sink. "I'm sure Detective Huxton is a great conversationalist. I bet I can get him talking."

She threw her hands up in the air and turned her drilling gaze on me. "You're not going to let it rest, are you? You may be my niece and I love you dearly, but sometimes you can be as annoying as a spoilt child. I'm sure I have a spell that will change that in a click of my fingers."

She looked so cute I squeezed my lips together to smother the laugh that itched to burst free.

"If you are trying to avoid the subject of Detective Huxton you're doing a shocking job. When I rang you from the police station earlier and mentioned he was back in town, you brushed it under the carpet as if it hadn't shattered you, but I could tell it had."

Her face fell, and I knew I hit the nail on the head. "You never did tell me what happened."

"Meow." Miss Saffron wiggled her way out of my arms and jumped onto the kitchen bench. Her sleek back arched as she stretched her long supple legs, then settled between the two of us. As if reading my mind, she also appeared to be waiting for Aunt Edie to continue.

Aunt Edie cleared her throat and rolled back her shoulders. "There's not much to tell. I thought we had something special and obviously he didn't. One day we were happy and the next he left with very little explanation. All he said was 'There are things happening at the moment and it has nothing to do with us. I have no idea how long it will take so...'"

"So?" I asked, rubbing my forehead, the skin so tight if the wind changed, I'd have a face as flat as a pug dog. I drummed my nails repeatedly on the kitchen laminate.

She shrugged coolly. "So, I stopped him and let him off the hook. He went his way, and I went mine and the rest is history. It's in the past. No harm done. Now." She folded her arms across her chest and relaxed against the bench. "Enough talk about that man. Why don't you and Miss Saffron go give Eli a hand in The Melting Pot? I believe he's due to knock off soon for a busking session."

Woah, that change of topic was nothing short of abrupt. I guess the subject is closed. For now.

"I'm sure Eli is doing a bang-up job by himself." I could have sworn I saw a twinkle in Aunt Edie's eye. *What are you up to?* A shudder tossed my stomach on its head. *Please don't play match maker.*

"Um, actually…soon I'll be heading to the airport to pick up Tyler." My heart longed to see my best friend, but my head was still annoyed with him for keeping me in the dark about his early return. "And just in case I'm not back in time, I'll message Jordi to take Harriet home to get her stuff."

Aunt Edie shuffled around in the pantry, for what, I had no idea. "I'm glad he's coming home," she called in a deeper tone. "That boy has been away far too long."

Tell me about it.

She reappeared her arms laden with jars of varying sizes with just enough clearance to peek over the top.

"Here, let me help." Rushing to relieve some of the load, my eye caught the label on the top two jars. "Mugwort? Sandalwood? Goodness me, what are you planning?"

Vacating her arms of the load onto the bench, Aunt Edie brushed her hair from her face with the back of her palm. "I'm concerned how Harriet will take the news of her new path in life, so I thought I'd whip up a little something to help smooth things over if needed. Mugwort does wonders to enhance psychic powers. It will be more like an incense than a spell, so she'll be none the wiser."

Aunt Edie's big heart never ceased to amaze me. "You're the best. Want some help?"

"Love some," she said with a quirky wink. "Can you get the blue blender out of the pantry? It's on the second bottom shelf right at the back." A brisk succession of taps rattled the door took us both by surprise.

I frowned. "The only visitor I'm expecting is Jordi and it's not like her to knock and wait."

"Let's not keep whoever it is waiting." Her head dipped toward the door. "You get the door and I'll get the blender."

"On it." I turned and Miss Saffron darted to the door knocking my feet out from underneath me. My breath hitched in the back of my throat as the corner of the table caught my fall.

"What on earth is wrong with you?" I scowled, rubbing my backside jerking away at first touch.

Aww, that's gonna bruise.

It was hard to stay mad at my beloved familiar, but today she was pushing the friendship. Reaching the door, she sat beside my leg, her long body hugging my calf. Another round of taps echoed as I flung the door open. The air escaped from my lungs in one swoop and I gulped.

Speak of the devil.

CHAPTER FIVE

"**D**etective Huxton," I said, my voice loud enough for Aunt Edie to hear. "Can't say we were expecting you."

"I'm sorry to rock up on your doorstep." The carved lines on his forehead had softened since this morning. His eyes held a clear apology and his voice sounded sincere. "But I figured I should inform Harriet of new developments as soon as they come to hand, and I believe she came here after the police station."

Developments? I hope this is good news.

"Of course, please come in," I said, stepping aside. I kept my eye on Aunt Edie as she stood stock still in front of the pantry, blender held tightly to her chest. Closing the door, Detective Huxton stood, his gaze focused on one woman in the room. No guesses who that was. "Aunt Edie, you remember Detective Huxton, don't you?"

"Of course," she said, plastering a platonic smile on her face. "How nice to see you again. It sounded like you have some information for Harriet?" She placed the blender on the table, a clear barrier between them.

He cleared his throat and flicked open his notebook. "Yes, is Harriet around?"

I shook my head. "She's sleeping and I really don't want to wake her. She's wiped out from the ordeal this morning."

He nodded, his lips forming a clenched half-smile. "Yeah, I guess I can understand that. I can come back later."

Aunt Edie's eyes widened. "Why don't you tell us? We'll be sure to pass on the information as soon as she comes downstairs. Surely, you remember how tongues can chinwag in Saltwater Cove. By the time you return she'll have heard it, but it will be the hearsay and we all know that can't be good for the girl."

He tapped his thumb on the notepad. "You're probably right."

"Would you like a cup of coffee?" The moment the words left my mouth Aunt Edie's voice echoed inside my mind. My head jerked back. It always startled me how she can project her thoughts into my head.

No! No. No. He does not need to stay for coffee.

I glared at her, but rushed to correct my blunder. "Although I'm sure with a fresh murder investigation you must have way too much on your plate to waste time. We'd hate to keep you from your duties."

He nodded, looking down at his notebook. A laugh resembling a bark caught my ear. "Yes, true. Very well, I can now confirm it was poison that killed Camille. We are still following possible leads on that front. We believe it to be cyanide, but we're still waiting official confirmation."

"Cyanide? I don't understand. How? Why?" My words rushed out. "How can you be so sure?"

"We're not 100% sure yet, hence why we need official confirmation." He said, returning his notepad to his pocket. "But all the evidence so far points to cyanide, especially since the scent of almonds was present at the autopsy."

"Almonds?" I asked, puzzled by his reference to one of my favourite nuts. "How can almonds indicate poison? I for one love the sweet nutty taste of almonds. Aren't they good for you?"

Aunt Edie's shoulders relaxed, easing the growing boulder in the pit of my stomach. "Yes, very good for you. However, the smell of almonds is a clear indicator of cyanide poisoning. Not everyone can smell it, but it has a distinctively bitter scent that cannot be missed once smelled."

Bitter scent of almonds = cyanide = death. Got it.

My mind refocused on the present and I looked up, the two older adults in the room locked in an intense staring competition. The air tensed. There's nothing like feeling like a third wheel. I shuffled from one foot to the other, the uncomfortable silence stretched thin like a pair of Aunt Edie's pantyhose. "Would you two like me to give you a moment alone?"

"No," Aunt Edie said at the same time as Detective Huxton blurted, "Yes."

My head zipped from one to the other like a rally in a Grand Slam tennis match. "Um…awkward," I muttered, unsure where to look.

Detective Huxton turned and took a tentative step in my direction, a nervous smile matched the hesitation in his gaze. "If you would see it in your heart to give me a moment alone with your aunt, I would be most appreciative. It's been a while since we've seen each other, and I am hoping she will give me a few minutes of her time."

Handsome and polite. I see why she fell for the man. Her jaw dropped and she stood stock still lost for words. "Aunt Edie?"

"Sorry?" she said, her unfocussed gaze looking straight through me.

"Detective Huxton would like a moment alone."

"He does?" she muttered, her focus now back on the man standing metres from her.

My body twitched in anticipation. If I didn't know better, one would think I was stuck in the middle of a love scene in one of those lovey-dovey daytime soap operas.

"I'll just go and check on Harriet," I said, moving toward the staircase. "Won't be long."

Bounding on my toes I shot around the corner and started my ascent up the staircase. I'd barely taken three steps when three words spoken in a sorrowful tone froze my feet to the step.

"I'm so sorry." The tone of his voice grabbed me by the throat like a claw. I could barely breath around the knot forming and moving was definitely out of the question. Aunt Edie despised eavesdropping, but each time I willed my feet to move they ignored me like a sulky child.

Silence filled the house. Had he left? I frowned, straining to hear movement, any movement that would give me an indication of what was happening.

He continued his words drenched with sadness. "I know you may not believe me, Edith, but I am sorry. I never meant to hurt you and the last thing I wanted to do was leave. I had no choice."

"Maybe so," Aunt Edie said with a sigh. "We'd been seeing each other such a short time, but I thought we had something special. At least, it was to me."

"Me too. So, so special," he said.

"Then why leave without so much as an explanation? Was it because I was a witch?"

I gasped and slapped my hand over my mouth. That was news to me.

"Of course not," he said behind a muffled chuckle. "You being a witch had nothing to do with it. In fact, it made it easier. But I didn't think the line 'it's not you, it's me' was going to work."

"No, I don't suppose it would have," she said calmly. "It not my place to judge why you left. So much time has passed, it's best we leave the past where it is. In the past."

"No," he snapped. "You're the reason I transferred back to Saltwater Cove, not Camille's murder."

"Me?" Aunt Edie's voice rose three octaves.

I shut my eyes and did an internal happy dance. My hand fisted and I punched the air above my head.

"Yes, you. But I do owe you an explanation. The short version is my brother was killed, actually murdered, and my father requested I come home and find his killer."

Oh my God, how horrible. His brother murdered. It was crushing enough when my parents died in a freak accident, I can't imagine what he must be going through knowing his brother was murdered.

"Oh, Micah. I'm so sorry. I had no idea."

The anguish in her voice guttered me and my backside found the carpeted step before my legs buckled beneath me.

She continued. "That must have been awful for you. I can understand why you didn't want me to know, but you have to know I would have understood."

"Thank you. Yes, I know you would have. It was my mother and sister who took my brother's murder the hardest. Remember, how I said you being a witch would have made it easier?"

"Yes."

Hesitating, he cleared his throat. "You see…I'm also a Leodian."

Aunt Edie gasped. "A Leodian? How can that be?"

A Leodain? How cool.

Talk about a diamond in the rough.

"A long story best left for another time. I was about to come clean when I lost my brother and my life fell apart."

Silence fell between them and I imagined Aunt Edie wrapping her safe arms around his tortured soul. Her love was unconditional.

"A lot of time has passed since you left, Micah. I'm not the same woman I was then." Her tone was a little on the abrupt side. "Do you expect us to pick up where we were before you left?"

"Of course not. I'm back in Saltwater Cove permanently. I had to make things right between us and explain why I left. I was just hoping we could be friends. We had a great friendship once and they are hard to come by."

Friends? Come on Aunt Edie, even I can tell you're still in love with the guy. Friendship is the first step.

After a long pause, she spoke in her soft welcoming tone I loved so much. "Of course. I can do friendship. Some say I'm pretty good at it."

Even though I wasn't standing in the room, I sensed there were smiles all round.

"Thank you and I promise this time friendship is forever. I'll be off now. I've taken up too much of your time already. I will need to see Harriet again, but maybe when she's feeling better. It was lovely to see you again, Edith."

"You too, Micah."

The sharp click of the door confirmed his exit and I jumped up dying to hear her thoughts. I reached the bottom of the staircase and a blood-curdling scream bellowing from upstairs turned the blood in my veins ice cold.

"Oh my God," I yelled as all thoughts of Aunt Edie's love life vanished and visions of Harriet laying in a pool of blood screwed with my mind. I shot up the stairs two at a time barely able to suck air into my starved lungs.

"Harriet? Harriet are you okay?" I yelled, bolting down the corridor to her room. I flung the door open to see a sweat drenched Harriet sitting up, gasping for air. Rushing to the bed, I grabbed her ice-cold hands and squeezed. Aunt Edie hovered in the doorway. "Harriet, can you hear me?"

She sat motionless, her eyes staring straight through me as if I were glass. "Harriet. It's me...Evelyn. What happened?"

Harriet gasped and gulped for air, her eyes blinking several times, then slowly refocussed on me. Her hands still shaking, she opened her mouth to speak but nothing came out. Finally, a soft whisper from her trembling lips. "Evelyn?"

"Yes, it's me, Harriet."

"I...I...she...Camille's been murdered and I'm...I'm next," she muttered. Her eyes were wide open and she kept shaking her head.

Her words sliced my heart as if a scythe wheeled by death himself. What did she mean 'she's next'?

"Harriet, you're not making any sense. We already know Camille's dead and you're fine. You're here with me and Aunt Edie in our house."

"I saw it," she said, and her gaze finally fully registering who I was. "Oh Evelyn." She threw her arms around my neck and crushed me, jarring the wind from my lungs. "It was awful. The worst nightmare of my life."

I rubbed a soothing hand up and down her back and waited a moment until her breathing calmed. "It's all okay. Are you feeling better?"

She pulled back and nodded wiping her hair from her face. "Yes, I think so."

Aunt Edie spoke for the first time, but I didn't miss the concern in her eyes. "Harriet love, I know you may not want to remember but do you think you can tell us what scared you?"

Harriet nodded and paused, bitting her bottom lip. "It was the worst dream I've ever had in my life. First, I saw Camille in her office, and she was eating one of Vivienne's pumpkin pies and everything seemed okay. I felt like I was a fly on the wall. You know, like I was floating above the scene. No-one could see me. Then, all of a sudden, she froze mid mouthful like she was one of those wax figures from Madame Tussaud's Wax Museum. The pie started to sparkle and float up in the air spinning faster and faster. It was like watching a flashing neon light show and then it vanished into thin air and another appeared in front of Camille in its place."

Harriet's hands began to shake uncontrollably, and her complexion turned ashen within seconds.

I frowned and my gut tossed back and forth. "Harriet, what is it? What can you remember?"

"I…I…she…she continued eating as if nothing had happened…and…it was horrible." Harriet scrunched her eyes shut and shook her head in short fast jerks. "She ate about three mouthfuls of the pie and then she started coughing and clutching at her throat. She gasped, trying to suck in air, but she failed. Her face turned red, her hands thrashing uncontrollably, knocking random things off her desk and then…"

I hadn't realised I was holding my breath until my lungs burned from the lack of oxygen. I gasped. "And then?"

"And then she started shaking, her whole body I mean. Like she was having a fit and then she collapsed onto her desk face first into the pie. It was horrible."

My gazed found Aunt Edie and she jumped into my head keeping Harriet unaware of our internal conversation.

There's an evil source at work here. A witch maybe, but whoever it is sounds like they poisoned Vivienne's pumpkin pie.'

"I think you're absolutely right and that means they know Vivienne delivers pies to the bank and will most probably take the blame. Looks like she's being framed for Camille's murder. But more importantly this means Harriet can see the past as well as the future."

"I guess I was more affected by finding Camille's body than I realised," Harriet said, flopping back on the bed and closing her eyes.

"But why do you think you'll be next?" I asked.

She sat up again this time leaning back on her hands. Little tremors coating her voice.

"Because in my dream they were after me, too. I was running for my life. My shirt was ripped. My hair looked like a bird's nest that had weathered a storm, make up streaming down my face and there was a gouge on my forehead with blood trickling down my face. Every time I looked behind me, all I could see was darkness. I somehow knew they were still behind me. I knew if I stopped running, they'd kill me. I just kept running, my surroundings blurring into one. Old boarded-up houses, forests, broken down warehouses, one foot after the next with no end in sight."

"But Harriet, remember Evelyn put a protective spell on the amulet she gave you, so as long as you wear it, nothing can hurt you," Aunt Edie said, moving toward the end of the bed.

Harriet rubbed her brow excessively, her gaze haunted. "That's why I was so freaked out, I wasn't wearing it. When I was running, it was gone. My neck was bare. There was no amulet and no spell to protect me."

Gone? No! How…when?

My eyes widened and I ran a shaky hand through my hair. "That can't be good."

"What do you mean?" Harriet asked, her voice on the edge of hysteria.

"Just that it can't be good that you are having such disturbing dreams," I said, covering up my blunder. I pointed to the amulet still adorning her neck. "And look. It's still there. Aunt Edie and I are here and as long as we are, nothing will happen to you."

Harriet's gaze darted between both of us several times and a hesitant smile broke out across her face. "Thank you. I know it was just a dream, but heck, it seemed so real."

"You're exhausted now more than ever. Why don't you see if you can rest up a little bit longer?"

Harriet paused, her tired eyes giving away her state of mind. "I know you're right, but I'm scared. What if I shut my eyes and it happens all over again?"

I squeezed her hands. "Aunt Edie and I will be here and Jordi will be back any time now. And if I know Jordi, she'll have gossip to tell and I know you'll want to be refreshed for it."

She nodded and slid down in the bed. "I do feel wiped out. Maybe I'll just rest and forgo the sleep."

I smiled and pulled up the bedspread, tucking it under her chin. "Sounds like a good idea. We'll be downstairs if you need anything at all, just call. Okay?"

She nodded. "Okay. Love you."

"Love you too." I followed Aunt Edie into the kitchen. The clarity of Harriet's visions knocked the air from my chest. The last one scared the bejesus out of me.

"This is worse than I thought," Aunt Edie said, wearing the floorboards thin with her pacing. "Harriet is in grave danger. Her visions are strong and it's best she finds out the truth sooner rather than later. Going forward, she'll be able to deal with whatever comes her way. That girl is going to need some loving guidance when she finds out she's a witch and her life is going to change forever."

"I agree." The time on the wall clock nabbed my attention and my jaw clenched. "Great, if I don't move my butt, Tyler will be waiting at the airport for me instead of the other way around." I gave Aunt Edie a hug and peck on the cheek goodbye. "Hold the fort down for me until I get back?"

"Of course, love."

I threw my bag over my shoulder and grabbed my car keys. "If Jordi gets back before me, fill her in and then we'll sort out what to do next after I get back."

"Will do."

She gifted me a smile that extended all the way to her beautiful honey-brown eyes.

"Give that young man a welcome home hug for me. There'll be a place for him at Saturday night's Halloween dinner at The Melting Pot and I expect him to fill it."

I giggled at her motherly tone. "I'll tell him. See you later."

CHAPTER SIX

Why didn't I just tell Tyler to catch a cab home?

I rose up on my tippy-toes to see over the waiting crowd as the passengers exited the plane one by one. The butterflies in my stomach fluttered, fuelling an overwhelming urge to flee. I rocked from foot to foot, my muscles twitching. It had been several months since I'd face-timed Tyler, had he changed? Or would he look the same as he did complete with tattered dreadlocks and unkept beard. Six months is a long time to be travelling a third-world country. I guess he had his reasons.

A buff, toned man strutted toward me and his gorgeous grin stole my breath right out of my chest. I didn't know where to look first. His broad shoulders, his humongous upper arms, his sexy square jawline or his dreamy cobalt blue eyes. Gone were the dreadlocks replaced with a short back and sides and not a hair in sight on his face. Smooth and sexy, sending my pulse into meltdown.

Tyler?

"Wow, Evie girl, aren't you a sight for sore eyes," he said lifting me into a bear hug and spinning, my feet dangling half a metre off the floor. "How's my favourite witch?"

I grabbed his shoulders and my palms barely fit around his tight bulge of muscle. The seductive scent of musk filled my nostrils and had my head spinning. What the hell happened in Nepal? Shock doesn't even begin to cover it. "Tyler, I hardly recognised you. What happened to the dreadlocks and beard?"

I found me feet firmly planted on the floor but his arms were still around me. "That was the Nepal, backpacker Tyler, and this." He paused and took a step back and steadily twirled. "Is the new improved Tyler ready to come home and start living back in civilisation."

"Wow, I had no idea the new and improved Tyler had changed so much, but then how would I, I didn't even know about you coming back early," I said in a sullen tone folding my arms across my chest.

"Yeah, sorry about that." He headed off toward the luggage carousel, my feet moving on rote beside him. "It was supposed to be a surprise. No-one was supposed to know expect Mum and Dad.

They're currently in Paris, so I figured it'd be safe to tell them. What I didn't account for was Mum's inability to keep a secret. Doesn't matter now."

He paused and his eyes ran over my body from my head to toe. He'd never looked at me that way before. His intense gaze sent pleasurable aches raging through me.

What on earth is happening? This is Tyler Broderick my best friend, not my boyfriend.

"Come on, you." I play punched him in his shoulder and gasped. I shook the pins and needles from my hand. "Aww. What have you been doing? Bench pressing Buddhas while you were there?"

He chuckled and my heart did a backflip. "Not exactly. I realised life was passing me by and it was time to step up and start living my true destiny."

"True destiny?" I watched him throw his backpack over his shoulder like it was a feather. I thrust my hands on my hips and squinted at him. "Okay, who are you and what have you done with my best friend?"

He threw his arm around my shoulder and we headed out of the terminal. "Oh Evie girl, I've missed your sense of humour. I've missed Saltwater Cove. I want you to fill me on everything, the old the new. All of it."

By the time we were on the road heading home it was like old times, except for my heartbeat, which was drumming my chest like a jackhammer. Gone was my favourite computer-crazed nerd replaced by a hunky male fit to strut his stuff on a New York runway. My phone vibrated on the console sending Dance Monkey barrelling through the car Bluetooth.

Saved by the bell.

"Hello."

The familiar tense voice of Harriet hit my ears. "Evelyn, they confirmed it was cyanide poisoning that killed her. Detective Huxton just dropped by with the news officially declaring it a homicide."

"Cyanide poisoning?" Tyler said, his widened gaze burning a hole right through me. "Homicide?"

"Tyler, is that you?" Harriet asked.

"Hey Harriet, yeah its me."

He kept his enquiring gaze glued to me as he spoke.

Harriet's tone took an upturn beat. "Welcome home, stranger."

"Thanks, now who was killed with cyanide poisoning?" He asked, a frown marring his perfect face. "And how long has Detective Huxton been back in Saltwater Cove?"

"Thanks for the update, Harriet. I'll take it from here. Bye, see you when I get home." I hit the end call button promptly. My chest tightened under Tyler's scrutinising gaze. "So, tell me about Nepal and why the early return?"

"Oh no you don't," he said, shaking his head. "You're not changing the subject. You can try, but I'm not leaving this car until you tell me who was killed with cyanide poisoning and no amount of deflecting is going to prevent that outcome."

I glanced sideways at Tyler and I was lost in his sexy, deep blue eyes. My pulse quickened and I blinked several times, returning my focus to the road. A much safer option. "I could, of course, put a spell on you and wipe your memory."

What the hell is wrong with me? In the last twenty-four hours I've been attracted to two men. The handsome new town busker and my best friend who I have never found attractive in my life. Until twenty minutes ago.

I squeezed the steering wheel and prayed Tyler mistook my growing libido for my reluctance to reveal information about Camille's murder.

"Yes, you could, but then you'd get in trouble for using your powers for personal gain." He tutted and shook his head. "There are very strict rules against it, or have you forgotten?"

Hardly.

"I'd advise against it. Remember we do live in Saltwater Cove where town gossip is broadcast in the local news twice a day, at least it used to be. So, if you don't tell me I'm going to find out anyway…unless its changed in the last few years."

I shook my head and sighed, my left eye started its annoying twitch. Something it did when I was out of all options.

"No, it hasn't changed. The condensed version is Camille Stenson, the loans manager and sometimes teller at the Saltwater Cove Bank, was found murdered this morning and it turns out cyanide was the poison of choice. Harriet found the body and she quickly became the prime suspect which is ludicrous and will never be proven. That's about it in a nutshell."

He sat in silence as if letting my words sink in, his eyes stuck on me the whole time. Heat rose up my neck to my cheeks and I hiked the air conditioner up another notch or two.

"Who is Camille Stenson?"

I veered the car left off the freeway. "She arrived in Saltwater Cove about six months ago and took up the job of loans officer in the bank. Camille only worked as a teller when it was busy. She quickly gained herself the reputation of the town grouch. Popularity was not on her agenda. I guess someone had a score to settle."

"There's something you're not telling me, Evie," he said, leaning across the console. In the confines of my purple Volkswagen Beatle his musky citrus aftershave wafted in my direction.

Mandarin and violet? Burberry Touch for men. My favourite. Did he wear it on purpose? How would he know, I've never told him? Get a grip woman, this is Tyler for goodness' sake.

"Your eye is twitching like crazy which means you're not exactly telling me the whole story. Out with it, Evie girl," he snapped.

The whole story? Sure, you walked off that plane looking smokin' hot and sexy as hell with muscles I'd like to run my hands over and lips that could take me to heaven ten times over. Yeah, like that's going to work.

"Well, there is one other bit of information that isn't common knowledge yet," I said, sucking in a deep breath and turning down the main street of town. "Harriet's a witch, a powerful one but she doesn't know it yet."

His jaw dropped. "Come again?"

"Harriet has been experiencing some strange happenings recently and Aunt Edie believes she's about to come into her powers. And you know as well as I do it's rare that Aunt Edie is ever wrong. It appears Harriet has the power to see not only the future, but the past as well. And while we're not a hundred percent sure, we think she can time travel."

He raised his eyebrows. "Woah. Time travel? Are you serious?"

I nodded. "Yes. Seeing the future is one thing, but knowing the past and the ability to time travel to change it could be a blessing, and a curse."

"Sheesh. I travel the world and the town falls apart." Tyler ran a hand through his hair, returning his gaze to the road ahead.

"I wouldn't exactly say it's fallen apart, maybe it's…" My words were suddenly swallowed up by the sight before me. A bright white beam of light jumped around in the bank. "How can that be?"

"What? How can what be?" Tyler asked.

"Look, there," I said, pointing to the bank. "The bank's supposed to be closed. The lights are off but someone's in there with a flashlight snooping around and it looks like they're in Camille's office."

Tyler's gaze followed mine and his eyes squinted for a clearer view. "I can't see anything except a bank in pitch-black darkness. Are you sure?"

"As sure as I am that Harriet is innocent." I swerved the car in the direction of the bank carpark hitting the curb and my stomach lurched into my throat.

"Woah, easy there," he said, his hands searching for something solid to ground himself. "It's not like you to drive so erratically."

It's not every day your best friend is accused of murder either. Adrenaline spurred me on and my mind zeroed in on the bank. "Sorry, but it could be someone searching Camille's office destroying evidence."

"What are you going to do…confront them? This is dangerous in anyone's book even for a witch. Why don't we call the police?"

I pulled the car up to a halt, slamming my foot on the brake, jarring both our bodies forward. "I'm going to look in the window, and if there's cause for concern, I'll call the police. Don't be a wuss, Tyler. You coming or not?" I didn't wait for his response. My feet hit the ground running and I bolted toward the unlit bank window, my breathing laboured.

I crouched down and peered in the window holding my hands against the cold glass in a cup shape squinting to see inside. Nothing but darkness. "No, this can't be right."

"What can't be right?" Tyler asked from beside me.

"It's all dark. I can't see a thing." *Was my brain playing tricks on me?* "No lights on and no beam of light anywhere in sight." I turned and Tyler's questioning gaze gutted me. "I'm not imagining it, Tyler. I saw a light in Camille's office. It might be gone now, but it *was* there."

He held his hands out in a placating manner. "I believe you. But it's not there now."

I ground my teeth together and fisted my hands at my sides before I throttled him. "I can see that. Thanks for pointing out the obvious. I know I wasn't imagining it. Something strange is going on and I'm going to find out what it is one way or another." I walked back to the car in silence, but very aware of the man next to me watching my every move.

"Count me in, Evie girl. If you believe something fishy is going on, then I'm with you." He opened his car door and slid into the passenger seat. "Harriet's one of my best friends too, so whatever you need just ask and if it's in my power to deliver, it's yours. It's not like I have anything better to do with my time except catch up with some family for Mum."

A smile stretched from one ear to the other and my body was energised by his words. "Thank you, Tyler. You're the best. I forgive you."

His brow creased forming a mini monobrow as I pulled away from the bank. "For what?"

"For not telling me you were coming back early. Imagine how I felt when Jordi let it slip at Harriet's birthday drinks last night."

"Oh." He bit his bottom lip. "Sorry."

I laughed at his pouting expression. "Forget it. Let's call it even after you buy my lunch tomorrow at the Four Brothers. Deal?"

He chuckled. "Deal."

I pulled up into Aunt Edie's driveway after dropping Tyler home and killed the engine. I closed my eyes and breathed a huge sigh, my head flopping against the headrest. "Maybe I am going crazy. I'm sure I saw a light in Camille's office as I drove by."

The soulful tunes of a deep male voice sailed through the air lifting me into a place of serene calmness. The seductive strumming of his guitar echoed through my mind soothing my scattered thoughts.

"Ah, Eli," I muttered, my head lulling to the side. Eli's sexy cobalt blue eyes smiled at me. My eyelids snapped open and my head shot up. "Eli? Why am I dreaming about Eli?"

I stretched my spine up and looked in the rear-view mirror. There he was on the other side of the road busking away. People gathered to listen, mostly women, and they walked by, dropping money into his open guitar case. He nodded in recognition of their support. I swear his gaze caught mine in a moment of connection and I dropped down low in my seat. "What is wrong with me? Fantasising about two men is crazy. One I barely know, the other since I was eleven. I really need to get out more."

The upbeat words of Hall and Oates hit my ears and I gasped. "Oh crap, he did see me, otherwise why would he be singing the song Private Eyes?" My phone buzzed and I snatched it up before Dance Monkey had a chance to deafen Eli's voice. "Hello."

"Evelyn, thank God I was able to reach you. You need to come home straight away."

The urgency in Aunt Edie's voice turned my squirming insides into rock hard knots. I bolted upright and grabbed the keys from the ignition. "I am home. I'm just getting out of the car now. What's wrong?"

"They've arrested Vivienne for Camille's murder just as Harriet predicted. Isn't that outrageous?" Her pitch raising with each word.

"Vivienne?" *What the?*

"They say her pumpkin pie was laced with poison making it one of the deadliest pies in the world. The pie was full of ground-up apricot seeds and they contain amygdalin. Once swallowed, it converts into cyanide."

"Oh my God," I said, all thoughts of Eli gone as I bolted up the front stairs.

My heart pounded inside my ribcage as I raced into the kitchen to find Aunt Edie wearing down more floorboards and Jordi and Harriet sitting at the kitchen table. Aunt Edie's troubled gaze found mine and my heart ripped in two. I dumped my bag on the table and flopped into a chair. "Okay, fill me in and don't leave anything out."

Harriet was the first to speak. Her voice quivered. "It was just like my dream."

"How could Micah think Vivienne would do such a thing?" Aunt Edie said, the heels of her shoes scuffing the floor repeatedly as she paced.

"Being able to shift into a small bird does have its advantages. I sat on their windowsill and they were none the wiser," Jordi said, a cheeky glint in her eye. "They confirmed Camille's time of death was 6:40 am give or take a few minutes. Death was pretty much instant."

Nausea rolled around in my belly and I swallowed hard to keep the disgusting taste of copper from working its way into my throat.

Jordi continued, "Before they confirmed poison was in the pumpkin pie, Detective Huxton got a call from Mrs Ady."

"Harriet's neighbour? The lady who works at the church?" I asked, puzzled.

"Yep," Harriet said, accompanied by a sheepish grin. "I totally forgot I slept through my alarm this morning thanks to one too many shots last night. Apparently, it was blaring through the entire apartment block. Mrs Ady finally pounded my door down around 6.30 am and I must have answered it and turned it off because once she heard they suspected me, she rang the police station and told them the whole story. I can't remember even talking to her. Remind me never to drink that much Tequila again."

I squeezed Harriet's hand and smiled. "I'm glad your name has been cleared. I'm just sorry their focus is now on Vivienne."

Aunt Edie huffed. "Well they can try to pin this murder on her all they like, but it won't work I tell you. We'll find out who did this. I'm not about to let my best friend rot in jail for a crime she didn't commit."

I stood and my pulse surged. "And neither will we."

Harriet nodded. "Absolutely, you can count on Jordi and me."

"Definitely. There are a few other bits of information I managed to get." Jordi paused, taking a gulp of water from a cup in front of her. "But I think it would be best to first talk about Harriet's dream."

It was then I noticed the bowl on the counter behind Aunt Edie and the mild scent of Sandalwood floating in the air. Aunt Edie nodded and her voice rung out loud and clear in my mind.

'It's time Harriet knew the truth.'

"I think that's a great idea." I turned to Harriet and held both her hands in mine. "Sweetheart, there's no easy way to say this."

Harriet paled. "You're scaring me."

"I'm sorry, I don't mean to. Your dream earlier today felt real, didn't it?" Harriet nodded. I took in a deep breath and forged ahead, my insides doing nervous somersaults like a beginner gymnast at the first Olympics. "That's because it was real."

Harriet's jaw fell open and she went completely still. "I don't understand."

Aunt Edie slid into the chair next to me and placed a hand on Harriet's forearm. "Believe me, I know how all this is going to sound but it's time you knew the truth."

Harriet's gaze flicked between the three of us. "The truth about what?"

Jordi smiled. "You're a witch like Evelyn and Aunt Edie."

Aunt Edie continued in a soothing tone. "It felt real because it was real. You have the power to see the future, a possible future and after your vision today, I would say the past as well. And if I'm not mistaken and I rarely am, I also believe that you have the ability to time travel."

She sat as still as a popsicle. Damn it, maybe we moved too fast.

"Are you serious?" She asked, bolting from her chair. "I'm a witch…are you sure? I mean absolutely positively sure?"

Aunt Edie nodded. "Yes love, I am."

Harriet threw her arms out wide and spun like a ballerina in the middle of the kitchen. "Woohoo, I'm a witch."

I looked at Jordi and she had the same concerned look on her face tightening my chest. Was Harriet losing her mind?

"Harriet, are you okay?"

"I'm more than okay," she said, stumbling to a stop. "I'm a witch. No longer am I the odd one out. The one who wasn't special, the one with zero ability."

"You were never the odd one out," I snapped, her words crushing my heart.

"You know what I mean." She gasped and ran her hands through her hair.

Jordi piped up. "Tyler's not a witch."

"He doesn't count. He may not be a witch but he's a whiz at computers which is sort of like a power." She paused and wrapped her arms around her waist. "Why are they showing now? How come I didn't get them earlier like you guys?"

"The witch world is a strange one, powers can be triggered by a person or incident. I expect you have witch blood a few generations back and with the appearance of the hooded man last night, it awakened your abilities. There will be lots to learn but know that we will be with you every step of the way."

Tears clouded her eyes and she wiped them away with her sleeve. "Thank you. At least now I know why no-one could keep a secret from me."

Her giggles were contagious and soon we were all wiping happy tears from our eyes.

Jordi stood with her arms folded. "Can we get back to discussing the rest of the information from my eavesdropping session this afternoon?"

"Of course," I said, sucking in deep breaths and grabbing the stitch stabbing my side. We all sat in chairs around the kitchen table waiting for Jordi to pick up where she left off.

"Wait," Harriet yelled, the colour vanishing from her cheeks, leaving a pasty white appearance in its place. "I'm going to die. In my dream, I mean, in my vision today someone was after me, trying to kill me. If I can see the future as you say, then I'm going to die. I saw my imminent death with no amulet to protect me."

Harriet's words cut me to the core. "You are not going to die. What you saw was one possible future. The future can be changed with a snap of one's fingers. You saw that vision for a reason. Now we have to work out what it means before it happens and with the three of us in your corner, we can't lose."

Harriet nodded, although her expression was unconvinced.

"We'll be here to help you." Jordi reaffirmed. "Back to my information. I thought it strange, but Huxton said they're going to keep the knowledge of the apricot seeds out of the press."

"Good heavens, why?" Aunt Edie asked.

"He reckons they'll have enough to hold Vivienne because the poison was found in her pumpkin pie. She was supposed to bring it with her when she had her appointment with Camille yesterday morning but forgot. She delivered to the bank later that afternoon giving her plenty of time to take revenge on Camille for not approving her loan by going home and adding the poison to it."

"I don't like to speak ill of the dead, but the woman was something else. She wouldn't give Vivienne a loan but still happy to buy her pumpkin pies." Aunt Edie growled.

"We need a plan of action," I said, taking the lead. "Aunt Edie, can you use your influence with your old pal, Micah Huxton, to get Vivienne released?" She nodded. "Jordi and I will take Harriet home to pack an overnight bag and on the way, I'll fill them in on the sexy new improved Tyler Broderick."

I stared at three gaping expressions and giggled as I exited.

CHAPTER SEVEN

*C*amille's untimely demise yesterday hadn't stopped the locals from gracing The Four Brothers for lunch. Thanks to the town gossip train, The Melting Pot had been extra busy this morning with enquiring minds interested in any scrap of information they could get their mitts on. Aunt Edie had to force me to take my lunch break and boy, am I glad she did. I skipped breakfast this morning and my growling hungry stomach monster just about turned me into the Hulk.

Thank goodness she was able to persuade Detective Huxton to release Vivienne last night. Insisting on going home, Vivienne wanted to keep her mind off Camille's death which meant cooking, lots and lots of cooking. Aunt Edie promised to update her with any new findings. Currently, the list was looking rather bleak.

Harriet gulped down the last of her lemonade and wiped the moisture from her lips with a drag of her forearm across her mouth. "Ah, I needed that. I'm so glad they kept the bank closed today. I wasn't looking forward to going into work. My mind's still processing all the new information from yesterday. With Mr Bain still out of town and all, I suppose they couldn't re-open until he returns. Means I can hang out with you at The Melting Pot."

I sipped my lemon, lime and bitters, the cold liquid chilling my insides as it slid down my throat sending ice shockwaves through my chest. "It was pretty cool of Mr Bain to let you take the time you need. He must have known you were pretty upset and needed the rest."

Harriet nodded. "He's good like that. He looks after his employees at the bank. Detective Huxton said he was pretty distraught when they told him about Camille, and he wanted to come back from the symposium early to make sure I was okay."

My eyebrows shot up. "Is that so?"

"Yep," Harriet said, the whites of her eyes glowing under the fluorescent lights. "The bank was a crime scene yesterday and they didn't know if it would be available to open today or not so he's coming back when the symposium ends which is this afternoon."

"I guess it was lucky Della Raymond was away this week visiting her new granddaughter."

"Oh my God, I feel terrible." Harriet's hands twisted with the damp serviette wrapped around her empty glass. "In all the kerfuffle of yesterday I totally forgot to call her and let her know about Camille."

"I'm sure someone would have told her by now. When is she due back?" I asked, popping another crunchy beer battered chip in my mouth. The salty taste pleasuring my taste buds one by one.

"Next week. She'll have missed the whole event." Lucky her. "Let's hope they've caught the real murderer before she comes back."

Yeah, me too. Aunt Edie mentioned Vivienne was surprisingly calm, almost too calm after she was released from the police station last night. I wonder if she even processed what had happened. My thoughts were interrupted by a deep authoritative voice.

"Evelyn...Harriet, good to see you're okay," Mercer said, pulling up at our table, a gorgeous, tall, leggy blonde with a smile as beautiful as Leslie Mann on his tail. "I'd like you to meet our new hotel manager, Florence Chesterfield."

Florence Chesterfield? Sounds like she's straight out of an episode of Downtown Abbey.

"Nice to meet you." I nodded. "Welcome to Saltwater Cove."

She grabbed my hand off the table and shook it. Continuously. "Thank you. It's so nice to meet you. I'm so excited to be here and so thankful to Mercer for giving me this chance of a lifetime."

Needles pierced my arm and it was about to drop off. She'd endlessly shook it this whole time. I couldn't help but giggle. "Do you think I could have my hand back now?"

"Oh my God, I'm so sorry," she said, dropping my hand as if it was infected with a deadly disease. "I'm not making a very good first impression, am I?"

"You're doing a great job," I said, trying to ease her apprehension.

Harriet's spine straightened and she thrust her hand out, Florence taking up the gesture. "I'm Harriet, so good to have you join our little town. I hope yesterday's murder didn't sway you from joining our little community?"

"Murder?" she said, the blood draining from her face. "What murder?"

"Thanks Harriet," Mercer said, his forehead creasing. "We'll catch you ladies later. We've some business to take care of." He guided her toward the back offices.

"That really was uncalled for, Harriet," I said, sighing. "It's probably the poor woman's first day in town and you hit her with a murder."

"What's wrong with that?" Harriet said, cocking her head to the side. "She'd find out soon enough. Besides, there was something about her that just didn't sit right with me."

"What do you mean?"

Harriet shrugged. "I'm not sure. I can't put my finger on it, but I got a cold shiver when she shook my hand. Maybe something, maybe nothing. I didn't have a vision or anything, it was just a feeling I got."

I drummed my nails on the table wondering if there was something she's not telling me. Her visions were still new to her, maybe she didn't know what to make of them.

"Are you sure?"

"Positive. Although I wonder how Prudence is going to react when she meets the woman who stole her dream job?" She looked at her watch and bit her bottom lip. "We still have forty-five minutes before we have to head back to The Melting Pot, right?"

I nodded, dipping a chip in some prize-winning garlic aioli sauce and popping it into my mouth.

"Great," she said hiking her bag up on her shoulder and sliding off the chair. "I'm going to pop down to Salty Snips and see if I can make a hair appointment with Misty. After yesterday I need a little pick me up. I promise I'll be back in time to make it back to The Melting Pot before the end of your lunch break."

"No problem, I'll be here." I continued munching away. The food at The Four Brothers never ceased to please my palate. My thoughts drifted back to Vivienne. Why her? Why would someone want to frame her for Camille's murder?

They did have a very vocal row here last night in front of a crowded room and they had a few choice words to say to each other before Camille stormed out. It doesn't look good for Vivienne. What was it again she said, 'I'll get the money and I will make you eat your words, if it's the last thing I do.' Well if the evidence is to be believed, Vivienne certainly made Camille eat her words in the shape of a poisoned pumpkin pie.

"Penny for your thoughts?"

I jumped in surprise, my heart catapulting out of my chest. The cheeky male voice caught me off guard and a half-eaten chip lodged itself in the back of my throat. Coughing and spluttering, I heaved and gasped for air, my windpipe semi-blocked. Tears blurred my vision. Searing heat flooded my cheeks and my pulse throbbed against my temple. Any minute my head was going to explode and bits of my brain would be cast in all directions.

"Jeez, Evelyn, I know you're happy to see me, there's no need to make a scene," Eli said as the palm of his strong manly hand thumped my back knocking the offending chip down my throat.

I gripped the edge of the table, sucking deep breaths in and out. I paused, wiping the tears from my eyes and saw Eli slide into Harriet's empty seat. "That's…not exactly…what I was thinking. But thank you, even though you were the reason I was choking in the first place."

"Me?" Eli said, his eyebrows shooting up. "All I did was ask if you wanted to chat and you just about keeled over in front of me. Luckily, I didn't have to give you mouth to mouth. Although, I am up on my first aid and people do say I'm very good at it."

Was he making a pass at me? Or diffusing an awkward situation with comedy?

I decided to choose the latter. "Oh, you're a real comedian today, aren't you? Remind me next time to make sure I look for potential hazards before I eat my lunch."

His playful grin eased the awkwardness that surfaced, and I breathed a silent sigh.

"Is this a party for two or can anyone join?"

I turned to see Tyler standing beside the table staring at Eli. Or was it glaring. One testosterone-filled male was enough, but two was a challenge I didn't want to deal with during my lunch break.

Tyler continued. "Are you new in Saltwater Cove?"

"Sure am," Eli said, extending his hand. "Eli Pruitt. I work with Evelyn and Edie at The Melting Pot."

"Is that so? News to me." Tyler dropped Eli's hand and turned his gaze on me. "Gee, Evie girl, I thought your friend here would have fallen under the banner on 'new in town.' You might have mentioned him yesterday."

Was that jealousy behind Tyler's sullen expression?

Eli smiled, catching Tyler's eye. "Oh, I'm sure she would have if not for the murder."

"Thanks," Tyler said, a smug grin on his face. "He's working at The Melting Pot with you?"

Now would be a good time for Harriet to return. "And Aunt Edie. In between his busking sessions. Eli's a singer. He's taken up residence outside the grocery store across the road."

"I see. The locals get free entertainment while they shop. I suppose that's one way to make a living. Beats poverty I guess."

What the...? My jaw clenched, and I pressed my hands together in my lap to stop myself from slogging Tyler in the gut. Although he deserved more than that.

Eli cleared his throat and stood. "Um...I think I'll shoot off, I have a few things to do. Catch you later." He turned to Tyler and his back stiffened. "Nice to meet you. I'm sure we'll see each other around town."

Tyler dipped his head. "Count on it."

I barely held it together. I watched Eli walk out of earshot before I let rip. "What the hell, Tyler?" His blank expression riled my insides. "You couldn't be anymore rude if you tried."

"What are you talking about?" he said, pulling back from the table.

I threw my hands up in the air. "Really? Could you not hear yourself?"

"What? I was making conversation with the new man in town." He took Eli's seat. "Which, if you had told me about yesterday, I would've known exactly who you were talking to."

I folded my arms across my tight chest and sat back eyeing my good friend. "You could have made a better first impression. I know you've been away for a long time, but the Tyler I remember wouldn't have been so rude."

He sat frozen, his lips opened a fraction after a sharp intake of breath. He squeezed his blue eyes shut and pinched the bridge of his nose. He sighed visibly, gnawing at his bottom lip. "You're right. You're absolutely right. That's not me. I'm sorry Evie. I was looking forward to spending some time with you and I guess when I walked in and saw you with a strange man, I kind of flipped."

"Kind of?" I snapped.

"I thought maybe he was your boyfriend you hadn't told me about." He paused, dropping his gaze.

Boyfriend? Oh my God, please don't tell me it looked like I was flirting with Eli? Note to self: Never be alone with a hot single man in public again.

"I'm sorry." His face fell and he shook his head. His hands toying with the salt and pepper shakers.

I leaned in and smiled. "It's okay, I forgive you, and for the record Eli is not my boyfriend. If I was seeing someone, don't you think I would have told my best friend?"

He shrugged. "I guess."

"But I think you owe Eli an apology. I'd hate for him to think my best friend is a grumpy jealous ogre," I said with a giggle. My eye caught Harriet as she stopped by the entry to chat with Mercer. Tyler smiled and the tension hanging over the table evaporated. "My lunch break is almost over. If I'm late, Aunt Edie will not be impressed. I know she wants to work out a plan of action to help clear Vivienne's name."

"Let me know if you need any help? I may not be able to cast spells like you or Aunt Edie or shift into an animal like Jordi, but no-one is better when it comes to computers than me."

"Thanks. I may take you up on that," I said, sliding my purse back into my handbag. "We'll catch up later, okay?"

"Definitely."

Harriet's voice rattled on and on about her upcoming hair appointment as we walked back to The Melting Pot four streets away. The details of the last twenty-four hours were having an all-out war fighting for place on honour in my mind.

Why did someone want Camille Dead? Harriet is a witch? Is Vivienne involved? If not, why frame her for murder? If yes…no way she would never stoop to murder…Eli's sexy singing voice…Tyler's very hot new buff body…Anyone would think I haven't had a date in a while. They'd be right.

I stepped onto the road and my head shot up at the blaring sound of a car horn. Searing fire ignited my forearm and I gasped. My vision blurred as Harriet yanked me clear of an inevitable collision.

Her hand squeezed my forearm tight. "Oh my God, are you okay? Do you have a death wish or something? Did you not see the lights turn green?"

I blinked several times, my hazy surroundings finally coming into focus. "Um, sorry. My mind was away with the fairies."

Harriet released my arm and I glanced at the growing red mark where her hand once was.

"I'm sorry. I didn't mean to grab you so hard, but I'd rather not have a squished best friend if it's all the same to you."

"Thanks. I owe you," I said, giving her a hug.

The green walk light flicked on and Harriet threaded her arm through mine and we stepped out on the cross walk together.

"Let's just make it back in one piece and I'll be happy. What were you thinking about anyway? I'm guessing you didn't hear a word I said."

I shrugged. "No, sorry, my mind was jam-packed with the events of the last twenty-four hours. I was trying to make sense of Camille's murder and why someone would want to frame Vivienne for it."

Best not to mention Eli or Tyler were floating around in there too. It's probably just my body reminding me my biological clock is ticking. Wait, I'm only twenty-three, my biological clock can take a hike for at least five years.

"I don't get it either. Why Vivienne?" Harriet said, opening the door to The Melting Pot. "If only I knew how to focus my powers to see the future I could help somehow."

"Give it time. You will. It's all still very new for you. We'll work on some focusing techniques Aunt Edie taught me." I followed Harriet inside and did a double take. "I would have come back earlier if I'd known it was this busy." I turned to Harriet and asked, "Can you clear the dirty dishes off the tables and pop them in the kitchen and I'll get to them after the rush?"

She nodded and I hurried to the counter. Throwing my bag underneath, I put my witch hat back on and pushed my sleeves up above my elbows. "Aunt Edie, why didn't you ring me if it was this busy? I would have come back sooner."

"No need," Eli said, walking from the kitchen with a tray of chocolate brownies for the display

126

cabinet. "I was in the neighbourhood and was happy to lend a hand."

Why do I run into this man everywhere I go?

"Sweetheart, I would have called you had Eli not been here." Aunt Edie took another order for two strong black Witches Brews and gave the woman her change and table number. "But I won't say no to you jumping on the coffee machine and catching up on the orders and delivering these two Witches Brews."

"Say no more." I shuffled past Eli and Aunt Edie and began working.

"Strong." She added with a grin and I nodded.

Aunt Edie stopped Harriet before she had a chance to go collect more dirty dishes off the tables. "Harriet love, I was hoping you might help me out by wrapping some more cutlery in napkins, we seem to be all out."

"Sure thing." Harriett shrugged and a huge smile donned her face. "Just point me in the direction and I'll get to it."

I stuck to the coffee machine. Harriet hid herself away in the corner out of sight behind the supply cupboard and wrapped cutlery. Aunt Edie dealt with the food orders, and Eli took over the counter. Things ran like clockwork for the next thirty minutes until I spied Harriet shrunk down in her chair waving her arms frantically trying to get my attention.

What is with her? She's either practicing a new interpretative dance or she's about to burst a blood vessel.

I squinted but trying to lip read Harriet's words was out of the question. All I could decipher was 'Tea are sweetness old tin the hair.' If it was secret code, it was lost on me.

I wiped my coffee stained hands on a pumpkin hand towel and grabbed a tray of clean forks. "I'm just going to pop these over to Harriet." Not waiting for an objection, I scooted across the room and into the empty chair beside her. "What is wrong with you?"

Harriet made a shushing sound with her finger to her lips.

I whispered. "Are you having a fit or something? You look like a deranged monkey flapping your arms around."

She rolled her eyes to the roof and pursed her lips. "Don't be ridiculous. I am not having a fit, nor am I a deranged monkey." Her eyes widened like she was about to share her deepest darkest secret with the world. "But do I have gossip for you that could change the world as we know it."

Who doesn't love gossip? My pulse sped up and I just about shot out of the chair. Keeping my voice low, I whispered, "Well, come on, out with it. Don't keep me hanging."

Harriet shuffled in her chair dragging the suspense out. "I was sitting here minding my own business wrapping cutlery as instructed when the two ladies on the other side of the supply cabinet started chatting and I couldn't help but overhear. I didn't mean to and they probably thought no-one would hear them."

"What are you talking about?"

"Wait for it…Camille…" She paused and she looked left, then right and behind, her head practically spinning in circles to check for eavesdroppers.

"Camille, what?" I asked, tapping my fingernails on the table.

"According to the two ladies behind me, Camille is…was…a witch and I bet they're witches too, otherwise how would they know?"

How indeed?

CHAPTER EIGHT

I froze and blinked several times, relieving the dryness in my eyes. Harriet sat, pleased as punch with her discovery.

"Well?" she said, her eyes bulging. "Camille was a witch and not a single person in Saltwater Cove knew about it."

"There may have been one person who knew…the murderer."

"The murderer?" Harriet paled and her shoulders slouched. "Maybe her murder had nothing to do with her being a witch."

"Maybe. Did they say anything else witch like?"

She shrugged and half nodded. "Possibly. They were talking about Camille's obsession with finding the truth and how it got her killed. They were hoping to step in where Camille left off before word reaches the other members of the Elder Flame."

No way! Members of the Elder Flame here...in Saltwater Cove and Camille Stenson was one of them?

My thoughts spun and a rush of light-headedness swept over me.

"Woah," I said, my hands holding firm to each side of my head to stop it exploding. If I wasn't sitting down, I'd fall down. My voice raspy, I asked, "Are you sure they said Elder Flame?"

Harriet nodded. "Positive. What is Elder Flame?"

Goosebumps slid along the base of my neck. "Only one of the most powerful witch covens in history."

Harriet's jaw dropped and the sparkle in her eye held a million questions. She mouthed, "O-M-G."

I rubbed my creased forehead. "Aunt Edie will want to know, but we have to be sure." My mind raced and a strategy slotted into place with each passing second.

"What do we do now?" Harriet asked.

"I don't think we can do much until your information is confirmed one way or another." If they are witches, then what better place to hide than in a witch themed café."

"Genius, right?" Harriet agreed. "Maybe we should just ask them?"

Sure, that'll work. Excuse me, my friend was eavesdropping on your conversation and we were wondering if you ladies are witches from the Elder Flame Coven? They'd probably run straight to the insane department of the Saltwater Memorial Hospital and have me committed.

"I'm not sure coming straight out with it is the best way, but I have an idea." I pushed the clean forks off the tray and onto the table. "Can you go and tell Aunt Edie what you heard, and I will be over as soon as I clear their table of dirty dishes."

Harriet's eyebrows squished together. "Um…clean their table?"

"Trust me," I said with a wink.

I picked up the tray and stood tall, rolling my shoulders back. Plastering on my best sweet and innocent smile, I headed for the table in question. They didn't look like witches, but then all witches don't walk around with black and orange striped stockings, a pointy hat, and a broom. That's just *my* work uniform. They look more like two country bumpkins with their mixture of taupe cowboy boots, plaid shirts, and faded denim jeans. Their outfits would be more suited to a rodeo.

I sucked in a shaky breath and willed the mass of butterflies in my stomach to quieten. I slid my tray onto the side of their table and started stacking their empty dishes.

"Afternoon ladies, I hope everything was to your satisfaction?"

The woman on my left raised her head and looked at me. A sharp intake of breath paused my actions mid-movement. Her black eyes momentarily paralysed me before she broke into a huge smile. "It was perfect, my dear. The food here is absolutely delightful, isn't it, Olive? My compliments to the chef."

I drew back, unnerved by the depth of blackness in the woman's eyes but continued to clear their empty dishes.

"Oh definitely," Olive said, delicately dabbing each end of her lips with a serviette then discarding it to the side. "It was the best chicken pot pie I've ever tasted."

I smiled. "I'll make sure I give your compliments to the chef. Are you interested in dessert, ladies? We have a special menu with a selection of delicious treats that might appeal to your heightened senses more than our standard cake range. One would say it's a magical selection."

Both ladies paused and looked at each other suspiciously. Now was my moment to strike. The butterflies in my stomach had quadrupled. I conveniently edged my tray further onto the table knocking Olive's discarded serviette sending it tumbling to the floor.

"Oh my gosh, how clumsy of me," I said, my hand clutched at my chest. "I'm so sorry."

The woman opposite Olive brushed her hand through the air. "Never mind, accidents happen." Olive bent down to retrieve her fallen serviette from the floor.

My gaze glued to the back of her neck and the blood froze in my veins. Unable to move, I stood there like a marble statue staring. Oh my God, Harriet was right. They are witches of the Elder Flame Coven. The intricate tattoo at the base of her neck proved it. I made a slow 'O' action while my mind blanked and all thoughts of what to do or say vanished.

"It's all right, Evelyn," said the woman to my right. "I'm sure our presence has come as a bit of a shock, but you really should breathe. We wouldn't want you passing out on us."

Breathe? Yes, breathing is good.

My chest burned desperately for air. It rose and fell with each long intake of breath. My voice quivered but worked all the same.

"You called me, Evelyn? Do we know each other? Have we met before?"

"Not yet, but we've known of you for a while now. My name is Aubrey Garcia," she said with a quaint nod, her golden curly locks gracing her shoulder. "And this is my sister, Olive."

I turned to the woman opposite and she gave me a gracious nod.

Aubrey continued, her voice sung in my ears calming my rampaging butterflies. "Judging by your reaction to Olive's tattoo, the cat is out of the bag so to speak. We were hoping you and your aunt might help us?"

"Help you? But you're members of the Elder Flame Coven, how can we help *you*?"

She squinted and pursed her lips in a thin line. "News obviously doesn't travel as fast in Saltwater Cove as it does in other parts of the world. We go by the Elder Flame now. We dropped the Coven from the title."

The tension fell away from my shoulders as the conversation took a casual turn.

"Really…why? I've always known the Elder Flame Coven to be the most powerful. Aunt Edie loved to tell me of your adventures and daring escapes."

Olive huffed and sat back in her chair, shaking her head. "Exactly. Do you know how hard it is to keep up that image 24/7? It's exhausting and some of us aren't exactly getting any younger. The new youthful members have so much vibrancy and tenacity we could see the future was with them, not us old fuddy-duddies. When we mentioned our retirement to the witches within the coven they decided, with our blessing, to keep the Elder Flame Coven going. But they wanted it under a new progressive title so they decided to drop the 'Coven' from the title and we decided to retire and take some time for ourselves."

"Retire? New name?" The words blurted from my lips louder than I expected.

A familiar arm eased around my waist and I turned to see Aunt Edie smiling at me. "Is everything okay, Evelyn?"

"I…we…yes…no…they…um…sure." The words jumbled in my mind. I wanted to scream, *How the hell can everything be okay when members of the most powerful coven decided to retire because life is too tough. Oh, and now it's a new progressive coven, minus the word coven. By the way Camille was a witch and belonged to said coven. Surprise.'*

Aunt Edie kept her smile targeted on me and her thoughts answered mine while the two ladies sat watching the silent interaction between us. *'It's okay, love. Harriet told me, and everything will work out. I promise.'*

'How can it be okay? Camille was a witch and a member of the Elder Flame Coven which is apparently not a coven anymore because these ladies in front of us want to retire. Can a witch even retire?'

Before Aunt Edie had a chance to answer, Olive interjected. "Edith Grayson, I am Olive Garcia and this is my sister, Aubrey. I have to say what a thrill to meet you in person. Camille, rest her soul, told us many stories about The Melting Pot and we knew if we ever came to Saltwater Cove this would be our first stop. I just wish it was under better circumstances."

Aubrey's vacant expression met Olive's words. Who was Camille to these ladies?

Aunt Edie nodded. "The afternoon rush has gone and I'm sure Eli can hold the fort for a while. Why don't you join us next door in our home, where the real magic happens?"

'Are you sure about this, Aunt Edie?'

A slight shiver ran up my arms and down my back. My gaze caught Aunt Edie's and she read my thoughts instantly.

'Absolutely, love.'

My mind was racing with excuses.

'But what about Eli? We can't leave him here by himself.'

'Eli will be fine. The lunch rush is over which leaves coffee and cakes and he's a wiz on the coffee machine.'

Both ladies stood and picked up their bags.

"Lead the way," Olive said, a little too cheerful.

Was it me or have I dropped out of reality into an alternate universe?

Harriet and I stood off to the side of the kitchen and watched Aunt Edie make herbal tea for our two esteemed guests. My mouth watered at the addictive aroma of lemongrass and ginger. They chatted and laughed and chatted some more. It was surreal in a bizarre kind of way.

My stomach clenched and I leaned in toward Harriet and whispered, "Is this at all strange to you, watching two witches of their status chatting with Aunt Edie like they've known each other for years?"

"I think it's positively wonderful." Her silly grin forced a cute dimple in her right cheek. "To think, two days ago I was a normal dull twenty-three-year-old looking at a boring life ahead of me, and now, I'm a new witch standing in my best friend's kitchen watching two witches from one of the most notable covens drinking herbal tea with Aunt Edie. Who would have thought?"

"Yeah, who would have thought? I see you skipped over the whole murder and finding Camille's body in that description."

"I didn't skip over it, I chose to address the positives," Harriet said, grinning.

She had taken to the witch world better than I anticipated.

"You know, I have to say I thought you'd freak out a little more."

She turned her emerald eyes on me and squinted. "What? Watching this historic moment?"

"No, silly." I giggled and shoved my shoulder up against hers. "Finding out you're a witch."

A huge grin broke out across her face that spoke to my heart.

"It was the best news I could have hoped for and I know I have a lot to learn and there will be training involved, but I always felt like the odd one out when it came to us three girls. You and Jordi have these extraordinary powers and here's little old me, a nobody."

"You were—" The knowing glint in her eye cut my words dead.

"You know what I mean. It was like I finally found my home and I want to embrace my new-found future with open arms and an open heart."

I glanced at Harriet and her eyes sparkled with unshed tears. My throat grew thick and I swallowed hard fighting back my own tears. "You're a dag, you know that?"

Harriet giggled and shrugged. "I know. But you love me."

"You bet your arse I do." We both fell into fits of laughter only to be scolded a moment later.

"If you two ladies are quite finished with your jibber-jabbing," Aunt Edie said, moving to the table. "Aubrey would like to fill us in on the missing pieces regarding Camille."

I wiped the moisture from my eyes and joined them, dragging Harriet along for the ride. Sitting around the table, the energy electrified the hairs on my arms. Aubrey placed her bone china teacup down on the saucer and paused, her gaze gliding from one to the other as if reading our minds. Maybe she was.

Aunt Edie spoke in a serene tone and smiled at Harriet. "I've explained to Aubrey and Olive about our newest recruit here and like Evelyn, I could not be more pleased to have her by my side."

"Thank you," Harriet said, all clogged up with emotion.

Aubrey took a breath and laced her fingers together around her china cup. "Ladies, it is of the utmost importance the real reason for Camille's presence in Saltwater Cove be kept secret."

Real reason?

"She was in town for one reason and one reason only…to find her sister's killer."

The air stilled and an icy chill caught my breath. Silence crushed the positive energy that existed a moment ago. Lost for words, I sat there absorbing each word Aubrey uttered.

She continued, her tone void of emotion. "I'm sure you weren't expecting me to be so upfront, but time is of the essence and we need to move on Camille's evidence before the trail gets overshadowed with her murder."

My brow creased. "Evidence?"

Olive placed a hand on Aubrey's forearm and a silent message passed between them before she spoke.

"The four of us had made the decision to retire, myself, Aubrey, Camille and her sister, Cynthia. She was the High Priestess. Cynthia was the one everyone held in awe. The one you measured yourself up to. The one everyone aspired to be. Stunningly beautiful, inside, and out. On our last night as official members of the coven we held a small celebration. Cynthia hadn't turned up. Camille went to look for her and stumbled across her lifeless body in the garden outside her house. The blood had been drained from her body leaving her skin pasty white. She lay peacefully with her arms crossed over her heart, dressed in a white lace gown, and surrounded by crimson rose petals. It held all the visuals of a sacrifice."

Aunt Edie gasped. "A sacrifice? Good lord."

"Are you sure?" I asked. I pressed the palm of my hand against the sharp pain in my sternum. The mere thought of a human sacrifice sickened me to the core.

What kind of human would do that to a woman? Maybe it wasn't a human at all, but something much more sinister.

"No-one can ever be sure when it comes to magic, but yes, we think so and Camille's murder confirms our suspicions."

A momentary pause stilled the air sending chills down my spine.

"All leads on Cynthia's murder led to Saltwater Cove, but then it all went dead," Olive said. "Camille insisted she go undercover. She made us promise if something ever happened to her, we would stop at nothing to find the truth."

"We weren't happy about it." Aubrey huffed and shook her head. "Camille has never been one to fit in and play nice. She wouldn't think twice about putting even the nicest people in their place, but deep down she did have a heart of gold. Showing it was the issue."

Aubrey added. "Yes, deep, deep down."

"I know this is a difficult time." Aunt Edie's reassuring smile cracked the tension hanging like a low storm cloud over the table. "But you will get through it and we're all here to help you anyway we can."

"Absolutely," Harriet said with a confirming nod.

"Thank you," Aubrey said, a cherry red blush warming her cheeks. "Camille spoke so highly of you all."

I eased back in my chair, the weight of Aubrey's words weighing heavy on my heart. My arms dropped into my lap and tension gripped me chest. No matter how I willed my eyes to look at the two women before me, my gaze glued to my hands planted squarely in my lap.

I'm sorry, Camille. I'm so sorry I was ever rude to you. I promise I will find your murderer if it's the last thing I do.

"Olive and I will gladly accept any help we can get. We have two murders to solve and stop a murderer in their tracks before the body count increases."

Aunt Edie cleared her throat knocking the stray thoughts from my mind in a snap. "Right, where should we start?"

Olive and Aubrey exchanged an odd glance. There it was again. The same look Aunt Edie has when she pops into my mind without warning. I'm not imagining it. I swear they can talk to each other or I'm not a graduate witch. Only one way to find out.

"I hope this is not too forward, but are you able to read each other's minds?"

"You're very perceptive, dear," Aubrey said, eloquently sipping her tea. "We certainly can."

"Wow, that totally rocks socks," Harriet blurted, bouncing her butt on her chair. "Can you read my thoughts?"

"Oh Harriet," I said, cringing and slapping a hand to my forehead. "You sure do know how to break the tension. Promise me you'll never change?"

A familiar cheeky grin I'd come to know so well gleamed at me across the table.

"Promise." She turned her eager gaze on Aubrey. "So, can you read my mind? Because I'm thinking something that no-one knows but Evelyn and me and if it were to come out, I think she'd kill me."

My jaw dropped. "What on earth are you talking about?"

Aubrey shook her head ignoring Harriet's badly timed attempt at humour. "No, we were only blessed with reading each other's thoughts."

I politely placed my hands down on the table and forced a smile. "I think we're getting a little off track here. Let's not forget we have a murderer on the loose in Saltwater Cove. I think finding out what Camille knew should be our priority."

"Agreed." Aubrey and Olive said in perfect unison. "Camille wasn't overly open with her findings. She said she didn't want to get our hopes up until she has concrete evidence. She did mention that she had the evidence under lock and key, wherever that may be."

Harriet clicked her fingers and gasped. "Oh my God, I've got it. Camille was a very secretive person. There can only be two places, her office at the bank or her house. I say we start with her office and even though it's closed, I have a key and I can go in this afternoon. If I'm caught I'll say that I came in to clean up so that Mr Bain didn't have to do it when he gets back. I'm sure Detective Huxton has finished at the bank and since I was Camille's assistant, it wouldn't be unusual for me to be in her office."

Olive raised an eyebrow in Aunt Edie's direction. "Detective?"

"Yes, Micah Huxton is the detective in charge of Camille's case and a good friend," Aunt Edie said, her matter-of-fact tone clearly meant to hide her emotional attachment to the man. Like that worked.

"And?" I goaded her, hoping she'd spill the beans.

"And." She paused, tucking in her upper lip, her gaze pierced my chest like a double-edged sword. "And he's a Leodian."

Wrong beans. I meant the ones where you still have feelings for the guy.

"Goodness me, a Leodian?" Aubrey said, eyeing Olive. "That is a stroke in our favour. Can he be trusted?"

Aunt Edie spoke without hesitation. "Absolutely. I would trust him with my life."

How about your heart?

Harriet frowned. "What is a Leodian?"

"Simply put, a Leodian is a witch who can read the past life of an object," I said.

Harriet's brow wrinkled and she scratched her temple. She grabbed the saltshaker and held it up. "What…like he can read the life of this saltshaker?"

"Not exactly," said Aunt Edie, replacing the saltshaker on the table. "When a Leodian touches a certain object, it can show a vision or a scene if you will, involving that object. For instances, if he was to hold that old picture of a tea garden on my wall over there." All eyes followed Aunt Edie's pointed finger. "He may see this scene right now or he may see something to do with the picture prior to me buying it. Although every Leodian's powers differ and as for Micah's, I am not exactly sure how his work."

"Wow." Harriet sighed and slapped her forehead. "I have so much to learn."

Aunt Edie patted her hand. "All in good time, love."

I looked at Aubrey and bit my bottom lip. Was it the right time to ask a personal question? If Camille knew my mother, maybe they do to.

"Is something else bothering you, Evelyn?" Olive asked.

My gut was telling me to speak up, but the pesky niggle in the back of my mind kept my lips sealed. I shook my head.

"If it's all the same with you, the longer we sit here the more time the police have to pin this murder on Vivienne. I say Harriet and I pop over to the bank as she suggested and see what we can find out."

"Splendid." Aubrey clapped her hands together. "Olive and I will go over to Camille's house and see what we can find."

Harriet frowned. Her expression resembled Aunt Edie's classic pondering look. "Are you sure that's wise? We wouldn't want the wrong person to see you. They may think you've broken into Camille's house."

"Pfft. Don't worry, they won't," Aubrey said, picking up her bag. "Olive can whip us in and out in the blink of an eye. Literally."

"Oh stop." Olive blushed and swished her hand mid-air casually dismissing Aubrey's comment. "Aubrey loves using my relocation spell to jump from place to place. I just think she hates the exercise."

"Except in this case it's necessary," Aubrey snapped.

Aunt Edie stood. "Why don't you ladies join us for dinner tonight?"

Aubrey's eyes softened and a warm glow radiated across the table. "Oh, what a lovely offer. Camille did say your food is some of the best she'd ever tasted, but we couldn't impose."

"No imposition at all, we'd love to have you join us. It will give us time to catch up on developments of the case and a chance for me to practice some new dishes I have planned for tomorrow night's Halloween dinner at the Melting Point. While you're out, I'll make a call to Micah and see if he can update me on any new developments from his end."

"In that case we'd love to," Aubrey said, standing up.

Aunt Edie followed our guests to the door. "How does seven sound?"

Olive squeezed Aunt Edie in a hug. "Perfect. See you all then."

"Bye," I called, followed by a warm farewell by Harriet.

"Well, that is a bit of good news if I do say so myself," Aunt Edie said, manoeuvring her way around the table and chairs. "If they can help clear Vivienne's name, I'm all for it."

I nodded and turned to Harriet and smiled. "Do you think you could go and check on Eli and see if he's doing okay? He's been next door by himself for a while now. Aunt Edie and I'll be there in a few minutes, I just have to take care of something first."

"Is everything all right?" she asked, an edge of concern to her question.

I rolled my eyes. "Of course, silly. I just want to run something by Aunt Edie."

She shrugged. "Sure, no problem. See you later, Aunt Edie," she called over her shoulder then trotted off through the door.

"Bye love." Aunt Edie stood, arms folded across her chest with her head tilted to the side. Her classic I'm-waiting-and-not-moving-until-you-spill pose. "Mm...take care of something?"

Before I lost my nerve, I dove straight in. "More like a question than anything else. The morning grumpy Camille turned into cheery Camille after eating one of your happy candies she said she never seemed to tell me enough how beautiful I was, just like my mother. How could she know my mother if Camille has only been in town six months?"

Aunt Edie's arms dropped and her eyes tightened. "She did?"

I nodded, my belly as tight as a nun's coif. "Yes, and I never got a chance to ask her. You had more interactions with Camille than me. Had she mentioned anything to you about knowing mum?"

"I had no idea. No, she's never mentioned her to me." Aunt Edie began her routine pacing cupping an elbow in one hand and tapping her lips with the other.

"What do you suppose it means?"

She stopped and her posture straightened. "I can't be sure, but now we know Camille was a witch of the Elder Flame Coven, it could mean a number of things. I suggest we ask Aubrey and Olive tonight. Let's hope they can give us some answers."

"You read my mind."

Aunt Edie let loose a warm, hearty laugh. "Not this time I didn't."

"Ha-ha, you are a funny one, aren't you?" I turned and grabbed my keys and bag off the counter. "If you'll excuse me, Harriet and I have an appointment with an empty bank."

CHAPTER NINE

I took six steps into the darkened bank and the stillness was more deafening than excited fans cheering a football match. I'd parked the car two streets down and we'd come in the side entrance, on Harriet's request. She insisted it would pose less chance of anyone seeing us since the door was disguised by overgrown Hydrangea bushes. The hazy glow of the emergency exit lights cast unnerving people-like shadows across the main floor. I shivered and goose bumps shot up my arms sending the hairs on the back of my neck to attention.

A scraping high-pitched sound grated on my nerves and sent shivers through me. "Aw, what was that?" I turned and squinted at the fresh rays of sunlight streaming through the window.

"Oops, sorry. I should have warned you," Harriet said. "I've been asking Mr Bain for a while now to get the curtain rods oiled. It makes that God-awful sound every time I open them."

Harriet grabbed my arm and dragged me through the staff barrier to the right of Della's desk and around hers toward Camille's office.

"Aw," I said, tugging my arm free from her grip. "I think I know the way to Camille's office. I may not have been in it, but I do know where it is located. This isn't my first time in the bank."

Harriet stopped and turned. "I'm sorry. I'm just so excited to be on my first secret mission as a witch," she said, barely able to stand still. She looked so adorable shuffling from one foot to another as if she had ants in her pants. I squeezed my lips together so the laugh barrelling up from my belly wouldn't escape.

We continued toward the back of the bank. Her bronzed bob bouncing with each step. "Tell me, how many secret missions have you been on…before you were a witch, I mean?"

"I haven't *really* been on any secret missions. I was just making a point." She huffed. Spinning on her heel, she stood with her hands on her hips. A suspicious glare pointing straight at me. "That is, unless you count the time in the eighth grade when you insisted on me sending secret love notes to Gabriel Maxwell pretending to be you."

I gasped and my jaw dropped. Heat flamed through my cheeks. "I can't believe you brought him up. It was the eighth grade for goodness' sake. I plead adolescence stupidity. Can we continue with doing what we came here to do? Search Camille's office."

I followed Harriet as she led the way. The distant memory of Gabriel Maxwell's rejection was a slap to my ego. Thank God his family left Saltwater Cove at the end of that year. But that didn't stop Prudence from rubbing my nose in it every chance she got.

"I can't believe the police left her office unlocked," Harriet said as she turned the doorknob and slid the door open, stepping inside Camille's office.

Neither can I. Detective Huxton is way too thorough to leave the door unlocked. Which leaves only two other possibilities I can think of. One, a policeman on the investigation left it unlocked...and two, another person has been in here after the police left and before we got here. But why and how did they get in?

I glanced toward the back door and bit the inside of my cheek. Harriet used her key to get in and there was no evidence of tampering, so they obviously didn't come in that way. Different scenarios ticked over in my mind as I searched the bank for possible entry points. It only leaves the front door. I made a mental note to check it on the way out. The quirky voice of Tones and I blared from my bag and my heart catapulted into the back of my throat.

"Oh my God."

"Are you all right?" Harriet asked as she moved to the other side of the office.

My hand flattened against my chest, my heartbeat wildly drumming my palm. "Sure, my head was a million miles away. Remind me next time we're on a secret mission to turn my phone on silent." I rummaged around in my bag searching for the incessant noise.

"Hello."

I stepped into Camille's office and froze as the picture before me rendered me speechless. I'd been transported back to Edwardian times as if I was standing in the office of George Bernard Shaw. A spectacular red oak desk filled the centre of the room with two matching wooden chairs occupying the customer spots. Camille's chair, a larger more sophisticated version with a plush green cushioned seat. A matching filing cabinet stood against the wall to the right and a long wall unit occupied the back wall topped with an impressive collection of books. Beautiful floral curtains adorned the windows either side of the wall unit. Open just enough the let a stream of afternoon sun light our way.

"Evie girl. What'cha up to on this fine Friday afternoon?"

It was the poshest office I've ever stepped into. Nothing like the ultra-modern décor of the rest of the bank.

"Evie? Evelyn, are you there?" Tyler barked, snapping me out of my daydream.

I cleared my throat. "Ah, yeah, course I'm here. What's up?"

"I was just ringing to see what you were up to this afternoon and to see if you wanted to grab a drink at The Four Brothers." He paused. "We've a lot of catching up to do."

"Yeah, we do." I watched Harriet siphon through the trays on Camille's desk, and not too carefully either. The last thing we need is her boss complaining to the police that they've had a break in. "Um, listen Tyler, I have to go. A drink sounds great. Why don't I swing by and pick you up in about an hour?"

"Evie, you don't sound like yourself today. Is everything okay? You not doing something dangerous, are you?"

Dangerous? Me...never.

I could imagine my nose getting longer with each lie giving Pinocchio a run for his money. "Of course not, as if. I'll see you in an hour. Okay?"

"Okay."

I hung up before he could get another word out. Shoving my phone back in my bag, I dropped it on one of the customer chairs.

"Harriet, wait a minute."

She stooped mid-shuffle. "Why? What's the problem?"

"I know you work here, and this may not be the first time you've been in Camille's office, but it is the first time after the police have been here. Do you really want it to look like an intruder has been ferreting about in her stuff? What do you think Mr Bain will say when he returns tomorrow?"

She straightened and looked around at her handy work, her brow wrinkled. "I hadn't thought of that. No problem, it won't take me long to fix it up." She flitted around straightening papers and adjusting the document trays on the desk and then stood back grinning with her arms wide open. "Good as new. No-one would ever know we were here."

I smiled. "Oh Harriet, you do keep things interesting. Okay, let's keep looking, but make sure you put everything back where you found it afterwards."

Harriet nodded, and we went to work lifting papers, checking documents, moving trinkets and office supplies searching for a lead.

"Tell me, how come Camille's office is filled with all this antique Edwardian furniture?" I asked Harriet as I sifted through another drawer. "It looks amazing, but it's so different to the rest of the bank."

Harriet shrugged. "When she arrived, I remember her and Mr Bain chatting, and she said she couldn't possibly take the job unless her office was one of style and sophistication. She offered to pay for it and arrange removalists herself."

"Really? What did Mr Bain have to say about that?"

"Yep." She nodded and began riffling through another cupboard. "He was pretty cool about it. The next day we came in to find she'd moved this entire office in overnight."

"Overnight? I'm guessing there was a little magic involved."

Harriet stopped mid-shuffle and glanced my way. "I always did wonder how she managed to do it so quickly. Now I know."

Thirty minutes later and still nothing. I ran a hand through my hair and let out an agonising groan. Half from frustration and half out of hunger. "This is pointless. Camille was meticulous at keeping everything in order. No post-it notes, no random names or numbers, no leads anywhere. Just all official banking stuff."

Harriet threw her hands up in the air and flopped into Camille's chair. "I know the only place I haven't looked is the filing cabinet, but it's locked."

"What are you talking about? I thought you checked it. You were searching that side of the room," I said, shaking my head.

"Na-ah. How am I supposed to look inside if I don't have a key?"

"I assumed you found it." Harriet shook her head and a sliver of guilt worked its way into my gut. So far, we've yielded nothing, zero, zilch. If we go back empty handed, they're sure to pin this crime on Vivienne.

I walked over to the filing cabinet and placed one hand on top of the cabinet and the other about six inches above the lock. I glued my eyes to the lock and the tips of my fingers began to tingle like a rush of pins and needles. "What once was under lock and key, with this spell I now set free. Once done with it then let it be, return it under lock and key."

I held my hands still as a rainbow of glittery sparkles danced around my fingers and over the lock of the filing cabinet. A sharp click pierced the air as the lock disengaged. There are advantages to being a witch.

"That is totally cool," Harriet said, rushing over, her eyes glowing with intrigue. "I love watching your magic in action."

I gently eased the top drawer of the filing cabinet open and caught Harriet's wide-eyed stare. Full of expanding files jam-packed with papers. "If Camille was hiding anything it's sure to be in here. Keep your eyes peeled for anything out of the ordinary."

Harriet nodded and I thumbed through file after file. The edge of an expanding file sliced my index finger and I let out a sharp gasp pausing the search.

"Aw, damn it," I said sucking the blood on the end on my throbbing finger. I stared evil daggers at the offending file. Why are the files laying down flat? Shouldn't files be standing up in a filing cabinet? I stepped back and looked at the other two drawers. I pulled each out and sure enough, both drawers had files standing up. So why not the top drawer?

Oh, you are a clever woman, Camille.

"Evelyn, why are you grinning? We haven't found anything," Harriet asked with impatience.

"If I'm right, and I'm pretty sure I am, Camille was one smart cookie, I mean witch." Harriet's brow crinkled and I could imagine the clogs in her brain turning over out of control. "I pulled the top drawer open and pointed inside. "Look."

Harriet peered over the edge of the drawer at the flat files and shrugged. "So?"

"So…" I smiled, and it quickly turned into a grin. I was grinning like I'd just won first place at the Saltwater Cove karaoke competition. "Don't you get it? Why have two drawers with files that stand up and one that doesn't?"

Harriet stood there with a blank expression on her face clearly befuddled by my question. Maybe showing her would clear the air. I pulled out the top drawer again and grabbed several handfuls of files and placed them on the desk, Harriet watching intently. I grabbed the last one and stood it up in the second and then the third drawer and it slotted into place perfectly. I opened the top drawer and repeated the action this time the top of the file cleared the top rim of the drawer by at least five inches.

Harriet's jaw dropped and I squeezed my hands into fists. It was all I could do to stop myself reaching over and lifting her jaw back into place.

"Oh—my," she whispered.

I reached in and fiddled with the bottom. I knew it was a false bottom, but it was stuck in there pretty good. Camille was certainly hiding something.

I turned and searched for something sharp. I spied the perfect object taking pride of place next to the antique inkwell on Camille's desk.

"Hand me that letter opener, will you?" I asked, nodding in its direction.

Harriet sprang into action. I jammed the letter opener down the side of the false bottom and gave it one almighty shove. The side lifted up giving way to the real base of the filing cabinet. My eye caught the silver mirrored box hidden towards the back of the drawer. I gasped.

"What? What is it?" Harriet asked.

Her eyes lit up and her gaze locked on mine. I pointed to the box in the back of the drawer and my pulse sped up.

Harriet's gasp echoed mine. "Oh my God, you did it. This is so cool. You found the missing piece we've been looking for."

"Maybe…maybe not. For all we know it could hold her makeup." I withdrew the box from its nestled spot at the back of the drawer. The fading sun streaming through the window caught the edge of the box, shooting a rainbow of angled reflections across the room. Shades of purples, pinks and yellows melded together like a garden of tulips in full bloom on a warm spring morning. "Everything in this office has to do with the bank except this box."

"Come on, don't keep me in suspense," Harriet said, flicking her hands as if she were covered in water.

"Okay, calm down." I placed the box on Camille's desk and my pulse doubled. Please be the answer we're looking for. I eased the lid open and my shoulders slumped. I pinched the bridge of my nose. More papers.

Is this all the woman had…papers? At this rate Vivienne will be making pumpkin pies wearing an orange jumpsuit and a grungy hairnet.

"I don't believe it," Harriet said in a whisper, her tone bathed in hope.

My head snapped up. Harriet stood wide-eyed, her jaw dropped, staring at an open piece of paper in her hands. "What?"

"Just the best lead…ever." Excited, she flipped the paper and the words jumped off the page.

I grabbed her hand to keep it still while I read. My eyes read each word with painstaking precision.

If you think you can come into my town and take what's mine, think again. It'll be a cold day in hell before I let you win this battle. I know all about your little secret. If you don't keep your hands to yourself, I'll broadcast it all over Saltwater Cove on the nightly news and I'm sure with the spin I'll put on it, no-one is going to believe your story. You'll be run out of town for sure. Stay away, BITCH!

"Told you so. This has got to have something to do with her murder, right?" Harriet asked, grinning like she just won the lottery. She picked up a handful of similar letters secured with an elastic band. "And look there's more."

Warmth infused my body. "It sure looks like it, but we can't know for sure." I pulled out a bunch of post-it notes with dates written on them and one lonely name. Grand Majestic.

Harriet looked over my shoulder and muttered, "Grand Majestic? Hey, isn't that the old closed hotel on the way out of town, by the turn off to the abandoned geological site?"

I nodded and frowned scanning each note for some sort of connection. "Sure is. It was quite luxurious in its time."

What's with the dates on each post-it notes and how do they relate to the Grand Majestic, if at all?

"Bingo," Harriet called triumphantly. "If the name Jeffrey Allan and the words fraud and theft written underneath doesn't scream motive, I don't know what does?"

"What? Are you serious?" I said, investigating the dog-eared paper in Harriet's hand. Something didn't sit right. My gut churned, a dozen questions on the tip of my tongue. "Three possible leads in one box, could it be that easy?"

"Why not?" Harriet trotted over and placed her elbow on the top of the filing cabinet. "Don't forget, it was hidden away here under lock and key in a mirrored box that looks like it holds makeup. You wouldn't even know it was there unless you were looking. The police probably don't know it exists which is lucky for us."

"I suppose so." I swallowed, a mass of uncertainty pushing against the back of my throat.

"Camille was the loans officer, so maybe this Jeffrey Allan guy was trying to rip the bank off or something. It's a place to start, at least," Harriet said, reaching over to grab some files. "Here, best we get these back in place."

I placed the post-it notes and dog-eared paper back in the box with the blackmail letter and helped restack the drawer. Adrenaline pumped through my veins the more I thought about our find. A knot stuck in my belly teasing my conscious. I'm never one to turn away from a challenge especially when I can prove a dear friend innocent of murder.

"I think you're right, Harriet."

"I am?" she asked, passing me the second last pile of files.

"Yes, I'm not entirely convinced about the ease of finding three leads in one convenient location, but as you said, it does give us a place to start. Three places actually. We'll need to keep our eyes and ears open and our witch skills at the ready just in case we run into any unwelcome surprises." Slotting the last file back in its rightful place I closed the drawer and held my hands over the top, my fingertips twitching as the lock clicked back into place.

"Sounds good to me. Ah, damn it," she blurted in a huff.

I turned to see a generous smattering of blue ink sploshed over Harriet's pale blue pants and a horrified expression on her face. "What happened?"

"Damn inkwell," she said, frowning and examining her damaged outfit. "Camille is old school and she insisted on signing all her documents the old way with ink and quill. I guess it was the witch way in the Elder Flame Coven. This looks ridiculous."

"Stop," I yelled. I surprised myself with the high pitch of my voice. Harriet froze mid-wipe of a tissue now covered in blue ink. "Don't wipe it, you're just going to make it worse. You really need to change."

"No kidding. Just call me Harriet the bubbling buffoon," she said, her cheeks flushing a ruby red. Struggling to wipe the remainder of the ink from her hands she gave up and threw the stained tissue in the rubbish bin beside the desk. "This is never going to come out if I don't get to a washing machine soon."

I smiled, keeping my lips sealed.

I hate to be the one to tell you, but that is never *going to come out anyway.*

"You're meeting Tyler for a drink at The Four Brothers, right?"

I nodded.

"If you can drop me home on the way, I'll find something a little less clownish to wear and then you can pick me up on the way back to your place. It will give me time to throw this in the wash. And since I'll be staying in your house for a few more days, I'll grab a few more things to tide me over. What do you think?"

"Are you sure that's wise? Being by yourself I mean after yesterday's nightmare?" A rush of nausea wormed its way into my belly. The last thing I wanted to do was relive the event, but the image of Harriet sitting on my bed drenched in sweat, fear screaming from every pore of her body would forever be etched in my mind like an unwanted tattoo.

Her expression became guarded. "There will always be an element of danger, Evelyn. In my vision I didn't recognise the location, I only knew I'd never been there before. It wasn't familiar to me therefore it can't be my home, can it?"

I bit my bottom lip, Harriet' words doing their best to convince me. "I suppose not."

"It's settled then," she said, sliding the mirrored box into my bag and holding it out toward me.

Damn knots. Go the hell away.

I hiked the bag up on my shoulder and rubbed my aching stomach. "Are you sure?"

"Positive," she said, leading the way out of Camille's office and out the side door we entered through.

"Hey, can you wait a minute?" I said, placing a hand on Harriet's forearm. "I just want to check something out."

She shrugged. "Sure."

I darted toward the front door and examined the lock. No tampering. Now, I'm really confused.

"Is everything all right?" Harriet called from the side entrance.

I nodded and headed back to join her. "Yes, I just wanted to see if the lock had been tampered with."

"And had it?"

I shook my head. "Listen, I was thinking, why don't I wait for you and you can join Tyler and me at The Four Brothers," I said, pleased as punch with my suggestion. Keeping Harriet safe was equally as important as proving Vivienne innocent.

A flush crept across Harriet's cheeks and I swear she muffled a laugh. What is that all about?

"It's fine, truly. I'm not keen on being the third wheel. Besides, I need to wash these pants asap."

Harriet locked the side door behind us and looked each way to make sure the coast was clear before we headed back to the car. The temperature dropped. I pulled my jacket tighter and hugged my middle. Still, the cool afternoon breeze was strong enough to make the hairs on my arms stand to attention. A shiver pulverised my body. Beginning at the top of my head and ending at my toes. The kind of shiver you get when someone has walked over your grave.

"Third wheel? What are you talking about?" I said, jumping in the car and roaring the engine to life.

"He's been away for a long time and I just reckon he wants some alone time with you, that's all."

Alone time with me? Surely, she didn't mean what I think she meant? We were friends and that's all. Even though he does look like a sexy super model. F-R-I-E-N-D-S.

My pulse raced and a steaming hot flush hit me. I wiped my brow and sat tall tossing my hair off my face.

"You are a real comedian today, aren't you? Alone time at the local pub, as if. One can never be alone at The Four Brothers." I drove, my eyes trained to the road. Harriet's words droned on like clanging symbols in my head.

CHAPTER TEN

I reversed out of Harriet's driveway and headed toward Tyler's house east of the church on the other side of town. Harriet's ad hoc comment regarding Tyler was now neatly compartmentalised in the deep recesses on my mind. Protecting those I loved most and proving Vivienne's innocence was my number one focus.

My only focus.

Where to start? I could, of course go to the police and declare what we discovered and ask for their help. But then I'd have to confess to using magic to open the filing cabinet and I'm sure that'll go down like a lead balloon.

I pulled up at Tyler's house and killed the engine. The answer was staring me in the face.

"Or I can use what I have at my disposal to solve the puzzle. The mystery of Jeffrey Allan." A stroke of genius, on my part.

I don't know what happened in Nepal to change Tyler's appearance or why he came back looking like a pumped Hugh Jackman in his Wolverine years. He's still my favourite nerd with spiffing computer skills that would rival any top-notch hacker. He used to be able to find information even the best police geek couldn't manage. Let's hope I can convince him to use his talents to help clear Vivienne's name.

Energy buzzed through my body and I jumped out practically skipping up his front stairs. The door swung open and I paused catching my breath. I inhaled deeply, soaking up the picture of divine goodness standing before me in a white polo shirt and brown chinos. Sexy nerd alert. Shaking my head, I cursed. Where were my thoughts headed, anyway?

Damn it, why does he have to look good enough to eat. Focus, focus on your goal.

"Evie, girl, aren't you a sight for sore eyes?" he said, play punching my stomach. "I'm ready. I just have to lock the back door."

Typical Tyler. I pushed past him and headed inside. "Actually, change of plans. I was hoping I could convince you to help me with a little problem."

His brow creased and his eyes narrowed. "What kind of problem? You're not in any kind of trouble, are you?"

"Pfft, no." I giggled and my stomach dropped as the omission flowed from my lips. "At least not yet, but the day's far from over. I'm sure I can find some given half a chance."

"Same old Evie," he said. A huge grin lit up his face as he ruffled the top of my hair like I was his twelve-year-old sister.

Ew, not cool at all. A shudder snaked up my spine. That would mean I was salivating over my older brother. My attraction to the new and improved Tyler began to lose its appeal.

"What do you need?" he asked.

I sat my bag on the kitchen table and fished out the mirrored box. "Harriet and I stumbled across this box of Camille's with some interesting information and I was hoping you might be able to help me track down a lead with your whiz-bang computer skills."

Tyler straightened his back and folded his arms across his chest. His pursed lips and glaring eyes were enough to make me break out in hives.

His tone was stern and commanding. "Stumbled? And just how did you 'stumble' across it?"

"Okay, fine. We found it in Camille's office."

His arms dropped and his eyes widened. "You what? What were you doing in Camille's office? Isn't the bank closed? Did you break in?"

The sharp tone in his voice grated on my nerves. "Geez, calm down," I said, jerking back. "Of course not, Harriet had a key. She does work there, remember? I promised Aunt Edie I'd do everything in my power to help clear Vivienne's name. A little visit to the bank proved rewarding and now we have three possible leads. You of all people should know I keep my promises."

The silence dragged between us and he stood staring as if he was looking straight through me. I cringed under his unsettling gaze. He'd been back less than forty-eight hours and I'd already pissed him off. My gut tightened and I sighed, "I'm sorry. That was totally uncalled for."

"Was that where you were when I rang earlier?" he asked.

I nodded. "In the grand scheme of things, it was just a short visit and it yielded some great leads I'm hoping my best friend will help me crack. What do you say?" I gave him my best pleading puppy dog eyes and pouty look I could muster up. A glimpse of a smile turned up the corner of his mouth and I knew I was cracking his macho protective barrier.

"You've a fierce loyal streak, Evelyn." He paused and rubbed his chin as if unsure how to continue.

Evelyn? He never uses my given name, it's always Evie girl. Why do I get the feeling this conversation is headed into awkward territory?

"You're my best friend, my closest friend witch or no witch, and I know you can handle yourself, but the thought of not having you in my life..." *Please don't get all mushy on me.* "...isn't something I want to contemplate."

Time to end this. We have more important things to do like finding a murderer. "You won't have to because I'm not going anywhere. I've managed to keep all my body parts intact while you were away, and now you're home I'm not about to let my guard down, but I will make you a promise. Right here, right now."

"Oh," he said, with a raised eyebrow.

I held my hand over my heart and spoke in a tone he couldn't mistake for anything other than sincere. My racing heart thumped against my palm.

"I promise to be true to myself and that means helping the people who mean the most to me. I will always be the fun-loving Evie you've always known, but I promise from this moment on to take all precautions necessary to keep myself safe. I promise if the situation warrants a protector or if I feel I need back up, you'll be the first person I'll call. Considering how buff you are, look out anyone who messes with me."

Tyler's shoulders softened and the tension dispelled leaving a comfortable mood between us.

"Thank you. Okay, what did you want help with?" he asked.

"Sweet, you're the best," I said, opening the box, taking out a piece of paper and handing it to Tyler. "Do you think you can find this man, Jeffrey Allan? I think Camille was investigating him for fraud or theft."

"No problem. Why don't you make some coffee and meet me in my office?" He paused and gazed dreamy-eyed at me one more time. "It's good to be home."

I watched his firm backside as he glided down the hallway toward his office. I turned and hustled toward the coffee machine cursing myself with each step. Get a grip. He's the same nerdy guy he's always been—just in a hot new body.

Note to self: You are not going to fall for your best friend and that's a promise.

I placed a steaming vanilla latte to the right of Tyler's keyboard and watched his fingers tap away at the keys as if performing an elegant dance across the letters.

"Thanks, Evie girl." He paused and sipped.

I bit my lip to keep from smiling. Hearing my nickname sent warmth and ease rushing into my heart. "Any luck?"

He shook his head but kept tapping away. "Not yet, but I've only just started."

"I know it's not my place to pry, but why did you come back early?" I asked, wanting to find answers.

He brushed my question away with a haphazard shrug of his shoulders. "I missed home I guess."

You guess? What's that supposed to mean? I know deflecting when I see it. Something happened in Nepal he's not telling me. This conversation isn't over.

"Anyway, Dorothy always said there's no place like home and she was right. What have I missed since I've been away? I noticed when I was in town earlier the Baker house was empty. When did that happen?"

"A few months back. Poor old Mabel," I said, fighting back tears. "It was heartbreaking. Her sister, Gladys fell and broke her hip about five or six months ago and since Mabel is her only living relative the job of looking after her landed on her shoulders. That woman has the purest most wonderful heart. She'd spend the weekdays with her sister and come home on the weekend to be with Henry. It was tearing them apart."

Tyler paused and looked my way, the comfort in his eyes went a long way to easing the lump in my throat. "That must have been tough. Henry and Mabel have never really been apart. True soul mates."

I nodded and swallowed. "It was. They lasted as long as they could and then Henry decided to go with her. Their final days in Saltwater Cove were rough. I'll miss them. I got a postcard from Mable about three weeks ago and they sound like they're having the time of their lives."

"I'm glad. They say every story has a silver lining." He took another sip of his coffee and returned to his computer search. "I apologised to Eli for my behaviour yesterday."

"Glad to hear it. Hopefully he doesn't think you're a complete jerk."

He gasped. "I am not a jerk."

Tight lipped, I raised an eyebrow at him, and he burst out laughing.

"Okay, maybe I was a little jerk," Tyler said, holding his thumb and forefinger an inch apart. "What's his story anyway?"

I shrugged and drained the last drop of coffee from my cup. Tyler's question stopped my thoughts dead. How much do we really know about Eli? I don't think I even know his last name. "I'm not sure. He's been in town a few weeks and Aunt Edie hired him to help at The Melting Pot and I trust her instincts."

She's a pretty good judge of character, but it wouldn't hurt to do a little investigating into Saltwater Cove's newest member just in case there are any skeletons hidden in the closest.

A trilling of beeps and bells boomed from Tyler's computer as the screen flashed a multitude of words. I jumped a mile off the ground and my heart kick-started into overdrive. "What's those noises mean?"

"Bingo," Tyler said, looking pleased with himself. A grin of triumph dazzled his expression. "You wanted to know where Jeffrey Allan was, and I found him."

"You did?" I held my fist out and he fist-bumped it just like we used to do in high school. "You're the man."

"Yes, I am," he said, his voice proud. "Do you want the good news or the bad news first?"

Bad news? I dropped my head forward into my palm and squeezed my eyes shut. The weight of his words baited me. "Please don't tell me he's dead. I'd rather not break witch law and have to resurrect the dead."

He ruffled my hair again, nudging me in the ribs. "Oh, Evie girl, I have missed your sense of humour. No, he's not dead, at least not all of them."

"How many are there?"

"According to my sources there are five. Two deceased, both kicking the bucket in their nineties. One lives in Wales. One resides Down Under and one…."

He paused and turned, branding a cheeky smile. Keeping me in suspense was not cool. My insides were about to explode.

"The last one lives in Noble Crest Assisted Living over in Hallows Creek."

"Hallows Creek? Are you for real? That's only thirty minutes away." I wanted to throw my arms around Tyler and kiss him. Instead I held my hand up for a high five. Tyler slapped his palm against mine and electricity bolted down my arm. High adrenaline I grabbed the mirror box in one hand and my bag in the other and headed for the front door. Not knowing how long this will take, I grabbed my phone and sent a short text to Aunt Edie.

Got to check something out. Start dinner without us if we're not there. I'll explain everything when I get home. Love you.

I glanced over my shoulder. "You coming?"

He frowned. "Where?"

"Noble Crest Assisted Living, where else?"

"I can't believe you talked me into this," Tyler grumbled, sitting back in the passenger seat.

"Me?" I feigned hurt. "It's not like I twisted your arm or anything. I'm just going to talk to the guy. See if I can find out some information, that's all."

"And what if he doesn't want to talk to you?"

Not an option as far as I'm concerned. The way I see it, Camille wouldn't have associated his name with fraud or theft unless she had good reason.

"I can only try." Change of subject would go a long way to settle my frenzied stomach. "Are you going to fill me in on why the transformation?"

Tyler sat staring out the front windscreen, his preoccupied gaze glued to the road ahead as if he was back in Nepal instead of sitting right beside me. He blinked several times and ran his hand through his short hair. "There's not much to tell. I knew it was time to do something with my life, but I had to find focus first."

"And did you?" I asked, turning down Fleetwood Street.

"Yeah, I did," he said, looking at me with his cobalt blue eyes. "Once I had the goal in sight, it was full steam ahead."

My gaze moved past Tyler and caught the Neon 'P' sign standing tall in front of the Petrol Station. I drove past and the information jumbled inside my mind started linking together. I can't believe I didn't think of it earlier. Jeremy Allan owns the petrol station and maybe he knows a Jeffrey Allan. I swerved the car and took a left down Tanners Drive to circle the block.

Tyler's hand flew to the dashboard and his nostrils flared. "Geez, Evie, what did you do that for?"

"Oops, sorry. I thought I'd get some petrol before we headed out of town." It wasn't exactly a lie. I had half a tank, but it can always use a top up. You never know where this meeting might lead.

"A little heads up next time would be great so I don't shave another five years off my life," Tyler said.

The vein in the side of his head twitched as he gave me his best evil stare.

"I am sorry. It wasn't my intention to send you to an early grave." Tyler's penetrating gaze sent the tightness in my chest bubbling to the surface. His frown deepened and his eyes had me shrinking in my seat. "The truth is I do need petrol, but when I saw the 'P' of the petrol station I remembered Jeremy Allan owns it and I thought he may know this Jeffrey guy. I mean it couldn't hurt to ask, right?"

"You could have just told me before you took the corner like a drag racer," he snapped, folding his arms across his chest, and returning his gaze to the bitumen ahead.

My heart sank. "I know and I'm sorry. If nothing comes of it, at least I can eliminate him. No harm in asking, is there?"

He shook his head and his arms relaxed. "No of course not. Just give me a warning next time, will you?"

"Sure," I said, pulling into the station and popping the fuel cap. "Would you mind filling up while I nip into the toilet? I'll pay for the fuel on my way out." I didn't need to go until I saw the toilet sign. My pelvic floor muscles were fighting a losing battle against the sudden pressure of my bladder.

Next time go to the bathroom before you start the journey.

He huffed. "And let you have all the fun? Not likely. I'll fill up and meet you inside."

"Okay…Thanks." I dropped the keys in his palm, grabbed my bag and headed inside the shop. It was unusually quiet for a Friday, albeit the store radio seemed to be ten decibels higher than normal. I paused and smiled at the fake witches' cauldron that held pride of place as I entered the store. Between the glittered pumpkins, scary fake masks, and handmade witches' brooms hanging from the roof, Jeremy had done a sterling job building the Halloween spirit.

Why is it when you see the ladies symbol your bladder decides to ramp up the urgency?

Dodging the shelves and food stands, my eyes focused on the back of the shop. I was one step away from total relief when a familiar voice froze me to the spot. My pulse sped up when I overheard six words that pricked the hairs on the back of my neck.

"I'll get the money, damn it. There was a delay…no it wasn't my fault," Jeremy said, in hushed tones.

A delay…did he mean Camille's murder?

"I said I'd have the money for you in forty-eight hours and I meant it. Keep your threats to yourself and you can tell Big Johnno what he can do with his ultimatum."

I bit the inside on my lip to stop my gasp from giving away my presence. Scuffing footsteps headed back toward the front section of the shop and I moved post haste into the ladies' toilet. Once inside, I let out one almighty breath of air.

"That was no innocent conversation. Sounds like Jeremy owes money, a lot of money, but the question is to whom and is it worth killing for?"

By the time I got out of the ladies, Tyler was standing at the front counter chatting away to Jeremy. I straightened up my top and pulled my purse out to pay. "Hi Jeremy, how much do I owe you?" I said, my casual voice was the total opposite to the jumping butterflies swarming around my gut.

"Hi Evelyn, twenty-three dollars and forty cents."

Is that tension I hear in your voice, Jeremy? You wouldn't be nervous by any chance, would you?

"I got this," Tyler said, opening his wallet.

"It's fine. My car, my petrol," I said, smiling, placing my hand over his, pausing his movement. Tyler's gaze stared at my hands and an electric current danced up my arm. I withdrew my hand, grabbed a packet of Red Rock Dell chips and threw them on the counter along with a packet of Honeycomb

Maltesers. "If you must pay for something you can pick up the tab for these snacks."

"No problem," he muttered, rolling his eyes. "They always were your favourite."

I spotted the picture on the counter of Jeremy huddled up to his beautiful wife at their wedding and the words flowed from my mouth like a waterfall on a hot Summer's day. "Oh my gosh, Jeremy, that is the most gorgeous picture of you and Darma. Is that your wedding day?"

A broad smile broke out across his face as he gazed at the photo. There was no mistaking the love in his eyes. The adoration for his wife hit me square in the heart. He smoothly ran his fingers across the photo and my fingertips tingled. I snapped my hands into fists clipping the sensation off in its tracks.

"Yes, my beautiful Darma. She's the best thing that ever happened to me." He smiled and picked the photo, keeping his eyes glued to the love of his life. "It was the best day of my life when she agreed to be my wife. I'd give her the world if I could."

I fidgeted from one foot to the other. This mushy love talk was more than my heart was ready for and was doing nothing to help Vivienne. I cleared my throat and forged ahead. "I suppose all your family were happy for you two. You know—your brothers and sisters and parents, I mean."

Jeremy replaced the picture and clenched his jaw, rubbing his nose several times. "Only our parents were present. Darma is an only child and my only brother was killed in a car crash when we were teenagers."

"I'm so sorry." Numbness invaded every inch of my body. A familiar void filled my heart, the same void that surfaced the day I learned both my parents had been killed.

Tyler nodded. "Me too, man."

Jeremy turned a blank expression my way. "Thanks, but it's all good. I learnt to deal with it a long time ago. Will that be all?"

My throat clogged with emotion, I simply smiled, turned, and left, Tyler following behind.

With each step toward my car, the void in my heart receded. Dragging up my old emotions are not going to do Vivienne any good.

"Do you still want to go to Noble Crest?" Tyler asked, sliding into the passenger seat.

"More than ever."

CHAPTER ELEVEN

*A*re we in an assisted living complex or a five-star luxury resort? If this is what they look like, sign me up right now.

Wow, this place is fit for a king. I am way underdressed. It was like I was standing in the centre of a luxury private resort. The kind you get in those expensive holiday deals where you get all the food you could possibly eat and massages every day. Wooden balustrades lined the porcelain tile staircase and the stained-glass windows at the top let in just enough light to appear as if God was looking in from above. Several lounge seats scattered among potted greenery gave the feeling of an indoor garden party. If this is what the foyer looks like, I can only imagine what's in store when you reach the bedrooms.

My gaze fell on the reception counter and it was just as grand as the rest of the place, complete with a shimmering white marble countertop. I pushed up on my tippy-toes and whispered in Tyler's ear. "Let me do the talking."

Tyler shrugged and his head tilted to the side. "Hey, this is your show, I'm just along for the ride."

Putting on a professional smile, Tyler and I headed toward the reception area. A young woman looked up from a collection of documents and her strained smile met mine. Flustered was an understatement, I'd say more like stressed beyond belief. She dropped the papers and her fidgety hands picked at her fingernails while her shoulders hunched forward.

"Welcome to Noble Crest, how may I assist you today?" Her voice cracked with each rehearsed word spoken.

"Good morning." I paused and looked at her name badge. "Isla, is it?"

The woman nodded and began sorting through the mess of documents on her desk as if they were confidential.

Poor girl looks like she'd rather be anywhere but here. "Are you okay? You seem a little under the pump?"

Her eyes glazed over and she fiddled with the necklace around her neck. "I...no...yes, oh gosh I'm so sorry. This is my first official day on the desk by myself and I guess I didn't realise how overwhelming it would be."

Tyler leant his elbow on the counter and flashed his pearly whites Isla's way. "I think you're doing an amazing job. I'm sure a smart, beautiful woman like yourself will have it sorted in no time."

Oh please. No female's going to fall for that line.

My eyes itched to roll at his corny attempt at flirting with the pretty redhead. I half turned my head his way when the redhead's sheepish high-pitched cackle froze my movement. You can't be serious.

"Oh stop, you're too kind," she said, blushing, her eyelashes fluttering double time. "Thank you for those nice words. What can I help you with?"

They continued smiling at each other. My jaw dropped and a sharp intake of breath dried my mouth. This is the first time I'd seen Tyler flirt, and I didn't like it one bit. Talk about awkward and uncomfortable, and that was just me. It took a moment for my brain to realise Tyler was now staring at me. "Oh sorry, we're here to see Jeffrey Allan."

She kept her puppy dog eyes glued to Tyler. "Are you relatives or friends of the family?"

"Friends of the family," I said as heat washed up my cheeks.

She picked up a blue sign-in book and handed it to Tyler. "If you wouldn't mind signing in and out in this book."

He took the book and gave her another million-dollar smile, this time with a wink. "Thank you, Isla." He signed in and slid the book across the counter in my direction. "You've been a great help and I know you're going to be fantastic once you get the hang of things around here."

Isla's cheeks grew an even brighter red than before. "That's sweet of you to say. It's afternoon activity time so if you head up the stairs and through the double doors to the nurses' station, they'll be able to tell you where to find Mr Allen."

My stomach was as hard as cement rocks. If I had to withstand any more of this flirting garbage I was going to vomit where I stood. "Thank you. Come on let's not keep the woman from her work." I smiled and pushed Tyler toward the double door entry.

"Bye," she called as we headed off.

I waved my right hand above my head in a goodbye gesture and hit the entry button. Once behind closed doors I turned to Tyler and he stood there, hands shoved in his pockets, a smirking bemused smile gleaming back at me.

"Seriously? You couldn't flirt any more if you tried?" His smirk reached his eyes and my hands ached to punch him one in the stomach. The nerve of the man.

"We're in, aren't we? And without any questions," he said, in a matter-of-fact tone. "What's a little flirting if it gets what you want…I'm not just muscle, you know? You needed in here and I knew a way to make it happen. It's not like it was real."

I pulled back, his words doing nothing to ease my hardened stomach.

You could have fooled me.

His tone grew serious and his eyes more a stormy grey than blue. "A relationship with the wrong woman spells disaster and she is definitely the wrong woman for me."

Wrong woman? What's that supposed to mean…he doesn't like cackle-laughing redheads?

He broke eye contact and turned away, his body all tense. Did he fall in love with a woman in Nepal and she broke his heart? Holy cow, that makes total sense. The new, toned, sexy tough guy image, haircut, and shave. Why else would he have returned early from a trip except to mend a broken heart?

"Do you want to do this or not?" he snapped, and his jaw tightened.

"Sure," I said, as we walked down the hallway to the nurses' station. "And thanks for getting us in without any questions. I really appreciate it. It's great to have you back home."

"No problem. Glad to help," he said, gifting me his warmest smile, the tension gone in a flash. He was back to his normal self.

There's the Tyler Broderick I know. Fire burned in my belly. I made a silent promise to myself. When this is all over, I will find out what happened in Nepal one way or another and if some woman broke his heart, she'll have my wrath to deal with and it ain't gonna be pretty.

"Can I help you?" A male nurse asked as we approached the counter. His name tag was covered in gold stars and I only just made out his name, Eric. Eric must have done something right to get that many gold stars.

"Good afternoon, we've come to visit Jeffrey Allan. Isla at the front desk said they were in afternoon activities and you would be able to point us in the right direction."

"Sure, he's in the library playing chess with one of the nurses." He smiled and pointed toward the open wooden doors. "If you go through those doors there and take the third door on your left, follow it to the end and take a right then second left, walk around the water feature in the centre and you'll find the library two doors down.

"Come again," I said, my brain hurt just contemplating his road map of instructions.

"First time here?" he asked.

I nodded.

He closed a book on the counter and popped the pen in his top shirt pocket. "Come on, how about I walk you down?"

I glanced at Tyler and his appreciation mirrored mine. "Thank you, that would be great." We followed along behind Eric and politely listened to his continual stream of heightened babble about the wonders of Noble Crest. I leaned into Tyler and whispered, "Jeffrey's lucky his family is loaded. Nice to be able to afford a place like this."

Eric stopped and turned, and my heart jump-started as I almost face planted into his chest. "Oops, I hadn't realised we were here yet."

"We're not, but I couldn't help overhear your comment." His gaze drilled me like an arrow claiming its bullseye.

Damn me and my big mouth. A hot flush hit me, and my entire body headed into meltdown. I'm not sure Tyler's flirting can get us out of this one. Discussing patient financials is probably a big no no. "I'm so sorry, I know I should keep my trap shut. It always gets me into trouble even when I try to do the right thing."

Eric's jaw relaxed and his right lip turned up into a smirk. "It's okay, I guess I can forgive you this time, just don't let Jeffrey's brother hear you talk like that. He's a nice guy and all, but a sore loser when it comes to money."

"How do you mean?" Tyler asked.

"Well," Eric resumed the journey and I kept pace, hanging on his every word. "Don't get me wrong, Jed loves his brother, but Jeffrey is the one with all the money and sometimes I get the feeling Jed wishes Jeffrey would throw a little his way. I'm sure he would if it wasn't all tied up in this place and his trust fund at the bank."

Bingo.

My heart nearly stopped when he mentioned the word bank.

"I'll be sure to keep my lips sealed." I made a comical zipper action across my lips and mimicked throwing the key over my shoulder and he burst out laughing. We all joined in and my verbal fumble trickled away into the ether.

A high-pitched beep screeched from Eric's pocket and he sighed. "Damn it," he said checking the number. "I have to go. The library is the last door down on the right just past the water feature." He turned and scurried back the way we came.

I looked at Tyler with renewed energy in my veins. "Did you hear what he said? His brother would like the money if it wasn't all tied up in the bank. Maybe whoever this Jed is found Camille and she refused to give him the money. Maybe he's a crook and needs the money to pay some sort of debt."

"Woah, ease up," Tyler said with a frown. "I think you're getting way ahead of yourself here. It could be just good old innocent sibling rivalry."

"I know, you're right," I muttered, deflated. "Let's just get this over with so I can get home and share my findings with Aunt Edie."

I walked into the library and lost my breath instantly in the magnitude of the room. Books of all shapes and sizes adorned all four walls. Some modern, but most resembled old-fashioned books like those you'd find in the Bodleian libraries in Oxford. I sucked in a lungful of musty air. The masculine scent of leather oozing off the Chesterfield couches hung in the room.

This is by far my favourite room so far.

I spied a lady and man playing chess in the corner by the window and my stomach did a nervous flip. I walked into the centre of the room with Tyler by my side. The nurse looked from their chess game and smiled, her blue eyes shining like tinsel in the sun. "Well, hello there. Look, Jeffrey you have visitors."

The middle-aged man swung around. The sparkle in his eyes and innocent smile melted my heart. Did he not get many visitors? He sat bounding up and down in his chair waiting for one of us to move. I stepped closer, wanting nothing more than to keep the smile on his face for as long as possible. "Hello, Jeffrey. It's Evelyn and this is my friend, Tyler."

He shoved his jittery hand out toward me and I shook it. "Pleased to meet you, Evelyn." Then repeated the action with Tyler. "Pleased to meet you, Tyler. Wanna play chess with me?" he asked, shaking Tyler's hand vigorously.

The nurse laughed and her smile soothed my squirmy insides. "Not everyone wants to play chess, Jeffrey."

"No, it's okay. I love chess," Tyler said, smiling at the man. "I'm pretty good at it too if I say so myself."

"Shotgun white, it's my favourite," Jeffrey called in a squeaky child-like voice.

Tyler glanced my way and the pained stare in his eyes matched my own guttered anguish. It may be a five-star luxury assisted living facility, but that wouldn't curb the loneliness Jeffrey must experience day in day out. I rolled my shoulders back and sucked up the tears that wanted to submit to his foregone predicament. I may have come to get information, but there's no reason I have to leave before making a new friend.

Tyler replaced spots with the nurse who came to stand by my side. "Chess is Jeffrey's favourite game in the whole entire world. I've tried Checkers, Snakes and Ladders, Monopoly and even Uno, but nothing works. He seems to come alive when his mind is active pondering up the next move."

"I've never been able to get a handle on it myself." I watched Tyler reset the board. The instant bond between the two men was like watching two big brothers hanging out together. "How is Jeffrey doing today?"

She folded her arms across her chest and shook her head. Sucking in a deep breath she said, "Today is a good day. He's doing well under the circumstances. His memory is as it always has been since the accident. His childhood memories come and go, but no short-term memory. He's lucky if he can retain tomorrow what happens today. That's why I like to make each day as wonderful as I can. A brand-new day." She paused and clenched her teeth together. "Drunk drivers should be hauled up in front of a firing squad as far as I'm concerned. Any person who can leave someone for dead in a hit and run should be shot in my book."

Hit and run...God no. That poor man.

Tears welled in my eyes as I watch Tyler come alive as the game continued, but poor Jeffrey probably won't remember it tomorrow. I looked at the nurse just in time to see her wipe a lone tear from her eye. I suddenly felt like the most useless witch in the universe. What good are powers if you can't take an innocent's pain away.

She cleared her throat and re-buttoned her cardigan. "My shift is almost over. It's almost dinner time, so you won't get a long visit, I'm afraid. Someone will come and find Jeffrey for dinner soon." She turned toward the door, pausing a moment. "They'll probably remember, but if they don't, remind them to take the box beside Jeffrey's chair. He may not have his full memory of his past anymore but what he has is in that box and he'll throw a fit if it's left behind."

"Of course. Thank you," I said, offering a loving smile straight from my aching heart. I walked over to sit on the arm of Tyler's chair, the quiver in my lips a dead giveaway.

Suck it up, woman.

I cleared the frog in my throat and joined in the fun. "Looks like a tough game, who's winning?"

"Me," Jeffrey called, jabbing his thumb into his chest. "I'm winning against my new best friend."

An audible gasp left Tyler's lips and he looked up at Jeffrey, a distant stare in his gaze. Tyler blinked several times and shook his head. "I think I'm the lucky one, Jeffrey. You're a pretty cool guy and an amazing chess player."

I clutched my throat with my hand trying to stem my eruption of tears and sentiment to destroy the beautiful scene. Looking away, my gaze caught the edge of the box beside Jeffrey's chair and I remembered the reason for being here. My muscles twitched as I stood. I have to see inside that box. It's the best chance I'm going to have of finding the link between Camille and Jeffrey.

With the boys focused on each other and the game, I pasted on a smile and stood edging toward the box. I kept my eye on the chess game and pushed the box around to the back of Jeffrey's chair and dropped out of sight. I placed a hand on the box lid and froze at the sound of Jeffrey's voice. My heart palpitations thumped louder than a baseball belted out of the park.

"Hey…what type of move do you call that?"

"Ah, that's the TT," Tyler said.

Jeffrey giggled like a child. "Huh, the TT? What's that mean?"

"The Tyler Triumph move," he said with a kick to his tone. "Want me to show you?"

Silence met Tyler's question and I sat still, my chest burning from lack of air. Dizziness hit me hard as the sound of laughter and giggles mixed with Tyler's instruction filled the room. I sucked in several short breaths and kept one thought in mind, proving Vivienne's innocence.

I eased open the lid of the box and scanned the contents. A twinge clawed at my heart knowing this was all that was left of Jeffrey's past. A well-used baseball and glove, a Coke-Cola yo-yo, a dog-eared magazine copy of Scooby-Doo and the Old Ship Mystery, a whistle, and a photo in a shabby wooden frame. I picked up the photo and love filled my heart. Two happy teenage boys standing with their arms around each other's shoulders, each holding a remote-control toy boat. Taken at what looked like a sizable lake and in summer judging by their singlet tops and board shorts.

The joy spread across their faces was contagious and I found myself smiling at the love flowing between them. Were they friends or brothers? I flipped the frame over, and my question was answered by the inscription written in blue cursive on the back.

To my dear brother, Jeffrey. Happy 15th birthday Bro. Remember this time at the lake three years ago? It was the best summer ever. Boat races, bonfires, swimming competitions and let's not forget the Tullison twins in the house down by the water. Let's make a pact to return every two years and relive the best time of our lives. I love you, always and forever. Love your big bro.

Such happy words of a time when they hadn't a care in the world. Who is Jeffrey's bro and how is this going to help solve the fraud-theft puzzle? I wonder if he's still alive. I bit my bottom lip. There's one way I could find out. Adrenaline coursed through my limbs as I inconspicuously peeked around the chair to make sure I hadn't been missed. I hadn't.

I held the frame in one hand and the other above the picture and whispered, "A picture tells a thousand words, I pray you let my voice be heard. With this spell show me how, what they're like here and now."

I held my breath and a glittering array of sparkles and mist floated over my tingling fingertips. The picture wobbled like rippling water and then transported the boys into men of today. My body was paralysed by the men's faces staring back at me. I squeezed the frame so tight my knuckles whitened under the pressure.

No way, are you serious? This couldn't be more perfect if I'd planned it myself. Which of course, I didn't. My head shot up at the jingle jangle of a bell in the distance. Sounds like dinner time. I whipped out my phone and snapped a few candid shots of the picture before it reverted back to the original image.

I placed the frame back in its original spot and slid the box back around beside the chair.

My pulse racing, I jumped up on my haunches and pretended to tie my shoelaces just as an orderly entered the room. Talk about good timing. I came with so many questions and found a murderer.

"Time for dinner, Jeffrey." The man said as he strolled across the room stopping by the chess table.

I joined Tyler again, sitting on the armrest of his chair. Jeffrey frowned and flopped back in his chair; his arms crossed over his chest. His pouty bottom lip a dead giveaway of a tantrum on the verge of exploding. "No, I don't want dinner, I want to stay and play chess with Tyler."

"Jeffrey," Tyler said in a soft calming tone. "How about I make you a promise?"

Jeffrey's back stiffened and his eyebrow raised. "What?"

"I have to get going now anyway because my mum will have my dinner ready at home, but what if I promise to come back soon and we can play chess again and next time I'll teach you the Tyler Turn Pipe move?"

Jeffrey's eyes widened and his smile was so big I feared his cheeks would crack. "You promise? People come and visit me, and they promise to come back, but they never do."

That's the memory loss talking. My heart wasn't going to last another minute before the pain of knowing he'd forget us by tomorrow broke it in two. "Me too, Jeffrey. I promise I'll come back and visit, and I bet I can play chess just as good as Tyler."

"Ha. She likes to think she can," he said, poking me in the ribs.

"Okay," Jeffrey said, giggling, he jumped up from his chair and grabbed his box from the floor. "I'll see you when you come back to play. Bye Evelyn…bye Tyler."

"See you buddy," Tyler said, holding his hand up for a high five.

"See you later, Jeffrey," I said, watching him return Tyler's high five. The room fell silent after they'd left, and I turned to Tyler. "Listen, I know we came here for information, but I am not going to wuss out on the promise I just made to Jeffrey. You may not want to come back, but the guy could use some regular company."

Tyler frowned and half pushed me off the armrest with a play punch to my arm. "My promises mean something too, Evie girl, and I made one with Jeffrey I intend to keep."

"Even if his brother is a murderer?" I said, my queasy stomach waiting for his response.

He shot off the chair and stormed toward the door. I hadn't taken five steps before he turned. "Murderer?" he said, his expression demanding an explanation.

I pulled out my phone and held up the photo I snapped. No-one could mistake it was Jeremy Allan from the petrol station standing arm in arm with his brother.

CHAPTER TWELVE

"What the..." Tyler said, his brows furrowed and his eyes frozen on my phone. "That's Jeremy from the petrol station standing next to Jeffrey. But how...where? I don't understand."

I looked at the photo one more time then dropped it in my bag. "While you were playing chess, I managed to get a look inside Jeffrey's box. And apart from a few childhood items I found a photo of two boys decked out in older style summer outfits in front of a lake. I knew one of them had to be Jeffrey and, thanks to the inscription on the back, the other was his brother. So, I did a little spell and voila!" I paused and snapped my fingers. "I asked it to show me the boys all grown up."

Tyler's jaw set in a hard line. "So, Jeremy lied about having a brother?"

My body infused with a new surge of adrenaline. "No, he didn't lie about having a brother, he lied about his brother still being alive. When you were filling up the car, I overheard Jeremy on the phone, and he didn't sound to happy."

"What do you mean?"

"If I remember correctly, he owed money and he said he'd have it for him in forty-eight hours. And there were threats and an ultimatum in there from Big Johnno, whoever that is."

Tyler rubbed his chin, his eyes wide. "He needs money and his brother has money. If he lied about his brother still being alive, he could have lied about anything. Maybe Camille stumbled across his plan to rip his brother off and he silenced her before she could out him and framed Vivienne."

I checked my watch and my blood ran cold. "Which means, we have exactly twenty-five minutes to get back to the petrol station before closing time and then who knows where Jeremy will be or who might end up his next victim."

Tyler offered to drive back to Saltwater Cove and the way my insides were jumping around like nobody's business, I was glad to hand the keys over.

I glanced at Tyler and his hands were clenched so tight around the wheel I could see every muscle in his forearm and hands pop. His eyes were focussed on the road ahead and he barely blinked. I sat with my phone to my ear, the dial tone drumming my eardrum.

Come on, Harriet, pick up…pick up…PICK UP. Why are you not answering your phone? Oh God, please don't have let anything happen to her. I'll never forgive myself if she's hurt or worse killed because I let her talk me into leaving her alone.

"Hello, this is Harriet."

Her chirpy voice was a vast contrast to the raging storm fighting it out inside my stomach.

"Harriet, where have you been? I've tried to call four times now. You had me worried sick. Are you okay?"

"I'm fine, Evelyn." Harriet paused and tutted down the line. "I was blow drying my hair. A woman is allowed to have a shower and freshen up, you know."

I ran my hand through my hair and pressed the base of my neck. "Of course, you are. Listen, I need you to do me a really big favour."

"Sure, what's going on?"

"I don't have time to explain now, but Tyler and I are on our way back into town—"

"What do you mean, on your way back into town? Where did you go? I thought you were having drinks at The Four Brothers." Harriet's voice lost its chirpiness and was now replaced with a wavering uncertainty.

"It's a long story and right now time is running out. I promise I'll explain everything when I get there, but I need you to do something for me no matter how strange it may sound."

"Does it have something to do with Camille's murder?" she asked.

"Yes, and I have to act quickly," I blurted.

"Okay, count me in." Her words were infused with conviction.

"I want you to go to the petrol station on Fleetwood Street and stop Jeremy Allan, the owner from closing up and leaving." My pulse was thrashing the side of my temple, it made it hard to concentrate. "It closes in about fifteen minutes, but Tyler and I won't get there in time. Whatever you do, do not let him leave."

"Why?"

An impatient huff escaped my lips. "I don't have time to explain now. Can you do this for me, please?"

"Okay, but how and I supposed to stop him leaving?" she asked. The reverberating sound of her front door closing echoed down the line.

"Anyway you can. Let one of your car tyres down, pretend you're sick, or better yet pretend to faint just make sure you wear the amulet so I know you'll be protected at all times and we'll get there as soon as we can."

"Okay, I have a plan. I have to go before I miss him. See you soon."

I dropped my hand in my lap and stared out the side window. Ouch, my damn chest hurt. Don't do anything silly, Harriet. Just stop him leaving, that's all.

"You didn't tell her Jeremy could be a cold-blooded murderer," Tyler said from his static driving position. I gazed his way. Nothing moved except his lips and the rise and fall of his chest.

I shook my head. "No, I decided not to."

"Why not?"

"The last thing I wanted to do was freak her out. If I had confessed our suspicions, she may have let it slip and that could have disastrous consequences. If she's wearing the amulet, she'll be safe." My entire body was as twitchy as a new-born colt.

"Fair enough," he said, turning down the highway toward Saltwater Cove. "Why didn't you magically transport us there? Surely you have a spell that would transport us there instantly? I mean what good is being a witch if you can't use your skills to your advantage every now and then?"

I sat frozen while Tyler's comment washed over me leaving my chest wrapped up tight like a coil which could explode any second. My mood matched the grey solemn sky clouds that had wiped away the setting sun. He was right, I should have been able to do a spell to transport us straight there. If it wasn't for the fact I was still a graduate witch. A shudder ran through my body at the memory of my last transportation experience.

"I'm afraid that's not going to be possible. You forget I'm only a graduate witch and until I am fully qualified the only transportation spell I can do needs a potion and I'm a little short on those at the moment."

His expression dropped. "Oh."

"Yeah, oh." My lips pursed tightly together. I was not taking a chance to blab. No way am I going to let Tyler know the last time I tried the Transportation Spell my measurements were slightly off and I ended up waist deep in the foul smelling cemetery pond surrounded by fish and all sorts of crawly creatures instead of the shoe shop across the road. I'm a graduate witch for a reason.

"How about we call the police?" he asked. "They could meet us there."

Tyler's stern voice knocked me back to the present. I shook my head. "No, not yet. Not until we get some hard-core evidence. We only have the picture on my phone which I sourced with a spell and the conversation I overhead and what's to stop him from denying it ever took place."

"All right. I'll be here to help out if the situation goes haywire. Let's not beat around the bush when we get there and above all else…don't provoke him into doing something crazy. Okay?"

"You don't have to ask me twice."

It seemed forever before the petrol station came into view. My back stiffened at Harriet's car parked out front beside one of the bowsers. I searched for any sign of Harriet and Jeremy. Nothing, the grounds were empty. Which meant they must be inside.

Tyler pulled up on the other side of Harriet's car. I jumped out, scanning the outside area once more for any sign of life. Zero. The street lights illuminated the pavement casting a mournful shadow over the sparse station grounds. With Tyler close on my tail, I scurried to the glass entry doors, but they didn't budge an inch. Locked. My pulse drummed in my head while a number of devastating scenarios ran through my mind, none of which ended in *happy ever after*.

"There," Tyler said, pointing toward the counter.

I followed his gaze to the chair beside the counter and my shoulders slumped in an exhale of relief. Harriet sat on the chair with a wet facecloth draped across her forehead held in place by Jeremy. Another male looking figure crouched down in front of her with their back to the door fanning her with a magazine.

Who is that?

I knocked on the door and waved my arm above my head until the muscle in my shoulder cramped. Jeremy said something to the man on his haunches and he turned. Eli? Of all the people in Saltwater Cove, Eli is the last person I expected to find here. Why is it he turns up at the most unexpected times? That's twice now. Maybe it was a good thing this time. We could use the extra muscle if the situation gets out of hand.

Eli bolted over and unlocked the door, his eyebrows drawn together. "Evelyn…Tyler, I'm so glad you're here. Harriet had a fainting spell and won't let us take her to the doctor."

The irony of the word spell was not lost on me. Keeping up the dramatic flair I ran over and crouched down beside Harriet. "Oh my God, Harriet, are you okay?"

"Um, I'm not sure." She stared blankly at me before here eyelids blinked rapidly. She took the wet face cloth from Jeremy, and he shuffled a few steps back. "Yes, I think so. I have been stressed since finding Camille and I haven't drunk much water lately. I suppose I could be dehydrated. But I seem to be feeling a bit better now."

Eli spoke from behind me. "When I came in, she didn't look the best. Quite pale actually."

Harriet looked at Eli and gasped. "I did?"

"Yes, that's why I suggested you go to the doctor," he said, shoving his hands in his pockets.

Seriously? She's a better actress than I thought. I covered my mouth and hid a smirking grin behind a forced cough as I stood up tall. "Thanks, Eli. I'll make sure she deals with whatever is going on as soon as possible."

Jeremy spoke for the first time. "What are you even doing here, Evelyn? It's after close."

My gaze found his and a quiver hit my stomach. I bent down and grabbed Harriet's hand and pulled her to stand behind me. Even though I felt sick to my stomach, with two muscle men and Harriet at my back I dived in, tackling my suspicions head-on. "It just so happens Tyler and I were out at Noble Crest today." I raised my eyebrows and waited. Please let him spill. Will he fess up on his own? Or will he keep lying?

Bingo!

Jeremy's eyes widened and he clutched his arms to his chest doing his darndest to erect a barrier between us. All eyes were on Jeremy and he froze, his pupils dilated.

"And I'm just wondering why you lied this afternoon about your brother, Jeffrey?" I said, pushing for answers.

"What? How did you find out about Jeffrey?"

My chest tightened as if being wedged in a vice. I forced myself to relax with a few calm breaths. "How I know is not important. It puzzles me that you have a brother so close yet when I asked if you had siblings today, you lied. You said he died in a car accident. Why is that?"

Tyler stepped up closer behind me, apparently his protective radar was on high alert. "Yes, tell us. Or maybe you could explain why Camille had a note with Jeffrey's name written on it alongside the words fraud and theft."

Harriet's sharp gasp pierced the sudden silence. "It was you. You murdered Camille. She found out about your brother and you killed her to keep your secret?"

"What…no," Jeremey said, his skin now as pale as the first fall of fresh snow before it's trampled into a muddy mush. "I would never hurt anyone. I didn't kill Camille. She may not have been my favourite person, but I would never hurt her."

Eli flipped open his phone. "I'm calling the police."

"No, wait." Jeremy shouted. He jerked forward and my heart jumped into my throat.

Male voices yelled over the top on one another and arms flew everywhere. The burn in my wrist skyrocketed up to my arm as Tyler pulled me back behind him. It all happened so quick my mind was still processing the kafuffle. I rubbed my wrist to relieve the ache. I found myself standing next to Harriet behind a pair of chiselled male shoulders. The speechless look on her face matched my own.

"I'm warning you. Don't even think of taking another step or you'll be sorry," Tyler spat.

I recoiled at the venomous tone in his words. I hadn't heard him talk that way since we were in high school.

"Please, you have to listen to me," Jeremy said. His pleading, high-pitched voice and flushed skin cut into my thoughts. "I don't know how you found out, but yes, I admit I lied about my brother Jeffrey, and I can explain if you'll let me, but I did not kill Camille. I wasn't even in Saltwater Cove when it happened."

He has an alibi? No, that can't be right.

"Wait a minute." I pushed through the male barrier and my eyes caught Tyler's cautious glare. I'm all for the protective older brother image. But something wasn't right. I just couldn't put my finger on it. I gave him my best 'trust me' look and it must have worked, because he gave a curt nod. I wasn't going to push my luck.

I stood beside Tyler and returned my gaze to the fatigued Jeremy. In the last few minutes he appeared to have lost the will to fight. I cleared my throat and he looked straight at me. In a soothing calm voice, I said, "Are you prepared to answer some questions, Jeremy or do we call the police and let them take care of it?"

He nodded. "Yes, I'll answer your questions. Just know that I did not kill Camille."

"Why lie about your brother?" Harriet asked before I had the chance.

His eyes focused on the floor in front of him as he ran a hand through his damp hair. "Do you have any idea what it's like to grow up knowing everyone looks at you like you're a piece of scum, like you're the worst person in the universe? Jeffrey's in that place with permanent brain damage because of me."

Keeping his head lowered, he glanced up and looked straight at me with pleading eyes. "I love Jeffrey. I was eighteen and I'd just got my licence. I took Jeffrey out in my jazzed-up car. I was showing him some tricks, doing burnouts and donuts that kind of thing. He wanted to go home, and I convinced him ten more minutes. They said the other driver was drunk and speeding, but if I'd gone home when he wanted to, we would have missed the car. Instead, we collided and Jeffrey's side took most of the brunt of the accident."

I swallowed hard to keep the rising nausea at bay. "So why lie about him?"

Jeremy continued. "After the accident, mum and dad couldn't handle it. Dad left and as much as I know mum loved us, she struggled with the stigma of having a brain-damaged child. I came home after work one day and found her cold body on the lounge with an empty pill bottle on the carpet beside her."

Poor man. What an ordeal he must have lived through. "Oh Jeremy, how awful. I'm so sorry."

He shrugged. "It is what it is. I don't blame her, or dad for that matter. I blame all the people who made fun of Jeffrey, the kids who taunted him, threw jarring puns his way and mine. He'd got a good payout from the accident, enough to live comfortably with assistance for the rest of his life. I wanted to look after him, but with working long hours and all, I just couldn't. I found a live-in nurse to help, but it didn't stop the sly looks every time I went into town. Finally, I couldn't take it anymore. We moved around a bit and then I found Noble Crest and it was like a blessing from God. No-one knew us there and it was easier for me to keep that side of my life a secret. I moved here and brought this place and it was easier to say he died in the car accident instead of the truth."

He paused, swallowed a few times, and ran his palms down his pants. A smile spread across his face. "And then I met my beautiful wife, Darma. It was love at first sight. She was visiting her mother in Noble Crest. Her father had passed a few years before. We fell in love and got married last year. I love Darma with all my heart. She insists on coming to visit Jeffrey with me."

"And you pretended to be Jeffrey to get access to his money so you could give her the life she deserves, and Camille caught you. That's why you killed her," I said, folding my arms across my chest.

He threw his hands up in the air. "Enough with the killing talk. I did not hurt Camille in any way."

"Explain Camille's note then?" Eli snapped.

"The only thing I'm guilty of is trying to please my wife."

My eyebrows shot up. "Come again?"

"It's our first wedding anniversary next week and Darma mentioned she wanted a puppy, but not just any puppy, a pure breed Frenchie. I was going to surprise her with one, but do you know how expensive those dogs are? There's no way I could afford it on my salary. The cheapest I found was six thousand dollars. I put up my motorbike for sale, but it hasn't sold. I was desperate and I knew Jeffrey had the money. Camille hadn't met Jeffrey, so I pretended to be him. I told her Jeremy was my middle name hoping she wouldn't look too far into it, but I guess she did."

"So, you committed fraud?" Harriet asked, her frown clearly showing her displeasure.

His back straightened and he held his chin high. "I'll gladly own up to fraud, but not murder."

He was doing a cracking job at poking holes in my murder theory. Could I have got it wrong? My stomach dropped at the thought. I have one last option up my sleeve. "Who is Big Johnno?"

Jeremy's brow wrinkled and he glared at me like I was a feral cat ready to attack. "How do you know about Big Johnno?"

"I overhead your conversation earlier today when I was on my way to the ladies. Sounded like you owed him some money and he wasn't too happy about waiting. Must have been serious if he issued you an ultimatum."

"Gee, nothing gets past you, does it?" he said in a grumpy tone. "If you must know, he's called big Johnno because that's exactly what he is. He stands two metres and ten centimetres tall, hence the term *big*. He's the one who owns the Frenchie. He told me he had another buyer and I promised I'd have the money for him so he wouldn't sell it. Tomorrow I intend to pawn my mother's diamond ring at *Heirloom Treasures Antique Shop* to get the money to buy the dog. All above board of course."

My mouth went dry and my words stuck in the back of my throat. It seemed everything I thought I knew was completely wrong except for the impersonating Jeffrey to get his money part. Where to now?

Tyler took over asking the one question that slipped my mind. "Tell us your alibi. You said you had one for the time of Camille's murder."

"Why do you even want to know?" he asked.

I stood tall refusing to let the tightness in my chest get the better of me. "Because Vivienne is being framed for Camille's murder and I made a promise to help clear her name and I never go back on my word."

"I was with Jeffrey," he said, smiling as his eyes glazed over. "Wednesday was monthly movie night at Noble Crest. Immediate family members could stay over. We watched the classics, Free Willy, Flubber, Incredibles and by the time Incredibles Two started, I'd crash on the roll out bed they put in Jeffrey's room. We had breakfast together and then I arrived home around ten Thursday morning. You can check if you want to. I'm really sorry about Camille and Vivienne, but I didn't have anything to do with either. Like I said, I will own up to pretending to be Jeffrey. That was just silly, but love will do that to a person. I'll head over to see Detective Huxton as soon as I leave here."

Great. A dead end. Now what?

CHAPTER THIRTEEN

I drove past Jordi's car parked on the street and pulled into Aunt Edie's driveway, turned the engine off and killed the lights. My head hurt from churning Jeremy's revelations over and over in my mind. By the time I'd dropped Tyler home and picked up Harriet after she'd dropped her car back at her house, I felt like I'd been through the wringer. Exhaustion invaded my body and my limbs were the weight of a ten-pound dumbbell. I rubbed my forehead, the brain strain stabbing needles behind my eyes.

"Are you okay?" Harriet whispered.

"Sure." I paused, the door half open letting the cool night air sooth my aching head. The sweet scent of cinnamon and lavender stormed my senses.

If that's Aunt Edie's cooking, then I just might make it through the rest of the night.

Harriet followed me inside, and while she dumped her backpack at the bottom of the stairs, I stood and let the delicious aromas from the kitchen breathe new life into my empty stomach. I laughed at the instant guttural growl calling from my belly. Glancing down, I shook my head and said, "Typical. As soon as you're in a nose whiff of Aunt Edie's cooking, you come to life."

"Who are you talking to?" Harriet asked, looking at me as if questioning my sanity.

"The growling hungry monster who lives in my stomach, who else?"

"Evelyn? Is that you, sweetheart?" Aunt Edie called from the lounge room.

"Sure is, and Harriet," I called back. I leant on the back of the kitchen chair and pushed my shoes off by each heel. My aching feet throbbed but thanked me for their new-found freedom.

Aunt Edie appeared from the lounge room with Miss Saffron snuggled in her arms. I always looked forward to Aunt Edie's loving smile whenever I walked through the door. I stroked Miss Saffron's head and she purred, licking my palm in gratitude. "Spoilt much?"

"Dinner is in the oven. I'm sure it's still hot enough. Jordi arrived not long ago so I decided to have dessert in the lounge room where she could get more acquainted with Aubrey and Olive. They hit it off, but there never really was any doubt about that." She adjusted the feline to the other arm, accompanied by an irritated purr.

"How's Vivienne?" I asked, keeping my hands tickling Miss Saffron behind her ear while my gaze and empty stomach focused on the oven.

"I've been in touch with her a few times and she's doing well, considering. I offered to come and get her, but she insisted on staying home. Vivienne always turned to cooking when life throws her in the deep end. I guess we'll all be getting pumpkin made treats for Christmas this year."

"At least we know she's safe at home."

Aunt Edie returned Miss Saffron to her bed in the corner and she wasn't too happy by the sound of it. A string of purrs mixed with cat-like grumbles filled the kitchen as she circled her bed five times before settling down to sleep with a big sigh. "Why not get your dinner and come in and join us. I'm sure you have plenty of news to share."

"That's an understatement," Harriet said, diving into the cutlery drawer for two matching knives and forks.

"Sounds good to me." I opened the oven and the succulent smell of a roast had my taste buds watering and my hungry monster flaring up again. "Man, am I going to enjoy this."

I sat next to Harriet on the main sofa in the lounge room eating away and listening to the spirited chatter between witches and shapeshifter. If you had told me two weeks ago two witches of the Elder Flame Coven would be sitting in our lounge room chatting away as if they were members of the family, I would have laughed. But here we are.

"Are you ready to spill yet, Evelyn?" Jordi asked, arms crossed in her normal impatient persona. "Some of us have been working all day instead of gallivanting around the countryside."

Harriet dropped her fork and the startling clatter of it colliding with her china plate made us all jump.

"We were not galivan…gallivanting around the…country…side," she said between chews.

"No, we weren't." I stared down at the gravy juices pooling in the base of my plate. If we didn't have company, I would lick the juice off with my tongue right here, it was that delicious.

I placed my plate on the coffee table, walked back into the kitchen and grabbed my bag. It will be easier to show them than explain in words. "As you know, Harriet and I went to the bank and it wasn't a total waste of time. Actually, it yielded an extremely important find." I paused and pulled the mirrored box from my bag. Gasps and wide eyes mixed with the flabbergasted expressions from the newcomers.

"Where on earth did you find it?" Jordi asked.

Her hazel eyes twitched and I could tell she itched to get her hands on the box.

"At the back of the top drawer of Camille's filing cabinet," I said, biting my bottom lip, waiting for the reprimand I knew was coming. Aunt Edie was against breaking the law and so was I. Normally. But sometimes using magic was more productive and this was one of those times.

Aunt Edie puckered her lips and glared at me and before I could utter an explanation, her voice rung out inside my head.

'And just how did you get into a locked filing cabinet, young lady?'

I was about to answer when Harriet took the words right out of my mouth.

"We were coming up empty and the only place we hadn't searched was the filing cabinet. Evelyn did an unlock spell. It was so cool. We knew you wouldn't mind since it was to help free your best friend from a murder charge."

I kept my eyes on Aunt Edie, waiting for the scolding. Even though I'd just stuffed my face with the best roast dinner ever, my stomach dropped through the floor.

Okay, give it to me. I can take it, but I'm not going to feel bad because it was the right thing to do to help Vivienne.

"But…" Harriet finished her last mouthful and placed her empty plate on the table. She shuffled to the edge of the couch, her jittery body adding to the tension in the room. "The best piece of news is the three clues we found in the mirrored box that make for the best motives for murder: fraud, jealousy and blackmail." Astonished mutterings flooded the room simultaneously.

"Blackmail? Are you serious?"

"…fraud…No way."

"…Jealousy. Oh my God…"

Harriet nodded. "We also found mysterious dates relating to the run down Grand Majestic hotel up by the old abandoned geological site." Harriet continued, dissolving the tension in the air with each spoken word.

Olive's grin spread from ear to ear. "You ladies have been busy. We're one step closer to finding Camille's real murderer."

Harriet flicked her legs underneath her on the couch, barely taking a breath between sentences. "More than one step. I'd say at least two. Thanks to

Evelyn and Tyler, we've already eliminated fraud as a motive. That just leaves jealousy, blackmail, and the Grand Majestic."

"Woah, back up a sec, you've lost me," Aunt Edie said, her eyebrows pulling together.

There it is again, her pondering expression. I wondered if she was pondering Harriet's words or the best way to throttle me.

"Thank you, Harriet. Your enthusiasm is to be commended and I know Vivienne would thank you if she could." Harriet's cheeks glowed and she returned Aunt Edie's words with a cheesy pleased-with-herself grin. "But I think Evelyn better explain everything from the start, don't you?"

I sighed and did as asked without omitting one skerrick of information. "And then Jeremy confessed everything. I think his heart's in the right place but blinded by love. I gave Noble Crest a call and they confirmed he was there on Wednesday night and stayed over in Jeffrey's room and left around nine-thirty Thursday morning. Which matches his description of the events. I think we can confidently say that the fraud angle is in the clear."

"What I don't get is what Eli was doing there?" Jordi said, her gaze wandering around the room.

Harriet cleared her throat and her ears turned a ruby shade of red. "That's my fault I'm afraid. The best way I could think of to keep Jeremy there was to pretend I was sick and going to faint. Problem was, I should have waited until I got inside instead of clutching my stomach. I stumbled from my car and Eli happened to be passing by at the exact same time and raced over to help. I guess I channelled my acting skills from school a little too well. At least it worked and I got Jeremy to stay put."

"That it did." Jordi laughed and soon the room was filled with relaxed chatter.

Aunt Edie cleared her throat. "I called Detective Huxton today." The chit chat ceased. "He wasn't much help I'm afraid. He did mention they were following up a lead or two and he would let me know as soon as he had information he could share."

"What about the letters, Evelyn?" Aubrey piped up. "Did you have a chance to look at them?"

I shook my head and opened the loose letter I had already read. The rough parchment brushed against my palms. It was an odd paper, not something you'd use for your everyday shopping list. Ignoring the irritating nag at the back of my neck, I said, "Not yet, but I have a feeling they're important. I'm not sure if they have anything to do with Camille being a witch or not. There's about eight and all are in the same handwriting. It's pretty, cursive and looks old school. I'd say she isn't my age, maybe someone older, but I couldn't be sure."

"Can I have a look?" Jordi asked, leaning forward on the couch.

I handed her the letter and watched a myriad of expressions pass as she read it.

"Okay, she says here...*If you think you can come into my town and take what's mine, think again.* What does that mean?" Jordi paused and glanced around the room.

Everyone looked as confused as I did.

Jordi continued. "She goes on to say...*I know all about your little secret.* Do you think that means they knew Camille was a witch? Being a witch or shapeshifter like me isn't a secret in Saltwater Cove, but maybe Camille was trying to keep her true identity a secret."

Harriet gasped, her jaw dropped and hands started flapping around like bird's wings. "I've got it. I bet Camille had a lover. What if she stole some other woman's man and these are letters to warn her to keep away, or else."

"A lover?" Aubrey and Olive said in unison.

Jordi giggled incessantly at Harriet's revelation. "Be serious, Harriet. A lover? As if."

Lover? Who in Saltwater Cove would be Camille's lover?

I gripped the edge of the cushion, irritated by Jordi's comment. "She may have been a cold woman to us, but regardless she was a woman with a heart and loved by many including her deceased sister. I hardly think she is going to show her true colours to a town when she was undercover searching for her sister's murderer. Do you?"

The room silenced and Jordi stopped mid-laugh and her face paled. Her gaze flitted from one person to another. She focused on Aubrey and Olive's stiffened expressions. "Oh God, I'm so sorry. I'm not normally that insensitive. I was remembering all the hard times she'd given me since she moved here when I should have remembered she was a member of your coven, and your friend."

Aubrey's posture relaxed and she placed a hand on Jordi's forearm. "We understand all too well. We love…loved Camille, but we also know she made it extremely hard for people to see past the brick wall she'd erected, especially if they'd only known her for a few months."

"Thank you," Jordi said, wiping her damp eyes. "I truly am sorry."

"It's all right," Aunt Edie said, handing her a tissue. "Harriet has made a point though. We have no idea of the real Camille, so how would any of us know if she had a lover or not? The answer could be in these letters, but they'll need to be studied."

Jordi gathered the letters off the table and held them tight in her lap. "I can do that. I'll take these home and scope them word for word and if there's clues in here that will lead us to the blackmailer, I'll find them. I promise."

Olive smiled and dipped her head at Jordi. "Thank you. We know you will."

Jordi pressed her fist against her thigh and sucked in a deep breath. "I know it doesn't excuse my 'foot in my mouth' moment, but it will show you I want to find Camille's murderer just as much as you all do."

"Thanks, Jordi," I said, sending my friend a reassuring smile. "That leaves the dates linked to the Grand Majestic and Harriet and I will tackle those first thing in the morning."

Aubrey squeezed Olive's hand, a moment passed between them and they nodded in unison.

"We're heading back to Camille's house in the morning. We didn't find anything of value this afternoon, but then again, we only scraped the surface. Maybe tomorrow we'll find something to confirm or dispel Harriet's theory."

"Who knows what we'll find," Olive said, leaning back in her chair. "She was smart enough to rent a house on acreage so we can take comfort knowing there are no pesky neighbours to question our movements."

"Well," Aunt Edie said, folding her arms and crossing her ankles. "This certainly is an interesting turn of events, but are we forgetting what day it is tomorrow?"

My stomach jumped and an electric current ignited my insides. "I sure do. Your favourite day of the year, besides Christmas, that is."

"Darn tootin' it is." Aunt Edie paused and the corners of her lips turned down. "However, considering the circumstances, I feel it might be best to cancel the Halloween celebrations planned for tomorrow evening."

Aubrey's eyes widened. "No, you mustn't."

"But how am I supposed to cook all day tomorrow for a celebration while my best friend is struggling to maintain her sanity under suspicion of murder? And you are all off putting your lives at risk trying to prove her innocence? There's more I could be doing."

Aunt Edie pinched the skin under her neck and a frown marred her expression. It can't be easy knowing Vivienne's livelihood is at risk. "However hard it may be, you must go on as normal and we'll keep you in the loop every step of the way. We can all meet back here at lunchtime to fill you in. How does that sound?"

"Evelyn's right," Harriet said, her strong gaze holding Aunt Edie to her chair. "If you cancel the Halloween dinner at The Melting Pot you might tip off the murderer and then they could change their plans or worse, leave Saltwater Cove. Then all of this will be for nothing and Vivienne is sure to go away for life for a murder she didn't commit."

Well, damn. Go Harriet.

I raised an eyebrow in Harriet's direction and the corners of my lips turned up. "What she said."

Aunt Edie's arms relaxed into her lap and she beamed at Harriet. "I can see you're learning fast, my dear. And you make a good point. I wouldn't want to tip the murderer off that something was up. But I will reserve the right to cancel if it becomes too dangerous or my help is needed."

There were nods and words of agreement all round.

"Right," Aunt Edie stood clasping her hands at her waist. "Who's for another round of pecan pie?"

Harriet's hand shot up in the air like a rocket. "Me please."

Jordi joined her with two arms reaching for the ceiling. "Me too."

Aubrey and Olive both smiled and stood. "I'd love to. But my waistline would not thank me in the morning," Aubrey said, picking up her bag. "We must take our leave. It has been a long day and I fear tomorrow will be even longer."

"Aubrey is right." Olive added, turning to face Jordi. "It was lovely to meet you Jordi."

"It was an honour to meet you. Us shapeshifters can never have too many witch friends, especially witches of your standing." Jordi threw each lady a warm smile, her earlier faux pas a memory in the past.

I watched Aunt Edie follow them out and my eye caught the picture of me huddled in my mum's arms on the mantle and pins and needles ran down my right thigh. My hand shot to my knee and I rubbed the sensation away. My stomach churned as the unanswered question locked in the back of my mind plagued me. How did Camille know my mother? I wondered if they had time to answer one more question.

I stood and brushed the wrinkles out of my clothes. "Do you girls want a hot Milo to go with your pie?" Nods and cheeky grins from both Harriet and Jordi were all the answers I needed.

I forced my feet to step one after another into the kitchen. I moved past Aunt Edie as she fiddled with scooping pecan pie into plates.

"Aubrey…Olive, I was hoping I might ask you one more question before you go?"

Olive stopped a metre from the door and turned. "Of course, dear."

"What is it?" Aubrey asked.

My stomach was in full hurricane mode and I looked down at my fingers twisting in knots. I squeezed them together, gripping hard to stop the chaotic movement. "Did Camille know my mother? The day before she was murdered, she mentioned I looked like my mother. Actually, she said she never seemed to tell me enough how beautiful I was, just like my mother. How would she know that unless she knew her?"

Aunt Edie was at my side, her body radiated warmth. Her arm eased around my shoulders and I knew she wanted to know the answer just as much as I did.

Olive and Aubrey looked at each other and their silent conversation taunted my shattered heart.

Please tell me. I can handle it. I have to know the truth.

Aubrey walked over and stopped in front on me, her black eyes gone, replaced by honey-brown. She placed a hand on my cheek, and I flinched. Her silky-smooth touch somehow eased the heaviness clouding my heart.

"I feel your pain and I wish we had more to tell you. As far as we know Camille never knew your mother; however, through her investigation she mentioned stumbling across a photo of your mother and father. I'm guessing she put two and two together and worked out who they were."

My breaths were coming hard and fast. "Do you know where the photo is? Do you have it? Did she tell you where she put it?"

Aubrey frowned and shook her head. Her hand dropped from my cheek leaving me longing for its comforting return "No, child. I know that's not the answer you were hoping for. If we come across it in our search you will be the first to know. I promise."

My insides wanted to scream, but what good would that do? It won't bring Camille or my parents back. I forced a smile, the muscles around my lips quivering. "Thank you."

A warm sensation grazed the side of my calf and I looked down to see Miss Saffron wrapped around my leg, her elegant neck stretched back and her golden eyes offering comfort.

Aunt Edie reached down and picked her up, cuddling her into her chest. She leaned in and whispered in my ear. "It's a start."

She was right. It was more than I knew ten minutes ago. I missed them every day, some days worse than others. I reached up and squeezed Aunt Edie's hand on my shoulder. "I love you."

"I love you too, sweetheart."

Miss Saffron joined in with a confirming *meow* which sounded a lot like *me too*. Her front paw worked its way down my forearm followed by a heartfelt purr as she rubbed her head against my arm, something she always did if she wanted a cuddle. I smiled and held my arms open.

"Come on then."

She jumped into my arms and the comforting warmth of her fur tickled my neck as she snuggled into my embrace. I giggled and plonked a kiss on top of her head. "I love you too."

Aubrey sighed and swished her shawl around her shoulders. "We must be off. Thank you once again for dinner and opening your home to us. We'll see you tomorrow."

"You're welcome—" Aunt Edie's words were interrupted by knuckles drumming on the door. "Goodness me, who could be calling this late at night?"

Miss Saffron perked up and her head turned toward the door, her ears pointed straight up. "Easy girl," I whispered, rubbing her silky-smooth belly.

Aunt Edie excused herself and opened the door. Her breath hitched and she stared dead ahead as if frozen in time. Needing no invitation, a familiar male voice spoke with harshness in his tone.

"I'm sorry to call so late," Detective Huxton said, clearing his throat. "May I come in? New evidence has come to light in the Camille Stenson murder."

CHAPTER FOURTEEN

"New evidence? What new evidence are you talking about?" Aunt Edie snapped. "Is this related to the phone call earlier?"

"Yes and no, but I'd really prefer to discuss it inside."

A moment of fleeting pain bared itself in her gaze and then it was gone. A strained smile welcomed him inside. "Of course, how rude of me. Please come in."

Huxton entered, passing by Aunt Edie into the kitchen where he stopped dead centre facing five pairs of inquisitive eyes. Jordi and Harriet flanked me either side as soon as they'd heard Detective Huxton's voice.

"Hell-oo," he said, his gaze acknowledging each one of us, stopping at Aubrey and Olive. "I don't believe I've had the pleasure."

Miss Saffron stayed quiet in my arms but kept an eagle eye on his movements. A shallow purr in the base of her throat vibrated against my bicep. Protecting me as always. One wrong move and Detective Huxton would know what it's like to be on the other end of a very riled up familiar.

Aubrey stepped forward and presented her hand. "Good evening, my name is Aubrey Garcia, and this is my sister, Olive. Pleased to make you acquaintance Mr…"

"Huxton…Detective Micah Huxton," he said, shaking her hand. He repeated the gesture with Olive then turned to Aunt Edie.

This visit must be about Jeremy. Pleased as punch with my afternoon's work, I couldn't wait to hear it from the man himself. My own detective work trumped his. A sudden thought had my stomach falling faster than the big dipper roller coaster. What if Jeremy lied and didn't go to the police?

"Detective Huxton, did you happen to get a visit from Jeremy Allan this evening?"

His brows drew together, the creases in his forehead showing his age. "Yes, I did but that's not why I'm here." His sombre expression focused on Aunt Edie. "I didn't realise you had company. I can come back."

He's not here about Jeremy and the expression on his face screams bad news. Oh no, Vivienne?

"No, it's quite all right," she said, moving to join the rest of us. "You mentioned new evidence."

Huxton raised an eyebrow at Aunt Edie and nodded in the direction of our guests. "Maybe we should talk in private."

"You may speak in front of us, Detective Huxton," Olive said, in a calming tone. "Camille was a close personal friend of ours and as you can imagine, when we heard about what happened, we came as soon as we could."

His eyebrows raised. "Close personal friend you say? From what I hear, Camille didn't have any close personal friends."

Aubrey sighed and pursed her lips. "Camille was an acquired taste, but nevertheless she was our friend and we would hate to see the wrong person convicted of her murder. Edith believes Vivienne is innocent and so do we. We'd very much like to hear your new evidence."

Detective Huxton didn't say a word. His eyes thinned and he kept his gaze concentrated on Aubrey and Olive as if trying to poke holes in their explanation in his head. He nodded. "Okay. But I would ask all of you to keep the information I'm about to share to yourselves. It hasn't been released yet, and we're not sure we will. I made a promise to Edith this afternoon that I would keep her up to date."

"I do appreciate it, Micha."

Detective Huxton turned around at the sound of his name from Aunt Edie's lips and his demeanour visibly softened when their gazes connected. "You're welcome."

Oh yeah, they've got it bad for each other. When this is all over and the rightful person is behind the bars, I think the girls and I should do a little match making.

"What is the new evidence, Detective?" I asked, ready to get this unexpected visit back on track.

He cleared his throat and his pitch dropped. "This afternoon it was confirmed Vivienne's bank account received an additional five hundred thousand dollars on the day of the murder."

Holy cow, where did Vivienne get that kind of money? Silence matched stunned expressions. You could have heard a hairpin drop.

"Pfft, that's ridiculous," Aunt Edie snapped, her arms crossing her chest, erecting a new barrier between them. "There must be some kind of mistake. Your whiz-bang technical people in the police department have obviously made an error."

"I verified it myself." He took his notebook out and flipped the pages to the one he was after. "A deposit of two hundred and fifty thousand was made before the murder and another of the same amount was deposited after the murder. The final payment for a job complete."

A glimpse of bewilderment filled Aunt Edie's gazed before it dissolved and was replaced with a glare even I wouldn't want to be on the end of.

"Do you mean to tell me you believe my best friend took money to murder Camille?" She stood and waited for his answer. As each second ticked over a rosy red heated blush was working its way up her neck.

His expression hardened. "I don't want to believe it, but I can't ignore the evidence."

"Evidence that someone planted," Harriet called, from my side.

"What makes you so sure someone planted it?" He asked, his gaze attentive to Harriet's answer.

"Because, how can you believe Vivienne would take a payment to murder someone? She is one of the nicest and most loving people in this town."

"That may be so but didn't you yourself witness an argument between Camille and Vivienne the night before her murder at The Four Brothers?" he asked.

His words were a crushing blow even I hadn't anticipated. The hairs on my neck pricked. I remember the argument as clear as day.

Harriet's jaw dropped. "What?"

He glanced down at his notepad and continued to speak. "According to my notes, you, Jordi and Evelyn were all at The Four Brothers on Wednesday evening along with several other people who witnessed the verbal disagreement between Vivienne and Camille where Vivienne was overheard saying…*I'll get the money and I will make you eat your words, if it's the last thing I do.* That sounds like a threat to me."

A heaviness filled my chest. I don't understand how Vivienne's words could be taken so far out of context.

Huxton stood his ground. "Some might say, the poisoned pumpkin pie and sudden influx in her bank balance is a clear indication of a guilty person."

"Some might, Detective," Aunt Edie said, her shoulders held stiff. "But we're not *some* people."

Jordi huffed. "Besides, most people in Saltwater Cove had choice words with Camille one time or another."

"If that's the case." Harriet stepped forward and held her wrists out toward him, palms smiling at the roof. "Arrest me too. I probably had many run ins with Camille, and they weren't always civil."

He shook his head and gave a wavering smile. If that's not the look of surrender, I don't know what is. "That won't be necessary, Harriet. For what it's worth I don't believe Vivienne is capable of murder any more than you ladies do, but I have a job to do and that job relies on evidence. I'm aware most of the town didn't see eye to eye with Camille, but then none of them have an additional half a million dollars in their bank accounts either. As yet, I am not arresting Vivienne, not technically."

"What does that mean?" Olive asked.

His gaze once more landed on Aunt Edie, his restless stance a giveaway to his conflicting emotions. "It means Vivienne is fully aware of my findings and she has agreed to stay supervised within the boundaries of her house."

"You mean under house arrest?" I blurted. This evening was going from bad to worse and the slight twitchy niggle behind my left eye had progressed to a full-blown headache.

He nodded. "Yes. By rights she should be charged with murder and be in a holding cell, but I promised Edith I'd leave no stone unturned. I'm still following up on a few leads. Something doesn't sit right with me and until I can get to the bottom of it, I've given permission for Vivienne to stay in her own home where she'll be comfortable. And where her friends will be able to contact her freely."

"Thank you, Detective," Aubrey said, offering him a smile. "We appreciate you bending the rules. If you don't mind, Olive and I will be on our way now. It has been a rather taxing day."

"Of course." He dipped his head. "Hopefully next time we meet it will be under happier circumstances."

"Yes, indeed," Aubrey said.

She and Olive gave Aunt Edie a hug and left. The door closing sharply behind them startled Miss Saffron in my arms.

"Meow." Her tail shot up straighter than a ruler. She twisted and turned in my arms. My grip slipped and she fell to the floor catching herself silently on all fours.

Rubbing the new scratch marks on my left arm, I glared at her standing tall as if she knew exactly what I was about to say. "Aw, next time you want to get down, just tell me." She splayed her front paw out on the ground and dipped her head in a bow-like action. I grinned. "That's more like it."

"Did that cat just bow to you?" Detective Huxton asked, an eyebrow raised.

"Yep, she did." I winked at Miss Saffron and she moseyed on back to sit by my feet. "Miss Saffron and I have a certain way we communicate."

Aunt Edie piped up. "Will there be anything else?"

My gut knotted at the wishful look in his eyes, as if he'd rather be with Aunt Edie the way things were before he left five years ago. He shook his head and took a couple of steps toward the door then clicked his fingers and spun.

"There was one more thing." He turned to Harriet. "I want you to stay away from the bank until I give the all clear. We had a tip-off regarding Camille's safe, so I called into the bank to check it out on my way over here and it looks like there has been a break in."

Jordi wrinkled her nose at Detective Huxton. "Camille had a safe? She was a woman of many secrets."

"Break in? What sort of break in?" I pried, but my breath hitched.

"Yes, although there seems to be no evidence of forced entry. It appears someone has gone through her stuff and we found an inked tissue in the waste basket that wasn't there previously."

Nausea clutched my throat and squeezed. The shiver of guilt stung my chest and worked its way to my belly. If I keep my mouth zipped there's no way Huxton can know Harriet and I were at the bank today. I'll make out it was their stuff-up.

"It was me. I spilt the ink," Harriet said, her voice thick and choked with emotion. "But I didn't break in, I swear. I have a key."

What are you doing, crazy woman? Do you want to get us both thrown in jail?

Huxton thinned his lips and said through gritted teeth. "Come again?"

I stared at Harriet desperate to get her attention before she blabbed, but she ignored my disguised eye gestures and kept talking.

"I'm so sorry." Her voice pleaded for understanding. "I had no idea I was supposed to let someone know. Camille had such a heavy workload and I know Mr Bain is going to be under the pump after being at the symposium and Della not getting back until next week. I thought I'd go in and pick up Camille's backlog of accounts and see if I can get a head start on them. I knocked over the inkwell and it went all over my clothes and I wiped it with a tissue." Harriet paused, tears welling in her eyes. "I have the damaged pants at home if you don't believe me. I didn't mean to cause you any trouble. I swear." A lone tear trickled down her pink cheek.

"Okay, okay it's all right. I believe you." He tutted and ran a hand through his hair. "I appreciate you coming clean, but in future check first before you go venturing into one of my crime scenes."

Harriet wiped her rosy wet cheeks with the back of her palm and nodded.

"Maybe I should post a policeman out front of my crime scenes from now on just in case anyone else gets a similar idea." He turned to Aunt Edie and smiled. "I am sorry for disrupting your evening. My promise still stands. I will inform you as soon as new information comes to light."

"Thank you. I appreciate it." Aunt Edie opened the door and he walked past brushing shoulders. "Good night, Detective Huxton."

"Good night, Edith,' he said, as she closed the door behind him.

Crisis averted, I turned to see Harriet rocking from side to side, arms swinging with a huge cheeky grin from ear to ear.

"I don't believe it. You were acting the whole time?"

"Me neither," Jordi said, lips pursed and hands on her hips.

PUMPKIN PIES & POTIONS

"While you ladies were off learning your witchy spells and shapeshifter tricks some of us were learning the important skills in life."

Jordi huffed. "Important skills like fake crying?"

Harriet shrugged. "Important skills like getting out of a tight situation with our limbs intact. Hey, there's always the need for one drama queen, so why not me?"

"It was an Oscar winning performance, Harriet," Aunt Edie said, doing her best keep a straight face. "Let's make sure we try to keep everything above board from now on. I do believe it's time to call it a night."

Jordi picked up her bag and the letters and hugged each of us before heading for the door.

"I'll search these and do my best to find any possible leads. I'll call you if I find anything. Night."

Aunt Edie looked exhausted. "Tomorrow is going to be a long day."

"You took the words right out of my mouth."

CHAPTER FIFTEEN

"Hold on," I screamed at the top of my lungs. Each word I spoke sliced my vocal cords like a shard of glass through skin. Crushing pain hit my lungs, intensified by the growing pressure of my chest flattened to the edge of a lone cliff. Harriet's life hung by a thread in my hands.

"Oh God, Evelyn don't let go. Please don't let me fall."

Harriet's pleading voice curdled the blood in my veins. Silent tears streamed down her face, a contrast to the violent thrashing waves beneath her dangling feet at the bottom of the cliff face. I squeezed her wrist tighter, my fingers cramping under the intense grip. My racing pulse boomed in my ears.

Oh God she's slipping. Come on Harriet, help me. I can't hold on any longer.

"Harriet, give me your other hand so I can pull you up," I yelled against the bitter-cold howling wind.

"I…I can't. Hel…help me."

Her voice crackled and disappeared as her grip loosened and she slid out of my hand free falling to her death.

"Nooooo," I screamed through the tears streaming down my face. My body frozen in the moment.

Snapping my eyes open, I shot up in bed, the air in my lungs so scarce I could barely breathe. I gasped huge breaths, sucking as much air as each gasp would let me. I scrunched my hands into fists, drawing the sheet into a ball in the process.

"What was that?" I muttered, my gaze searching for the cliff. The comforts of my bedroom replaced the nightmare. My bedside clock read two-thirty in bright red neon numbers. The silence of the darkened sky outside my window goose bumped my entire body. I ran a hand through my damp hair. Drenched with cool moisture, I grabbed the sheet and wiped the back of my neck and forehead. I closed my heavy eyelids a moment and focused on returning my breathing to its normal.

Why would I be dreaming about Harriet dying? God, I hope I don't have the power to see the future otherwise I'm locking her in a cage for the rest of her life.

"Why Harriet? It has to mean something, doesn't it?"

Drained from the emotional onslaught, I slid my legs over the edge of the bed. I cringed and rubbed my heavy chest with the palm of my hand. Pain ripped through my heart as if it had been torn in two. Maybe Harriet is in trouble. "I already know that piece of information from her own nightmare."

Sleep is not going to come easy now. A warm Milo usually does the trick when I can't stop my mind from racing. I blew out a heavy breath and slipped into my dressing gown. The eerie stillness of the house was a little unnerving. I crept downstairs careful not to disturb Harriet or Aunt Edie in the process.

I switched on the kitchen light and turned to see two golden eyes within arms-reach glowing under the bright light. I sucked in a sharp breath and my hand shot to my chest. My racing heart beat a relentless drumming against my palm.

"Far out, Miss Saffron. You sure know how to scare the bejesus out of someone." I scooped her up in my arms and she nuzzled into my neck, purring her pleasure. I smiled. "All right, you're forgiven." She turned her elegant face to mine and her whiskers curved upwards into a smile.

Cheeky girl.

I placed Miss Saffron on the counter next to the kettle. Sitting on her haunches, she steadily scrutinised my every move as I made a Milo.

"I guess I could talk to you about my dream." I leant against the kitchen bench and by the time I'd relayed the entire dream to Miss Saffron, a slow growl hung low in her throat. "I totally agree with you. And it's my job as her best friend to protect her. She's so new at being a witch, who knows what powers she'll end up with? I know she has the amulet but…" I paused, taking another sip, my insides doing a happy dance as the chocolate milky liquid worked its way down to my stomach.

I snapped my fingers, the answer hit me like a bolt of lightning. I looked at Miss Saffron and her inquisitive frown was just the cutest. "She needs a get out of jail free card." Miss Saffron tilted her head and her elegant tail whipped from side to side like a slithering snake.

"Don't you get it? The amulet will protect her but what if she needs to escape in a hurry? She'll need an out and I have the perfect solution." My body buzzed knowing she'd have an added level of protection. Miss Saffron nodded and stood tall, her back legs higher than the front showing her power and agility. She sprung through the air from the bench to the table like a panther in the wild and sat on the table ready. She loves it when I do magic. Sometimes I think she even understand the spells I'm casting.

I turned, grabbed a plastic bottle of sparkling water from the door of the fridge and re-joined her at the table.

Perfect. No-one will suspect this bottle has a freeze spell on it. Especially the person who opens it.

I opened the lid and held the bottle in one hand and the other floated above the top. I concentrated my focus on the cool liquid. I whispered, "A moment in time is what I seek, if you open this bottle all will go weak. With this spell a statue you'll be, until such time as I set you free." My fingertips tingled and a string of sparkled energy circled my hand and dove into the open bottle.

Replacing the lid, I smiled at Miss Saffron, who sat with beady eyes hanging off my every word. I sucked in a breath and a yawn scrunched my face into a thousand tiny lines.

"I think bed is calling, Miss Saffron," I said, picking her up and placing her comfortably back in her bed. I grabbed the bottle off the table and headed for the stairs. I called over my shoulder, "See you in the morning."

I looped the final twist of elastic around my ponytail and grabbed my pink cardigan off the bed. I looked at my ordinary reflection in the mirror. Not a bad look if I say so myself. Three-quarter cut-off jeans, aqua blue Grecian long-sleeve style top and white wedge sneakers. "Happy Halloween, Evelyn Grayson. Just another day in the life of a witch except this Halloween, I plan on catching a murderer before the holiday is totally ruined."

As I headed downstairs, my nostrils were accosted with the sugary scent of cinnamon. "What is that most delectable smell?" I said, entering the kitchen.

Harriet stood next to Aunt Edie by the stove, both deep in concentration, looking at a sizzling pan on the stove top.

Aunt Edie was the best aunt any girl could ask for. I loved the way she included Harriet and Jordi as part of the family. It seems I walked in on a cooking lesson in progress.

"Ah, hello? Are you having a cooking party over there or can anyone join in?"

Harriet spun and the animated sparkle in her eye had me smiling from ear to ear. "Evelyn, you're up. Aunt Edie's been showing me how to make fluffy cinnamon pancakes."

"So, I see." Thank goodness Harriet was wearing an apron. I think there was more batter on her than in the bowl.

"Are you hungry? I've made enough for everyone." She turned around and lifted the plate stacked high with delicious looking pancakes. Her brow creased as she looked at her handywork. "Actually, I think I've made enough for the whole town."

A hungry guttural growl worked its way up from my stomach to my throat. "Looks like my stomach has spoken and it says." I held my hands out toward the plate. "Gimme, gimme, gimme."

A cheeky giggle came from Aunt Edie's direction. "Now, now. There's plenty to go around."

She joined me at the table with a warm smile that lit her face up. "I was impressed with how quickly Harriet picked it up. Maybe I should train you as a cook and then you can take over The Melting Pot with Evelyn and I can be a lady of leisure."

What? Aunt Edie retire from The Melting Pot?

My chest tightened as her words sunk to the bottom of my stomach like a ten-pound stone. "Aunt Edie, are you thinking of leaving The Melting Pot?"

"Good gracious no," she said, amid a gasp or two and patted my wobbly knee.

A woosh of heat raced through my body and planted itself in my chest. "That's a relief."

She continued, her eyes subtly diverted from mine.

"But a woman of my age does need a rest every now and then. I wouldn't mind doing some travelling and if you had someone to help you run the place on a regular basis it would put my mind at ease."

Harriet clapped her hands together at her chest and her widened gaze caught Aunt Edie's eye. "O-M-G, you really think I have what it takes to be a good cook?"

"Of course, with the right training," I said, taking another bite of her mouth-watering pancakes. "Are you sure you want to be a cook?"

Harriet shrugged. "I'm not sure, but what I do know is I don't want to work at the bank anymore. It was okay and all, but after what happened to Camille," she paused and I saw a physical shudder run through her body. "I'm not keen on working in a place of death. Besides, now I'm a witch, I've a lot of years of training to catch up on and I'll need all the help I can get. I do love to cook and I love food, especially eating it. This way, I can learn to cook and train as a witch. Aunt Edie will be able to take some time off and I'll get to work with you and eat at the best café in town. Win-win for everyone."

I looked at Aunt Edie and she stared blankly back at me as dumbfounded as I was. "Did you accidently employ a new apprentice cook?"

"It appears I did." She leant over smiling warmly and squeezed Harriet's hand. "Welcome to The Melting Pot."

Harriet's excited high-pitched squeal shattered my ear drum, but I couldn't help the broad smile painted on my face. I looked at Aunt Edie. "Are you sure you know what you're doing? Harriet and I working together on a daily basis could be a recipe for disaster."

"It could also be a triumphant winner. Just imagine all the new fresh ideas your creative young minds will bring to the table." She stood and began clearing the breakfast mess. She placed the dishes in the sink and turned, standing with her hands on her hips. "And I think your training should start right now. It is the responsibility of every cook to clean their station after the cooking is complete and that includes breakfast." She grinned and spun on her heel toward The Melting Pot. "I'll be next door working on preparations for this evening. Don't forget to meet back here for an update at lunchtime."

The wooden door slammed shut behind her and I blinked at the echoing noise. "Not sure what's gotten into her this morning."

Harriet sprang off her chair and moved double time to clear the rest of the dishes. "I don't care. This is the best day ever. I have a new job. Goodbye bank and goodbye Mr Bain."

"Hold that thought," I said, putting my plate in the dishwasher. "Can you quit after you get me back into the bank?"

Harriet paused and her forehead creased like a crumpled-up chip packet.

"What are you talking about? I thought we were heading over to the old Grand Majestic to have a look around."

"We were…are, but I want to have one more look in Camille's office for her safe. Detective Huxton mentioned a safe. Did you know she had safe?"

Harriet shook her head and continued to rinse the dishes before stacking the dishwasher. "No, I had no idea. We've already searched her office and came up with the mirrored box. I can't see where she'd have a safe hidden away."

Do you have more secrets to reveal, Camille, or will this be a dead end? Can I really afford not to find out?

I shook my head and headed back to the table to grab the empty pancake plate and maple syrup. "I really don't think we can chance it. If there is a safe, what is in there could exonerate Vivienne of mur—"

The thunderous clap of shattering crockery bellowed from the sink and I spun to see Harriet sliding to her knees as if her legs were void of bones. Her shaking hands were holding her head as she rocked back and forth. She was gasping for air, her mutterings were rushed and garbled, and I could hardly make out a word.

Bile burned in the back of my throat. I crouched in front of her and held her shoulders, the vibration coursing through them shaking my own hands. "Oh my God, Harriet…Harriet?" She sat rocking back and forth, her body shaking uncontrollably.

"Harriet? Talk to me. Harriet, what's happening?" My heart beat so chaotic in my chest I thought it was going to jump right out of my skin.

Her elbows pulled into her side and she rolled her torso forward into a tight ball and as quickly as it started, it stopped. I gulped a lung full of air and sat paralysed waiting for her to register her surroundings. Minutes passed, although they felt like hours and she slowly unfurled her body. She looked straight through me and my heart clenched at the torment embedded in the depths of her eyes.

"Harriet, what happened?" I asked in my most calm voice, which was totally opposite to my insides. They were screaming like wildfire.

She squeezed her lips together, the corners turning down. She tensed and my gut knotted when fire worked its way into her eyes. Her monotone voice had an alarming chill to it.

"If this is what happens when I see a vision, you can take the witch powers back. I don't want them."

"You saw something?" I asked. She nodded slowly taking several breaths. Unsure what to do, I pushed up off the floor. "I'll get Aunt Edie."

"No," Harriet said, grabbing my wrist and yanking me back down. "I mean, please don't bother her, she's busy."

Aw, no need to rip my arms out of the socket.

I paused. Harriet loosened her grip and I held her cold hand in mine and offered the warmest smile I could muster.

"She's never too busy to help. That's what we're here for."

Harriet shook her head and her focus dropped to her hands. She picked one cuticle then another then another.

"I'm okay, really."

"Can you tell me what you saw?" I waited patiently.

She cleared her throat and began to stand. "It was the same as my dream, I mean my vision where a guy is chasing me, and my head is all bloodied. I guess this is what it feels like to have a vision when I'm awake."

Harriet's watery gaze tightened my throat. I've had years to come to terms with being a witch and how to focus my skills. Poor Harriet has been thrown in the deep end, and in the middle of a murder investigation no less. It's my job as her best friend to make sure she gets through this.

I threw my arms around her and squeezed as much love into them as I could manage. She tensed under my emotional onslaught. "You are going to be fine and I'm going to make sure of it."

"Huh…Evelyn?" she winced.

I pulled back and stood eye to eye, her agitated gaze understandable. "You're new at this, but you're not alone, Harriet. Aunt Edie and I will help you, well mostly Aunt Edie. She's a wonderful teacher and being a master witch means she knows a lot more than most witches. We'll help you hone your witch skills so that you can control them and learn how to turn them into an asset rather than a disability. Which is what I'm guessing they're feeling like right now."

Harriet's widened gaze stared at me like she'd missed every word I said.

"Harriet, did you hear what I said?"

She nodded. "Yes, thank you. I guess I was all caught up in the glamour and excitement of finding out I was a witch I wasn't really prepared or maybe I didn't believe it was true. Now, I know it's true and anything you or Aunt Edie can do to help me deal with the ambush of visions, I'll gladly take it."

"Are you sure you're okay?" I asked, a twinge of uncertainty niggled my gut.

"Yeah, I think so," she said, picking up the dropped dishes and placing them on the side of the sink. "It's not like I saw anything new."

I took over stacking the dishwasher while she rested against the kitchen bench. "Do you remember what happened just before you saw the vision? How did it make you feel?"

She nodded and ran her hand across her brow. "It was the weirdest feeling like I was wrapped up in a woollen blanket in the middle of summer. It covered my mouth and nose and I couldn't breathe, I couldn't move and my arms were strapped down. Fire ignited from my feet up and the heat was unbearable like I was cooking from the inside out, burning under the most intense heat. My skin pricked as the fire licked up my body and all I could do was scream and hope someone would hear me and then it seemed to level off as the vision emerged."

"Well, damn, that is one intense way to see the future," I said.

"Yeah," Harriet crossed her arms. "Wasn't the best way to start the day."

I hit the start button on the dishwasher then returned my gaze to Harriet. "But now you know what it feels like, you can sense a vision coming on. You'll know what to expect next time. For the time being, maybe we should have a word or signal that lets me know you're about to have a vision then I can be there to help you come out of it."

She pushed off the bench. "That is such a cool idea. How about…I'll ask for cinnamon pancakes."

"What?" I looked at her and a familiar zesty energy buzzed in her expression. "Why on earth would you choose cinnamon pancakes?"

"Because they were the official first meal I cooked as the new employee of The Melting Pot, so why not? If I get the sensation again, I'll try to say I need some cinnamon pancakes and you'll know exactly what I mean," she said in a matter-of-fact tone.

"Sounds good to me." I threw my arm around her shoulder. "I gotta say life is never boring when you're around."

"Pfft," Harriet said. She brushed my comment aside like the wind. "Boring is for dead people. Now we have a bank to visit, do we not?"

"We sure do, but before we head off, I made something last night I'd like you to keep in your bag." My stomach fluttered as I took the water bottle out of my bag and placed it on the table. The inside had turned a violet shade as it should.

Harriet's eyebrows squished together in a frown. "Um, Evelyn you do know you don't have to make bottled water, there's plenty in the fridge."

Cheeky sod.

"Oh, you think you're funny, don't you?" I said, poking her in the ribs.

She giggled and jumped out of the way. "I thought so."

"This is no ordinary bottle of water." I paused and watched my words work their way into Harriet's mind. The penny dropped and her gaze glowed like an inquisitive child in their first science lesson. "I want you to have this bottle of water and keep it with you at all times."

"Me...why?" she asked.

"This bottle contains a freeze spell and once opened, it will freeze the person who holds the opened bottle in their hands. Frozen like a statue.

Only for about thirty to forty seconds, but enough for you to make an escape." Harriet picked up the bottle and held it like she was cradling life itself. "Or dong them over the head with a heady object, whichever is required."

"This is so awesome, thank you." She looked up, a flash of trepidation crossing her expression. "But why?"

I shrugged and my stomach rolled like a brewing storm. "I was worried about you and I know you have the amulet on, but I wanted to make sure you had another way to protect yourself. Something that no-one would suspect. Just promise me you won't get it mixed up with a normal bottle. Just remember it's a violet shade."

She smiled and hugged the bottle to her chest. "I promise."

"Excellent." I glanced over at the wall clock and my jaw dropped. "Crap, we're already running late. Do you think you can be ready in ten minutes to go to the bank?"

"If I'm not..." She grinned and bolted toward the stairs. "I'll do the dishes every night for the next week."

CHAPTER SIXTEEN

"I don't believe it," I said, driving past the bank and watching the security guard fiddling with his phone. Huxton was true to his word.

"What don't you believe?" Harriet asked.

"Huxton said he'd put a man outside the bank, and he did. I guess we'll have to go to Plan B."

"Plan B? I didn't know we had a Plan B."

I smirked and turned the corner. "Give me time, I'm working on it. We need a way to get in that won't cause suspicion."

Harriet slapped her forehead. "I've got it. I don't know why I didn't think of it earlier." Her hand pointed dead ahead two streets past the bank. "Park there, behind the big oak tree."

Trusting Harriet's instincts, I swerved and parked on the other side of the tree, the low, leafy branches semi-masking my car from street view. Killing the engine, I turned to Harriet.

"What's Plan B?"

"Plan B is where I walk around to the front of the bank and convince the security guard to let me in so I can do some catch up work. Then I meet you at the side door and let you in and he'll be none the wiser. He won't even know you're inside." Harriet sat gleaming, chuffed with her idea.

"I love how your devious mind works." I held my hand up for a high five. Harriet's palm met mine sealing the plan of action. "You my dear, are going to be one handy witch to have around The Melting Pot."

Her eyes widened and she bounded out of the car. "You think so? Once I can learn how to control my visions, that is."

Harriet's upbeat energy was contagious. "Right, you go and wait behind the Hydrangea bushes and once I'm in I'll come get you."

We headed down the path and I stepped onto the grass pathway toward the side door. "I suppose you'll be drawing on more of your acting skills?"

Her head spun in my direction and she gave me a cheeky wink. "Well, we can't possibly have the bank open on Monday as normal when we're so backlogged with work. Imagine the trouble I'll get in? Besides what's a few tears if it helps get us the answers we need?"

"You're incorrigible. I'll see you soon."

Harriet nodded and took off, her bronzed bob swishing from side to side in the morning breeze. She walked with confidence and enough swagger to convince me.

I paced the ground behind the Hydrangea bush, a million and one reasons why she wouldn't be able to get in running through my mind. The powerful stench of a nearby Jasmine tree fought for pride of place, beating down the subtle scent of the Hydrangeas. My stomach churned from its sickly scent assaulting my senses or the possibility I could get caught breaking into a bank.

Come on Harriet. How long does it take? I must admit, she has some pretty snazzy acting skills but are they good enough to convince a lone security guard to let her in?

I kept my gaze alert, scanning a three sixty-degree area around me. It would be just my luck to have Detective Huxton out for a Saturday morning stroll. I jumped at the click of the lock on the door behind me and my heart kick-started into spasms. I turned and saw Harriet leaning against the open door, arms folded across her chest and a huge smile on her face. She waved me inside.

I guess her acting skills did the job. I really must get her to give me a few pointers on the acting front. You never know when I might need them. I raced up the stairs and followed her inside. "What took you so long?"

She rolled her eyes to the roof. "Mr Stuffy-pants out there was tougher than I thought." She dipped her head and then tossed her hair in one big swoop upward just like the runway models do to the camera. "He was no match for me. Once I teared up and explained how much trouble I was going to be in when Mr Bain returned if I didn't catch up on the backlog of work since Camille's murder, he softened a little and then I went in for the kill."

I raised an eyebrow. "The kill?"

"Huh ha," she nodded and headed toward Camille's office dumping her bag on her desk as she went by. "The tears were free flowing by then. I told him how Detective Huxton said it was okay to come in as long as I let someone know and if he didn't believe me to call him. But I pointed out I'd hate to be in his shoes when Huxton goes off his head for having his Saturday morning interrupted to ask a stupid question. Then he asked me where my car was."

"And what did you say?" This story was getting better by the second. Harriet should write a soap opera. I bet she'd sell it to a television network easy.

She grinned and her cheeks glowed a rosy pink. "That's the best part. I told him I walked to town because I was getting a head start on exercise. That way I could let loose tonight with the chocolates while trick or treating. I asked if he thought I looked fat in this outfit. I did a few twirls and catwalk struts. He must be trained well because a smart man never tells a woman she looks fat no matter what outfit she's wearing, or how much she's baiting him, and he was a smart man."

"Harriet, you didn't?" My jaw dropped.

She scrunched up her face and nodded gleefully. "I did. I know it was probably over the top, but after that he was putty in my hands and I kept telling myself it was for Vivienne. In the end, he said as long as I stay at my desk and away from Camille's office I was fine to come in. I'm not sure if he's going to call Detective Huxton or not so let's make this search as quick as possible."

"I agree," I said, easing her door open. It looked exactly how we left it yesterday minus the ink-stained tissue in the bin. "We're looking for a safe so it won't be in any ordinary place. Check behind wall pictures, cupboards, the floor for moved or replaced carpet, places like that."

Harriet moved to the other side of the room and began searching.

"Wait," I called and she spun, her eyes ringing with concern. "Leave everything exactly how you found it and I mean exactly."

Her brow creased and she tilted her head to the side. "I think I've learnt my lesson on that front."

I noticed Camille had no personal mementoes anywhere in her office. A dullness filled my chest as I remembered the smile on her face when she was under Aunt Edie's happy candy spell. I wish I had known the real Camille. I eased my fingers behind an antique-style painting hanging above the filing cabinets and pulled it forward. Squinting, I flattened my cheek to the cool wall and looked behind. Nothing, nada, zilch.

Harriet's whispered voice echoed around the wall. "Found anything?"

"No, you?" I asked.

She shook her head and frowned. "No. I can't find any secret safe or anything else secret for that matter."

Garbled noise resembling voices came from the front door. I clutched the edge of the filing cabinet while my stomach took a walloping from the butterflies dancing the quickstep inside my belly. Harriet's eyes widened and she pressed her fist to her mouth. Gate crashers were not in the plan.

What if it's Detective Huxton here to boot Harriet out? Maybe the security guard summed up the nerve to call him. This is not going to go down well. I'm not sure how we'll be able to talk our way out of this one.

Harriet moved to the window and peeked through the vertical blinds. She gasped, loud enough whoever was at the door could have heard. She spun, her face white as a sheet of paper. "It's Mr Bain," she mouthed. "What is he doing here? I didn't expect him to come in until Monday."

We were sitting ducks. "I have to get out of here. You might be allowed in the bank, but I'm certainly not."

"No." Harriet shook her head and her gaze wondered frantically looking all over Camille's office. "There's no time. By the sounds of his high-pitch annoyed tone he'll be walking through the front door any minute."

Any minute? My head swam and the light-headedness hit me at once like a gush of warm air. "What are we going to do?"

Harriet's hand held her forehead while she glanced around at the office once more. Her arms flew open and she thrust her hand out toward Camille's desk. "Get under there?"

I raised my eyebrows. "Under where?"

Harriet gritted her teeth and rolled her eyes. She grabbed a bunch of files off Camille's desk. "For heaven's sake, hide under Camille's desk. I'll tell him I'm catching up on Camille's work."

"And leave me stuck under the desk...no thanks."

"Have you got a better idea?" Harriet's gaze shot to the door and back again. "We're out of time. It's either under the desk or get caught in here, which will probably end both of us in a nice padded jail cell for a while."

The blood drained from my face and I knew in my heart Harriet was right. "Okay, okay, but how am I going to get out of here without you getting into trouble or blowing your cover?" I said as I rushed toward the cramped space, my heart thumping my chest wall.

Harriet winked and straightened her shoulders. "Don't worry, I'll get you out somehow. Now stay here until the coast is clear. Got it?"

I nodded and crouched down in front of the opening, my trembling hand gripping the edge of the desk and I looked up into Harriet's animated expression. "Thanks Harriet. I owe you."

"Nonsense, that's what best friends do for each other."

She turned sharply on her heel and exited Camille's office. I caught a glimpse of the morning sunlight stream through the front door of the bank as it opened before I held my breath and twisted my body into a space the size of a dog kennel. With my legs bent up and my knees around my armpits, I wrapped my arms around my legs and bent my neck forward so my forehead was almost kissing my knees.

Great, I'm definitely going to need a massage when I get out of here just so I'll be able to stand up straight.

I closed my eyes and focussed on the strained voices coming from the main area of the bank. Their chatter was full of distorted sentences, but a few words stuck out like an out of place jar in Aunt Edie's pantry. Backlog…Dawnbury Heights…last night. Dawnbury Heights? Isn't that where the banking symposium was being held?

Aw…Aw…Aw. No, no, no not a cramp in my hip. Why now? Why choose now to cramp up?

I held my breath and slapped my hand over my mouth, biting down on the inside of my index finger. A holler of pain tickled the inside of my throat and I squeezed my entire body tight like one of those stress balls you crush in your hand when you want to scream. If I didn't move there was going to be hell to pay and I'd be the one paying for it. I'd be walking like the Scarecrow from the Wizard of Oz for days.

As noiseless as I could, I dropped sideways onto my elbow and manoeuvred my hips around so I could drop my knees forward. The instant relief in my hip was akin to winning the hundred-metre sprint against the world number one. My head dropped back as I let out a silent exhale.

What the heck is that?

I locked onto the dark object taped to the underside of Camille's desk. It blended seamlessly with the dark wooden underside of her desktop. A place no-one would look unless they were hiding. Guess this is my lucky day. As lucky as one can get scrunched up like a crumpled piece of paper hidden at the bottom of the rubbish bin.

I reached up and the rough edges of metal scrapped along the edge of my skin. I ran my fingers along the outline and a new spur of adrenaline ignited my insides.

"A key?" I whispered. "Is this the key to open your safe, Camille?"

With my fingernail, I managed to peel the sticky tape back away with one hand and the other caught the key as it dropped like a deflated basketball. You're the answer, but to what, I'm not sure.

The stark cry of Harriet's voice bellowed from the bank and I just about smashed my head against the side of the mahogany desk. "Evelyn…NOW. Get out now."

"Now," I repeated as I clutched the key in my hand and scrambled to my feet ignoring the lingering pain in my hip. Bolting from my hiding place, I ran out of Camille's office, my pulse racing. I stopped when my gaze landed on Mr Bain crouched down on one knee on the ground beside Harriet with an open water bottle in his hands.

Harriet beamed. "Thanks for the frozen spell. Worked a treat." She grabbed the bottle and replaced the lid securely.

I had never seen Mr Bain on his knees before, let alone frozen at Harriet's feet. "The mind boggles. I don't have time now, but you are going to have to fill me in later why your boss is frozen down on one knee beside you looking like he's about to propose."

Harriet's eyes widened and she looked into his eyes and shivered. "Ew, don't even go there. How am I supposed to get that image out of my head? Since the bank didn't open yesterday, he stayed an extra night in Dawnbury Heights and came back last night. He came in today to get a head start on sorting stuff and then he began asking all sorts of question about the murder, Vivienne, and then he was going to ring Detective Huxton to find out the latest. I couldn't chance him telling the detective I'm here, so I faked a panic attack and asked him to get me my water bottle. My hands were shaking so much I couldn't open it so he said he would."

"You are positively sinful, Harriet Oakley," I said, so proud of her on-the-spot thinking. "I have to get out of here before the spell wears off. I've found another clue, but I don't have time to tell you now. I'll call you from the car and explain everything."

"A clue?" Harriet's eyes shone like glow worms.

There is no use having a clue if I don't know what it means. I tapped the first four digits of Harriet's number into my phone only to be interrupted by a photo of Jordi and me laughing at Graduation flash across the screen. "Hi Jordi. I—"

"Hi Evelyn," she said in a downward tone. "I'm really sorry, but I cannot find any clue or hint of anything in these letters. I know it was a threat to Camille and it must be staring me blindly in the face. I'm not giving up though. I will look at these until the next full moon if I have to, I will find something."

A ball of excited energy had my mind going faster than I could gather my thoughts. I held the rusted key up and my mind focused on one path.

Finding the answer must lay with this key. "Jordi, forget about the letters for now. I need a favour."

"Name it."

"I can't go into all the details now," I said, my mind moving faster than my mouth could keep up. "But I found an old key taped to the underside of Camille's desk. I'm sure it holds the answer to the puzzle. I want to get Tyler's help, he's got the computer connections to identify it, I hope."

"Way to go," she said with a renewed upbeat spring to her voice. "What do you need me to do?"

"Can you pick up Harriet from the bank? We were supposed to go over to the Grand Majestic to check it out. If you two could do that while I head over to Tyler's, we can knock two things on the head before we have to meet back at Aunt Edie's at lunchtime."

"Sure, no problem. I can be there in about fifteen minutes."

I dropped my head back and sighed. "Perfect. Have I told you lately that you're the best?"

Jordi's cheeky laugh warmed my heart. "Not in the last twenty-four hours but I'll forgive you. Want me to give Harriet a quick call?"

I shook my head. "No, it's cool. I promised I'll fill her in on the key. I'll tell her to be waiting out front of the bank in fifteen minutes."

"Sounds good to me. Keep me posted. Later," she said and hung up.

That woman sure does have a way with words. Short, sweet, and straight to the point.

I redialled Harriet's number and she picked up with two rings. She must have been sitting on the phone. "Harriet, are you okay?"

"Oh hi Evelyn. Yeah, I'm at work trying to catch up on some of the backlog."

Harriet's placating tone sent a warning shooting through me. "You can't talk, can you? I assume Mr Bain is in ear's reach."

"You got that right. I'm not sure how we'll get it all done."

I paused and bit my lip. "Okay, the shortened version is I found an old rusted key taped underneath Camille's desk. It has to be a clue of some sort, so I am heading over to Tyler's place to clean it up and pick his computer's brain to hopefully find an answer. Jordi is going to come by and pick you up out the front of the bank in fifteen minutes and then you two are going to check out the Grand Majestic. I'll take screen shots of the post-it notes and message them to you. Got it?"

She sighed. "Yeah, you're probably right. I have been a little off since this whole murder happened. Maybe I should head home after all. You're a good friend, Evelyn."

That's my girl. Keep that façade going for as long as possible.

"Use the panic attack if you have to just meet Jordi out front in fifteen."

"Okay, maybe I'll chat with you later after I head home and go back to bed for a few hours," she said.

Her sombre tone even convinced me.

"I'll be in touch if I have any news and likewise. Call me if you find anything out of the ordinary."

"Of course, I'll take some Panadol. Bye."

"See you later." She hung up. I threw my phone and the key back into my bag, turned the engine over and took off toward Tyler's. Please, please, please, make him find me some answers.

CHAPTER SEVENTEEN

Are you for real? How long does it take to open a damn door? "Tyler...Tyler come on open up," I called even louder. My knuckles numbed from the continual beating they were receiving against the hard wood.

The door flew open and my eyes were treated to a half-naked Tyler sporting a pair of pyjama bottoms and nothing else. I swallowed the hard lump in my throat.

He rubbed his sleepy eyes. "Is there a fire or something? A flood maybe? What is with pounding the door this early on a Saturday morning? Have you no consideration for people who may be suffering a hangover?"

A hangover? I've no time for self-inflicted dramas especially from a half-naked man resembling a Greek God. I pushed past and stormed into the kitchen.

"You have exactly ten minutes to make yourself respectable and be back in the kitchen and that includes a shower."

He followed me, dragging his groaning alcohol-induced lazy body behind. "Ten minutes? Come off it, Evie girl. You can't be serious?"

I spun and stood as still as a statue with my hands on my hips. My eyes thinned. Heat rose up my neck and a blaze of warmth planted itself in my cheeks.

He recoiled and took a step back. "I may have been away for a few years, but I could never forget that look. Ten minutes…you got it." He turned and bolted toward his bedroom.

I held back a giggle. Nice to know I can still scare the pants off him. Just like high school. I passed the time brewing two much needed coffees. Leaning against the kitchen bench, I sipped the steaming hot liquid. The sweet aroma bled into my veins and soothed the tension slowly building in my chest. Just as the clock struck ten, he reappeared fully clothed.

"Is one of those for me?" he asked.

I smiled and handed his coffee over. "You know I love coffee but if I have two of these in a row,

I won't need a spell to climb the walls, I'll be scaling them from caffeine overload. Why the hangover?"

Tyler shrugged and took a seat at the kitchen table and hesitated before speaking. "Nothing special. Just me and my old mate Jim Beam spent the night together watching some old classic movies." He paused and took several mouthfuls of the steaming elixir. "I'll be right as rain after I get this coffee into me."

"Glad to hear it." I wasn't convinced by his explanation but there were more pressing matters to attend to. I locked it away in the back of my mind to revisit when this nightmare was over.

"What's so important you had to bash down my door so early on a Saturday morning?" he asked between sips.

I opened my bag and pulled out the key and placed it in front of him on the table. "This old rusted key and the fact half a million dollars has mysteriously turned up in Vivienne's bank account."

His eyes widened as he picked up the key turning it over a few times then handed it back. The weight of it burned my skin as if I were holding a hot iron rod in my bare hand.

"I might be able to help trace the money, but what's with the old key?"

"It's where I found it that's interesting." He tilted his head as if he were about to give me another lecture on safety. "I found it taped to the underside of Camille's desk. Yes, I went back into the bank with Harriet this morning, but this time there was a security guard standing watch. See, no danger."

"If you say so," he muttered under his breath.

My skin caught along the rough edge of the raised surface of the key. There's something under all this rust. "Do you think your parents would have something to clean this up? You know, take the rust off so we can see what's underneath?"

He gave a half-hearted shrug. "Beats me, cleaning isn't my number one forte. If they do it will probably be in one of the laundry cupboards." He stood and picked up his coffee. "You want me to try and trace the money in Vivienne's account?"

I nodded. "Yes please. If anyone can do it, you can. While you look into the money, I'll give this beauty a clean."

"Sure. Is Vivienne's phone number the same?" he asked, standing, and shoving his chair in.

I nodded.

"I'll give her a call and grab some details before I get started. I'll leave you to your cleaning duties." He headed toward his office, leaving me ogling his coffee infused energetic strut.

Right, cleaning duties. I rummaged through drawers and opened doors in the laundry searching for the right stuff. If I hadn't known Tyler' parents were out of town I would have thought they'd been robbed. But then again who would break into a house just to clean their laundry cupboard out of supplies?

A cleaning fairy, that's who.

"Surely, there's something in this house to clean old keys? If I were at home, I'd have a pantry full of supplies to whip up a cleaning spell within minutes." I glanced down at my watch and bit down on my lower lip. Have I got enough time to pop home and clean it?

"Don't be ridiculous, Evelyn," I scolded myself. "You're a resourceful woman, use your talents." A few seconds passed. My back stiffened and my brain ignited by a lightbulb moment. I pulled out my phone. "The internet. Best place to find any answer."

"How to clean rust off old keys," I muttered as I typed waiting for the search engine to kick into gear.

Soak in Coca-Cola for twenty-four hours. That's twenty-four hours more than I have. Ah-ha. Household vinegar. The Brodericks are sure to have vinegar in their pantry.

"Gee, who knew vinegar would come in handy for something other than cooking or spell creation?"

I said, heading back into the kitchen. Hunting through the pantry shelves I moved bottles and jars. Bingo.

"Thank goodness the internet has step by step instructions." Careful not to burn myself, I simmered enough vinegar to cover the key. My insides bubbled as I poured it over the rusted object. "Now I have to wait thirty minutes. I wonder if Tyler is having any luck?"

My phone buzzed dancing on the counter from the vibration, the familiar face of Jordi flicked over the screen. The sudden drop in body temperature hit me and my head spun in dizzy circles. Woah, what was that? I grabbed the bench, squeezing to steady my jelly-like legs. My gaze landed once again on the phone picture of Jordi and me laughing at graduation. "Hello, Jordi, is everything all right? Are you and Harriet okay?"

She laughed. "Of course, we're all right, we're standing in the carpark of the Grand Majestic. What is with you?"

I ran my hand across my forehead and leant against the kitchen bench. "Um, nothing. I had the weirdest sensation a moment ago. Are you sure you and Harriet are okay?"

"Evelyn," she said sternly as if I was being told off by my mother. "If we weren't, I swear I would tell you. There is something weird going on with this place though."

I knew it. "What do you mean?"

"I bet it was a masterpiece in its day. There's no-one here but by the looks of it someone has been visiting recently. Exactly why, I'm not too sure."

The spooky edge to her tone had the hairs on the back of my neck twitching. "I don't follow."

"The place is locked tight and windows on the lower level boarded up with planks of wood. It's hard to see in except for a few gaps here and there, but there are fresh tyre tracks of no more than a day old. We found an old bonfire out back on the old grass tennis court, but it didn't look like an ordinary bonfire, the rocks surrounding it formed an unusual shape. Almost ritualistic in formation, but none I have ever seen."

"Evie girl, you gotta get your butt in here. I think I've found something." Tyler's voice rang out from his office.

A shiver ran through me from head to toe. We're getting close, I can feel it. "Is that all? Tyler has found something," I said, heading toward his room.

"One more thing, on the drive out, Harriet and I were discussing the dates on the post-it notes and there was something familiar about them. I knew I'd heard a few of them before but I couldn't place where, so I called my mum. She said they were all coinciding dates with annual events in the witch calendar."

"You're kidding. Which ones?" I plonked myself down in the chair next to Tyler and scribbled down the events as she rattled them off. "I'm still at Tyler's so we'll do a little more digging. You've done a great job, but maybe you should come home now?"

She tutted. "Not yet, I'm just going to shift and take a closer through a couple of the higher placed windows."

"Okay, but please be careful. Call me if you find anything." My gut was screaming like a bear with his leg caught in a trap.

"Will do," she said, ending the call.

"What was that all about?" Tyler asked, his gaze planted heavily on me. "Are they okay?"

Oh God, I hope so.

I nodded and picked up the paper with my hurried scribble. "Rise of the crescent Moon...Beckoning of the Harvest...Celebration of the Goddess of Life."

"We're going to one of your witch celebrations again, are we?" He grimaced. "Please don't make me dress up in weird colourful outfits like you made me do when we were younger."

I rubbed my forehead and looked over as Tyler's fingers tapped away at his keyboard. "You said you had something?"

"Yeah, I do but can you give me a few more minutes? I think I may have found something even better."

"No problem." I spotted one of his spare computers on the other desk was already switched on. Why someone needed four different computers beats me. Must be a nerdy thing. During school, Tyler had been the go-to man for anything to do with computers. I loved watching the buzz he got from doing his kind of magic. I wonder how he went in Nepal without his posse of technical backup?

"Do you mind if I use your other computer?" I asked, moving over to the other office chair. "It would be easier to search these events on a bigger screen than my phone."

"Go for it." He reached over and typed his password in. "You're all set."

I looked at the waiting keyboard and squeezed my hands into fists then wiggled my fingers ready to find answers. My fingers didn't move as fast as Tyler's, but I wasn't the slowest typist. Seems I didn't completely waste my time in IT at school and that A is really coming in handy right about now.

Come on, what have you got for me?

PUMPKIN PIES & POTIONS

It took me a few frustrating minutes then success.

'Witch Rituals? The secrets even the most powerful witches won't reveal?'

This should be good. I scrolled the page and it was like I was back taking witch lessons from Aunt Edie. Textbook witch knowledge in its simplest form. I paused and a pop-up button appeared on the bottom right of the screen. I read each word and my back stiffened ram-rod straight.

Real Witch Rituals, not for the faint hearted. Are you prepared to risk it?' Ha. I've seen some beauties in my time. Let's see how they go for scare factor.

I clicked and a question flashed up on the screen in bold red letters. To enter, answer the following question. Name three of the ingredients used in the Portinius Padliate spell.

Is this a joke? Why on earth would they want to know the ingredient for the itchy spell?

I guess to tell the real witches from the wannabes. My chest tightened as I typed pig's toenail, sprout of a baby scodonya flower, liquid of isle.

A dazzling array of colourful sparkles scattered across the screen dissolving into a list of rituals. Some I'd heard of, but there were many that were new to me. Why haven't these been in my teachings? Graduate witch or not, shouldn't I know about potential rituals that could have devastating consequences? Aunt Edie is definitely going to hear about this.

I scanned the list and my eyes nearly popped out of my head. My breathing quickened to the point of pain as one ritual in particular jumped out at me like a neon sign.

Resurrect a Loved One. Use this spell carefully as once started it must be finished or the past soul will stay dead for all eternity.

My eyes widened as I continued to read. Ritual One: Rise of the Crescent Moon, Ritual Two: Beckoning of the Harvest, three: Celebration of the Goddess of Life and the last one: The Final Awakening. To bring the deceased soul back to life, the last ritual must take place on Halloween and no less than two years of their passing and before the twelfth strike of noon.

"Oh my God, no, no, no. This is worse than I could ever have imagined." My voice came out in a scratchy whisper.

It all adds up now. It's dark magic, it has to be. Blood of a high Priestess...a ritual burning...heart of a new witch mixed with the old.

Shivers flooded my entire body while goose bumps riddled my arms. I could barely breathe around the bile burning the back of my throat. "Harriet's in danger. She was right all along."

"What are you mumbling about?" Tyler asked, his fingers paused. The air void of any clicking noise.

I turned to Tyler, my whole body shook and my ears filled with the thunderous noise of my heart thrashing inside my chest. "Harriet's in danger. If I read this right, someone is trying to bring a loved one back from the dead. Those dates Jordi rattled off are all dates that coincide with one of the rituals and the final one takes place today before the twelfth stroke of noon and the final ingredient is the heart of a new witch. Harriet's a new witch. This information combined with her vision of being in danger makes perfect sense."

His eyes clouded over. "You really think someone is trying to bring someone back from the dead? Has that ever been done before?"

I nodded and shrugged at the same time. "I'm not sure, it's black magic. Aunt Edie doesn't talk about it much. She likes to steer clear of it. I've never ever heard of it happening, but yes I think someone is trying to." I sucked in a long deep breath. "Camille was in Saltwater Cove because her sister was murdered. She was working undercover at the bank. She was trying to find the murderer and I bet my life on it that's what got her killed. Her sister was a high priestess and one of the rituals, The Beckoning of the

Harvest requires the blood of a high priestess mixed with the blood of the deceased."

"Okay, but what about the money? Do you think it's important who transferred it into Vivienne's account?" Tyler asked, turning back to his computer.

"Maybe, but making sure Harriet and Jordi are safe is way more important at the moment." I whipped out my phone and dialled Harriet's number. With each ring the clamp in my chest turned another clog tighter.

No answer.

My jaw clenched and I dialled Jordi's number. I was on the verge of hyperventilating. A soft hand brushed my shoulder and Tyler's soothing voice challenged my thumping pulse.

"Deep breaths, Evie girl. You'll be no good to them if you pass out. You're no good to me for that matter. I might have the computer skills and know how to hack a few websites, and a little bit of muscle, but when it comes to this witch mumbo-jumbo, that's where you come in. You can do this."

I looked into Tyler's eyes and the soft reassuring inner glow was overwhelming. I gifted him a smile, closed my eyes and focussed on my breathing.

I'm breathing in two three four and out two three four. In two three four and out two three four.

It kicked over into Jordi's voice mail. "Jordi it's me, Evelyn. It's important you call me as soon as you get this message. Please let me know you're both safe. Please call me."

Okay, now I'm really worried.

Ending the call, I stood and grabbed my scribbled note. "I have to go out there, to the Grand Majestic and make sure they're okay. Do you want to come?"

Tyler nodded and pointed to his computer screen. "Try and stop me, but first take a quick look at this."

My hands shot to my hips and my head tilted back. I couldn't help but grit my teeth. "Tyler, can't this wait? They could be in trouble."

"It'll take two minutes tops. Promise. I haven't got to the exact location of the bank the money was transferred from, but I did find out it came from an account name with the initials GM."

"GM? What does that mean?"

"Not sure, but it gets better. After I got through all the fake names it turns out the account is owned by Saltwater Coves' very own Stanley Bain." He hit a button and Mr Bain's face popped up on the screen. He swivelled in his chair and grinned like a Cheshire Cat. "Bet you didn't see that coming?"

My jaw slackened and you could have heard a toothpick drop. "Nope, you got me a good one there. Let me get this straight. Are you telling me Mr Bain, the manager of the Saltwater Cove Founders Bank is responsible for transferring the money into Vivienne's account?"

"Yep, and that's not all." Tyler turned back to his computer and punched away again on his keys and a load of other bank accounts filled the screen with Mr Bain's name and lots of big numbers followed by a row of zero's in the balance columns. "He has at least another six or seven I found. Looks like he's been doing a little withdrawing of his own."

"He laundered money from the bank and Camille caught him, he killed her and framed Vivienne." Even as the words came out of my mouth, it sounded way too simple. "That has to be the oldest crime in the book. And if that's the case maybe the black magic and rituals has nothing to do with Camille's death."

"Maybe, but you can't ignore someone is doing black magic in Saltwater Cove."

I ran a shaky hand through my hair. "You got that right. If the two crimes are separate, we could be looking for two different people. A murderer and someone undertaking an extremely dangerous ritual. Mr Bain wasn't even in town the morning Camille was murdered. He's been at Dawnbury Heights since Wednesday and only got back last night."

"Wait, what?" Tyler said, shaking his head. "No that can't be right. I saw him in town yesterday morning. He was driving out of the cemetery as I pulled into The Esplanade Café for a coffee."

I slapped my forehead and huffed. "Okay, this is getting more confusing by the second. On one hand we have an unknown who has been partaking in dark magic rituals to bring someone back from the dead. And all along we thought this had something to do with Camille's murder, it still might." Tyler nodded in agreement. "Then on the other hand we have Stanley Bain who has been stealing money from the bank, transferred half a million dollars into Vivienne's bank account and also lied about the time he returned to town."

Tyler stood, grabbed both coffee cups and headed out to the kitchen. "Sounds about right. If he lied about the time he returned, he could have lied about being in town at the time of the murder."

"The two might not be connected and it still leaves Harriet and Jordi out at the Grand Majestic in possible danger," I said as I emptied the vinegar out of the saucepan and grabbed the old key. I squinted and examined its indented surface barely making out the remnants of a logo. I shoved it in my bag. "Mr Bain and his laundering millions can wait, my number one priority is to get to Jordi and Harriet and make sure they're safe."

I turned on my heel, my gut knotting with each step toward the front door. Behind me the familiar metal on metal jingle of Tyler's keys sounded.

"I'll drive," he called out. "My 4WD might be old, but it's a lot tougher than that VW Beetle of yours...and faster."

I couldn't ague with him there. "Fine by me. It'll give me a chance to keep trying the girls." I followed Tyler down the back of his driveway to the garage, my mind preoccupied with thoughts of Harriet's vision. The chilled air shot straight through me like an icicle dagger.

His smooth smile softened my focus. "And while we're on the way why not give Detective Huxton a call. Maybe he can follow up on the Stanley Bain angle while we go get the girls."

"Good idea," I said and dialled the Saltwater Cove police station. "You're not just a pretty face, are you?" As soon as the words left my mouth, my entire body went into statue-like mode. I chanced a glance at Tyler as he pulled out of the driveway and headed for the Grand Majestic. The corner of his lips turned up into a smile.

Cheeky sod.

CHAPTER EIGHTEEN

"How do you know all this?" Detective Huxton's gruff voice grated on my nerves.

"I don't have the time to explain now, but you're going to have to trust me on this. Stanley Bain is a bad egg," I said, pausing. "He's involved with Camille's murder and if your computer techs do some digging, I'm sure they'll find he's been doing some laundering, some really expensive laundering if you know what I mean."

"Okay, we'll look in it. Why do I get the feeling you're not telling me the whole story?" he asked, a suspicious edge to his tone.

"When it comes to Stanley Bain, I am telling you everything I know. I swear." It wasn't a lie. I was telling him everything I knew when it came to the good old bank manager.

"Okay, I'll look into it. I'd like to chat about this further."

Time was running out and I still hadn't heard from Jordi or Harriett. Tyler upped his speed as we hit the highway and my right hand started shaking. "I'm sorry I'm busy right now, but I promise I'll be in touch soon." I ended the call and clenched my hands together in my lap squashing the jittery spasms.

Tyler glanced my way and his warm hand covered mine. "Hang in there Evie girl, we're almost there."

There it was again, Tyler's unconditional support. Tears blurred my vision.

"Hey, no crying. They'll be okay. We're almost there," he said.

Focus, damn it. I blinked away the tears and picked up the phone to dial. A tingling vibration shot through my hand and Harriet's cheeky caller ID grin was a welcome relief.

"It's about time I heard from you."

"Oh God Evelyn, you have to help us...please," Harriet said in a forced whisper.

The sheer terror in her tone sent my blood curdling. I pushed up in my seat, my back stiffening. Nausea knotting my insides. "Harriet, what's wrong…what happened? Where's Jordi?" I held my breath as Harriet's words shattered my heart.

"It all happened so fast. Someone is after me just like my vision predicted. I'm…going to…die," she said between whispered sobs.

I squeezed the phone in my hand until it matched the stabbing pain in my chest. In the background Tyler's blurred voice was competing for my attention. I zoned in on Harriet and willed my voice to stay strong. "You are not going to die. We're almost there. Where is Jordi?

"He caught us snooping in the old living room."

"He? Who's he…who is after you?" My heartbeat was out of control, thumping so hard inside my chest I thought it would burst.

"I don't know if it's a man or a woman, but it sounded like a man. The windows are all boarded up so I couldn't see their face, the only thing I'm sure of is they're bloody strong and tall and trying to kill me," she blurted in a brusque whisper. "He came after me and Jordi saved me. She pushed me out of the way and tried to shift but he got to her arms…Oh God…" Her voice trailed off.

"What happened, Harriet?" I asked, the words flew out of my mouth. I gripped the edge of the seat, my eyes barely able to focus.

Please don't be dead. Oh God, please don't be dead Jordi. My heart will never survive if I lose a part of my soul.

"She protected me, she told me to run, to get out. There wasn't much I could do except get both of us killed so I did. I hid in the next room, but I could hear his voice. I'll never forget it. He knew, Evelyn, he knew Jordi used her arms to shift, how would he know that?" The rising fear in Harriet's voice sent nausea bolting from my stomach to the back of my throat.

The only way he could know is if he knew Jordi personally. My gut tightened to the point of unendurable pain. Tyler pushed the accelerator to the floor, and it was as if the car and my racing pulse were fighting for pole position in the Formula One Grand Prix.

"Is Jordi alive, Harriet?" I squeezed my eyes shut and held my breath, the pain in my lungs burned hot like a sizzling bush fire.

"I think so, I don't know." My chest caved at the sound of Harriet's tortured sob. "It sounded like they struggled and then it went silent then a deep sinister voice said, 'Why waste my energy killing you, when it's your little companion I'm after'. He's after *me*, Evelyn. What the hell for I have no idea, but it's not for banking advice I can tell you that."

Tyler turned down the street and the threatening image of the Grand Majestic came into view in the far distance. It stood with fields of blooming flowers to its right and lush green forest to the left. A haunted vision surrounded by beauty and tranquillity. My chest seized. "Listen to me Harriet, we're almost there. You do whatever you have to do to stay alive, you hear me?"

"Yes," she said, her voice shaky. "Oh God, I have to go, he's coming."

The click of the call ending unleashed a torrent of expletives in my head I daren't say out loud for fear of it being my undoing. I quickly redialled her number and it went straight to voice mail. This is not good, not good at all. I could feel it in my bones.

"Tell me what is going on, Evelyn," Tyler said, pulling onto the verge outside the Grand Majestic. "I can tell they're in trouble but how bad is it?"

Bad, real bad, but that's not going to stop me going in there.

I tuned to face him, my entire body spiked with adrenaline. "It's bad. I'll give you the abridged version. Harriet is certain someone is after her, she's not sure who it is but they're strong and tall and their voice was deep and sounded male. Jordi pushed her out of the way and told her to run and she did."

His eyes widened and his shoulders tensed. "Black magic? This must have something to do with that ritual you were talking about. Right?"

I nodded. "Yes, and we know the ritual needs a new witch's heart for the final awakening spell and that makes finding Harriet the number one goal. Jordi was just collateral damage. I just pray she's still alive. She said they went straight for Jordi's arms which means they knew she uses them to shift. It's someone we know or at least knows she's a shape shifter."

"Well, come on," he said, jumping out of the car. "Let's get in there and see what we're dealing with."

I couldn't have said it better myself. Bolting up the steep gravel driveway, a plummeting wave ambushed my jittery insides. The old run-down hotel was the perfect place for a ritual. High on a hill, surrounded by land and no houses for miles. The rainwater-stained white paint was peeling off the walls in scattered strips. The gardens that once held pride of place lining the driveway, now in ruins. A few broken windows on the top floor rooms screamed haunted house to any tourist passing through Saltwater Cove. With each step toward the ominous looking building, my pulse jacked up.

"Let's not make any rash moves, okay?" Tyler said, glued to my side as we approached the façade.

My gaze caught sight of a hole in the boards of a lower left window and I marched in its direction. I paused at the fresh, clean circle smack in the middle of the grubby window. I dropped my gaze to the deadened garden bed.

Soil disturbed and fresh footprints. This had to be the spot the girls used to look inside.

"This looks like it's where one of them stood to look in." Tyler watched on with interest as I stood in the exact same spot and pushed up on my tippy-toes.

"Be careful, Evie girl." Tyler's tone warned.

Like I wouldn't be careful. I cupped my hands, interlocked my fingers, and pressed them above the newly cleaned circle. Squinting, I held my breath and peered in. Blinking a few times, the distorted view righted itself and my heart catapulted into the back of my throat and my entire body went numb.

"Oh God, Jordi…No." I swear the high-pitched squeal leaving my mouth belonged to someone else. The image of her twisted body, hands and feet bound will stay with me forever. "I'm coming, Jordi."

I backed out of the garden bed and turned my pleading gaze on Tyler. "It's Jordi, she's tied up on the floor. It looks like there was a struggle and there's blood. Harriet was right."

Tyler pulled out his phone and swallowed several times. "This has gone on long enough. Time to call the police."

He may as well have taken a sword to my heart. I grabbed his hand before he could punch in any numbers.

"No, there's no time to call the police. We have to do this. You and me."

"What?"

"More me than you. There's no time to call the police. Think about it, Tyler," I said, releasing his hand. I stepped forward and with all my will power igniting my belly, I begged him to listen. "Don't you remember?"

"Remember what?" he asked, his nostrils flaring.

"The final awakening spell needs the heart of a new witch and must take place before the twelfth stroke of midday. It's eleven fifteen now. If we wait for the police, Harriet will surely die, and God only knows what life-threatening injuries Jordi has suffered."

He shook his head. "But…"

"But nothing. We…I have to do this. I *can* do this. I need you to trust me." I paused and looked into his confused eyes. "Can you trust me, Tyler?"

He stared at me as if reading the very depths of my soul. He brushed his knuckle down my check and my breath hitched. His touch was so soft it spoke to my heart.

"You never have to doubt my trust in you," he said, his jaw jutting out strong. "All right, what do we do now?"

There was no end to his support but this time there's no way I can chance the life of another best friend. My gut tightened as I forced the words out. "*We* don't do anything…I go in after her."

His jaw dropped. "Are you out of your pretty little mind? There's no way in hell I'm letting you go in there alone. Witch or no witch, you'll get yourself killed and I am not having that on my conscience."

"And I can't protect you and Harriet at the same time," I blurted.

"Who said you had to protect me?" Tyler's expression grew dark and his lips thinned. "I'm a big boy and I can take care of myself, besides I wasn't exactly doing nothing while I was in Nepal."

"Tyler—"

He folded his arms across his buff chest and tapped his fingers against his skin. His posture upright, he stood ready for a fight.

"Are we going to waste time arguing or are we going in to save our friends?"

"Okay, but stay close at all times," I said, bypassing him and heading for the ornate wood carved front double doors.

"You don't have to ask me twice."

Tyler stood inches from my side. The electricity firing off his body combined with the adrenaline coursing through mine had me on high alert. I reached for the door handle praying my hand would be steady so I wouldn't give away just how freaked I was with what we were about to do. I gave it a turn.

"What are you doing?" Tyler asked, one eyebrow raised.

I shrugged. "It was worth a shot." I placed one hand flat on the lock on the door and held the other above it and whispered, "What once was under lock and key, with this spell I now set free. Once done with it then let it be. Return it under lock and key."

My fingers goose bumped and tingled as swirls of glittered colour materialised around my hands swirling in figure eight's through my fingers. A sharp click echoed from inside the door and my heart skipped a beat.

I gripped the door handle and turned to Tyler. "You ready for this?"

He nodded and sucked in a deep breath. "Ready as I'll ever be. Let's do this."

I held my breath and slowly turned the handle easing the door open enough to slide through. The gush of eeriness seeping from all corners of the interior sent shudders up my spine. The tattered geometrical black and gold art-deco style interior, a worn skeleton of its former days. What once was a striking, bold, sophisticated interior now dulled with the evidence of decaying years gone by. Sparse furniture lay broken and upturned covered in a thick layer of dust. A joyous place of yesteryear now lay in ruins.

We crept further into the silent structure and with each step my danger radar increased to a distressing level. I looked toward the living room where I saw Jodi and caught a glimpse of her bound feet.

"Jordi," I said, my voice weak and cracking. I bolted toward her. Please God, let her be alive and I wasn't too late. Tyler placed his fingers on her neck and my chest tightened, waiting. He nodded and mouthed 'unconscious but alive' and my lungs screamed for air from lack of oxygen. I ran my hands over her body looking for broken bones and untying the ropes bounding her feet as I went. Tyler took care with the ropes restraining her hands.

I glanced at Tyler's concerned eyes and breathed a sigh of relief. "On the outside it looks like nothing is broken, but she could have internal injuries." My eye dropped to a shiny object laying behind Tyler's feet. A shiny pink object. My hands grew clammy at the sight of Harriet's pink amulet on the floor.

"Tyler," I whispered, pointing past his left shoulder. "Can you get that pink stone necklace just beyond your feet." He nodded and turned to retrieve it. Knowing Harriet wore the amulet gave me comfort, but now she was out there unprotected with a crazed lunatic after her heart. I gazed down at the stone burning a hole in my palm and I snapped my fingers closed around it and pressed it to my chest.

Hang in there, Harriet I'm coming.

With trembling hands, I secured the necklace around my neck and reached over and grabbed Tyler's forearm. I placed my hand on the necklace and focused my energies into his questioning gaze.

"Tyler, I gave this amulet to Harriet for her birthday on Wednesday, I put a protective spell on it. Now I'm wearing it, nothing can happen to me."

Tyler nodded and I could see his shoulders slump slightly knowing I was safe. "Time is running out and you said you trusted me."

"I do," he whispered, his brow furrowed.

"Okay, then I have to go after Harriet alone." His back stiffened and he opened his mouth to argue. "Tyler, listen to me. I know it goes against everything you believe in, but there isn't time to debate it. I'm wearing the amulet so I'll be protected, but I can't look for Harriet, save her and you and defeat whoever is behind this nightmare. I'm a pretty good witch but I'm not that good."

He shook his head and a lone bead of sweat trickled down his cheek. "But?"

"No buts about it," I snapped and looked down at Jordi's limp body. "I can't lose you Tyler, and Jordi needs your help. I know we shouldn't move her until an ambulance gets here, but God only knows what this crazed psycho will do so you have to get her out of here. Call an ambulance and call the police. We know this is related to the ritual and although you're big and strong muscles might be useful in a normal fight, they aren't going to be any use to me when it comes to the supernatural. I will find Harriet and I'll do whatever I can to stop him."

"I don't like it, I don't like it at all, but the last thing I want is to put your life in danger, so I get it." He eased one arm underneath Jordi's knees and the other under her torso and lifted her off the cold floor. She flinched at the slight movement and her body crumpled against Tyler's, her head nestled into the crook of his neck. A gasp and muffled groan of pain reverberated against his skin.

He headed toward the front door. I followed and pulled it open. He paused and turned his blue eyes on me, and it was as if he sensed the inevitable uncertainty of our situation.

Tyler's shoulders moved up and down coordinated with his heavy breathing. He leaned in and whispered against my ear. "I still don't like it, but swear you'll come back to me, Evie girl. If you don't, I'm coming after you. We have unfinished business."

Unfinished business?

My jaw dropped open and warm air from his lips skimmed my skin as he kissed my cheek. Tension cramped my gut.

"Swear to me," he said one more time, his words coated with determination.

I could hardly speak, fear gnawing at my windpipe. "I swear."

He threw me one last classic Tyler smile, turned and walked down the front stairs heading for the open grassed area to the side of the driveway.

I closed the door and flattened my stiff body to the wood. Sucking in a deep breath, I hoped I could make good on the promise I just made. Harriet's bloodied vision exploded in my mind under the weight of the amulet pressing against my chest. There was no time for weakness. I pushed off the door and commanded my body to ignore the terror racing through my blood. I brushed my sweaty palms down my thighs and muttered, "Let's do this."

I walked stealthily through the main part of the building examining side rooms as I went. I was the only one who could hear the loud thrashing of my heartbeat. My eyes adjusted to the darkened interior and with only the sunlight streaming through the broken windows I had the element of surprise to my advantage.

All right Mr Baddie, where are you keeping my friend?

My body flinched at the sudden breeze that rustled through the building. A swirl of dust circled up from the hall table straight up my nose and I gasped, clamping my hand over my mouth and nose before a sneeze could erupt. I held my breath and squeezed my eyes shut tight, pinching the familiar tickle in the top of the bridge of my nasal passage.

One white elephant, two white elephants, three white elephants. Why did I have to be allergic to dust?

In slow motion I eased my breath out, opened my eyes and released my hand. I waited for the sneeze, but it was gone, thank goodness. Back on my mission, I crept toward the kitchen area, rolling my feet silently through each step as I went. There's no way they're going to hear me coming.

With each step I took, the atmosphere thickened and I knew I was close. The dilapidated kitchen door looked like the hinges would give way any second. Thankfully, there was a peep hole in the centre. It wasn't huge, but enough to see in. I pushed against the doorframe for support and eased up on my tippy-toes.

A dimly lit light flickered through the room and I blinked several times until the picture came into focus. A violent shudder seized my chest and raced through my body like scorching lava. I drew in a quick breath at the sight of Harriet alone, tied to a kitchen table, her clothes torn, her stomach exposed, head limp to the side and her beautiful bronzed bob smeared with blood.

Oh no! I'm too late!

CHAPTER NINETEEN

My legs wobbled like a perfectly cooked Pana Cotta, but I forced them through the door and bolted toward Harriet, the air burning my chest as I breathed. I kneeled beside the table and every muscle in my body trembled. The smothering coppery stench of blood filled the room and I dry retched several times as it seeped into my chest. Swallowing back the bile, I brushed the blood-stained hair from her face. I whispered, "Harriet? Harriet can you hear me?"

The ten seconds she took to answer me were the longest ten seconds of my life.

"Evelyn? Is that you," she whispered in a croaky voice.

I breathed a sigh and my head spun with relief. "Damn right it's me. I told you I would come and get you. You've bailed me out enough times, now it's my turn to save you for once."

Her lashes flickered open and tremors shook her body as she pulled against her restraints. She looked at me, her eyes coated with pure fear. "It was just like my vision. He caught me and we struggled but I got away and he chased me down. I couldn't win against his strength."

"Who chased you?" I held my breath waiting for the final piece to the puzzle.

"Stanley...Stanley Bain."

This is getting weirder by the second. I raced to untie her feet. There's no denying the murders and ritual is all linked together. Retaliation would be sweet once Harriet was safe.

"Stanley Bain, are you sure?" I gasped and bit my bottom lip as the skin on my fingers ripped against the rope shackles.

"Positive. I couldn't exactly miss his face when he was tying me to this table." Harriet grunted as she pulled at her hands. "It's not working, they're too strong. Can't you do your unlock spell on them?"

I shook my head, my jaw clenching. "I can't, that spell only works on a lock and key, not rope, but don't worry I'll find something." Scanning the old run-down kitchen, I pulled drawers and cupboards open. Scantily filled with pots and cooking utensils, but nothing sharp enough to cut the ropes.

It's a bloody kitchen for God's sake, why are there no knives in here?

I moved to the old pantry looking side cupboard and continued searching, my patience running very low. "Don't worry I'll have you out of there before Stanley comes back."

"Evelyn." I gripped the edge of the cupboard as the fear in Harriet's voice seized my heart. I spun and gasped. A caped Stanley stood behind Harriet. His eyes drawn and darkened, and the corners of his mouth turned down.

"Too late."

His sinister giggle curdled my blood.

"Well, well, well, if it isn't little Miss Nosy Witch herself."

The sunlight streaked through the porthole window above the old stove and caught the edge of the knife resting on Harriet's belly. The long blade ran horizontally from one side of her waist to the other.

Hold on Harriet. We've come this far, I'm not about to let you fall victim to this man's deluded mind.

My stomach clenched. "Stanley Bain, who would have thought you had it in you."

"I know. Harriet thinks her acting skills can compete with mine, but I have to say, she can't hold a candle to me," he said as he picked up the blade and ran it up and down Harriet's stomach. His threatening eyes salivated as he watched the blade skim her skin. "But the time is now, and all will soon be as it should."

Please God, let Tyler have called for help. Harriet's gaze caught mine and the stream of tears trickling down her temple broke my heart. Time was the key. I had to buy some. "Who is it, Stanley? Who are you trying to bring back from the dead?"

His head snapped up and it tilted giving off a zombie-like appearance, his pale skin accentuated by his sullen eyes.

"That is no concern of yours."

"Are you sure about that? I think it's only fair. I mean, if you're going to take the heart of my best friend, the least you could do is tell me who you're trying to bring back from the dead."

"What?" Harriet shrieked. "Oh, hell no, you're not using my heart. I'd like to keep it inside my chest for the next hundred years, thank you very much."

I kept talking. "If I'm guessing right, I don't think you're exactly going to let me live either so tell us why. I know you killed Cynthia for the blood of a high priestess, but why kill Camille? She has nothing to do with the ritual."

He aimed the knife toward me and bared his teeth like I was the evil spawn of the devil.

"Because that stupid cow couldn't leave well enough alone," he yelled, his nostrils flaring. "She had to go and stick her nose where it didn't belong."

My gaze fell on the stainless steel antique candlestick laying on top of the cabinet to my right, and a sliver of hope filled my heart. The clogs of a plan formed in my mind and I knew if I could keep him talking and get to the candlestick, I could disarm him with a paralysing spell.

My pulse raced as I crept in baby steps to my right, keeping my hands hidden behind my back. "She followed you to Saltwater Cove, didn't she? She knew, or suspected you killed Cynthia."

He threw his head back and laughed. "Bingo. Well done, bonus points for the graduate witch. You got it in one." He held his arms out to the side in a cross like pose and dipped his head back. He yelled at the top of his lungs. "I killed Cynthia."

His head jerked down, and his reddened face and glaring eyes pierced right through me. His eyes flashed cold and hard.

"For her blood?" I asked.

He ran his finger up the edge of the blade and my own blood ran cold. "Yes. I had no choice."

"When it comes to murder, you always have a choice," I said as my right hand clung to the icy candlestick behind my back.

"No, I didn't," he yelled, the veins in his neck bulging. He paused and an unnerving stillness filled the room. A smile worked its way across his face as if his thoughts were elsewhere. "I didn't have a choice. My beautiful wife paid the price with her life for my mistake."

Harriet's eye caught mine and she opened her jaw to speak and I shook my head. I had Stanley exactly where I wanted him and any movement or noise from Harriet could provoke him. She gave me a curt nod of understanding.

"What mistake?" I asked.

He spoke in a daze, his haunted gaze focused on the knife blade. "There was a disagreement you see, and one thing led to another and a gentleman was killed. I thought I covered all my bases, I made it look like a mugging. The authorities would come, and it would be an open and shut case. How was I supposed to know my lovely Serene would make an unexpected appearance? If only she hadn't pulled the knife from his back in a bid to save him, there would have been no fingerprints. She was in the wrong place at the wrong time and paid with her life."

In another time when he wasn't holding Harriet hostage for her heart, I may have felt sorry for the guy.

"I get that you're using the resurrection spell to bring Serene back, but why kill Camille?"

"She thought she was better than me, that's why," he said, smugly lowering the tip of the knife to Harriet's chest once more.

I sucked in a quick breath coinciding with Harriet's distorted gasp.

"She thought she could threaten me," he said, his eyes narrowed, and a flash of anger washed across them. "If I didn't turn myself in and face the consequences of my actions, she was going to report me. Report me? Ha. There is no way I was letting that stuck up pompous know-it-all stop me from bringing Serene back to life. One way or another, Camille was a dead woman."

Harriet looked straight into his eyes and her jaw dropped. "It was you outside The Four Brothers. You're the one I saw arguing with Camille. The evil I felt."

His vengeful gaze turned on Harriet and he moved threateningly, leaning his shoulders forward so his lips rested an inch from her face. He placed the blade of the knife across her neck and my vision tunnelled on his face inches from hers. He toyed with her battered body taunting her with the knife. I couldn't watch, but I couldn't look away.

Time to end this. I squeezed the candlestick in my hand held my other hand above it and in my quietest voice I gritted my teeth together and whispered, "Motion be that as it may, with this spell I put to stay. As still as one and all can be, from this moment on so shall he." My fingertips tingled and with Stanley's attention on Harriet he had no idea the sparkled show that took place behind my back.

I chanced a glance at the wall clock above the old stove and if it was correct, I had minutes left before it struck twelve.

"So, you killed Carmen and framed Vivienne by poisoning one of her pies? You transferred half a million dollars into her account and at the same time created a bunch of fake accounts stealing millions of dollars. What better scapegoat could there be than Vivienne, especially after their argument at The Four Brothers?"

He held his place, a hair's breadth from Harriet, but his gaze flicked up and caught mine. "Brava, well done," he said. His unblinking eyes unnerved my soul.

"Why apricot seeds?" I asked.

"Why not?" His face reddened. "We all know Vivienne doesn't just cook with pumpkins. Adds to the authenticity of the set-up, don't you think?"

The faint whirr of sirens in the distance penetrated the air. The realisation they were getting louder buckled my knees and I slumped against the side cupboard for support.

Fierceness rooted in Stanley's eyes and he let loose a guttural bellow just as the old wall clock stuck the first chime of twelve.

"Nooooooo, what have you done?" His hands started shaking and his flushed face looked from the clock to the final ritual display to his right and back again.

The sirens grew louder as though they were almost upon us. The second chime pierced the tense air.

"No, no, you're too late. By the time they get here, Harriet will be dead," he screamed, spittle flying over her body. "You will not defeat me. I will have my love, my beautiful Serene back with me. Enjoy watching me kill your friend."

"No, stop." Harriet screamed and her gaze stayed trained on the knife. She pulled and tugged at her restraints with all her power. "Please don't do this," she pleaded, free flowing tears streaming down her face.

He gripped the handle of the knife with both hands, the blade pointing down and raised it above his head. He mumbled a chant repeatedly, but it could have been in Greek for all I heard. The silver edge of the blade was on a direct trajectory with Harriet's heart.

A scorching blaze of heat barrelled through me, battling with the increasing volume of the shrieking sirens ringing in my ears. Every muscle in my body shook against the pulsating roar of my heartbeat. An animalistic growl roared from Stanley as he lifted the knife higher.

"No," I yelled. Holding the candlestick high above my right shoulder I pitched directly at Stanley's heart.

A shattering explosion of sparkled light ignited the room as the candlestick collided with his chest. He gasped and sucked in a lungful of air as though he'd been winded by a mammoth jab to the chest. The spell was working. I held my breath as his body began to paralyse itself from the collision point working its way to his extremities.

His eyes bulged and the corner of his lips turned up in a smirk just as his hands flew open and the knife descended downward toward Harriet aided by the pull of gravity.

CHAPTER TWENTY

"No," I screamed, the blood rushing to my ears. With Stanley's body completely paralysed in position like a marbled statue, I bolted toward Harriet.

Oh God, please don't let me be too late.

"Harriet...Harriet?" My voice vibrated through my head. My heart lurched as blood oozed from a fresh cut down the side of her abdomen. "Don't you dare die on me."

Harriet's head rolled from side to side, her eyelids flickered open and she let out an agonising gasp as though reality had set in. She panted and sucked in short breaths squeezing her eyes shut against the pain. "That scumbag cut me. Evelyn, you have to get me out of here."

"I will, hold on." Ignoring the rolling heat that circulated through my body I searched the floor for the knife. My hand shook as I picked it up. Harriet's blood coated the shinning silver surface. Shaking off the hellish bout of nausea that was minutes from surfacing, I worked double time sawing through the ropes. First her hands and then her feet.

A ghostlike silence fell over the house and I realised the sirens had stopped and it was only the thunderous beat of my pulse that I could hear. If they stopped, why hadn't they come in?

Harriet gritted her teeth and cringed in pain as she pressed her hand to the open gash. "Roll to the side and put your arm over my shoulders and I'll help carry you." It was slow going but adrenaline pumped me into action and within seconds we were both hobbling out of the kitchen with one focus in mind; to get the hell out of here and as far away from Stanley as possible.

"God, it hurts," Harriet said, between panted breaths.

If I thought of the depth of her injuries, it would be the end of me. "I know, but just think of the stories you'll be able to tell your kids when they ask what your first memory of being a witch was." Harriet's glare would have exploded my head then and there if she had the power to shoot lasers from her eyes.

She sucked in another painful breath. "Not exactly what I was thinking."

We turned the corner toward the main entrance and came face to face with the barrel of Detective Huxton's gun. Two policemen flanked him either side. They paled and their jaws dropped as they stared at both of us. My throat clenched and Huxton holstered his gun, took his jacket off and rolled it up into a tight ball.

"What the hell happened?" he blurted. He replaced Harriet's hand with his jacket and kept it pressed to her side. He pulled Harriet's other arm over his shoulder and all three of us hobbled out the front door.

"Long story short, Stanley Bain from the bank killed Camille. I put a paralysation spell on him, but I'm not sure how long it will last. He's in the old kitchen." We eased Harriet down on the front step, her back up against the pillar. I kept my eyes glued to the rise and fall of her chest while Huxton rattled off instructions.

I sat down and brushed the bedraggled blood-stained hair from her face. My pulse quickened again as I paused and took in her battered body. I ripped the bottom half of my pants off and tore it into strips and wrapped her bleeding wrists, my hands shaking the entire time.

Her eyes opened and her lips pressed together in a slight grimace. "Stop looking at me like that," Harriet said.

"Like what? I'm not looking at you in any particular way," I said, back-peddling.

"Like I look an inch from death." Harriet's breathing seemed to regulate, and her cheeks now flushed ruby red. "I know I look like I've just gone ten rounds with a heavyweight champion, but I think I look pretty darn good for someone who fought with a crazed lunatic, was tied to a table and had a knife slice through her side."

"Damn straight." Impressed by her strength, tears glistened in my eyes and my chest tightened. "It'll take a lot more than one psycho to keep you down."

"Okay, they'll take care of the situation until I can get in there." Detective Huxton crouched down and checked Harriet's wound. She gasped as he lifted his bloodied jacket. "You're a very lucky young lady."

Harriet's eyebrows raised. "I think we have different definitions of luck."

He looked up at Harriet's blank stare. "Lucky, because it appears the knife hasn't sliced any major organs or arteries. There would have been a lot more blood. But mostly you're lucky you have a friend willing to put her life on the line to save yours."

Harriet squeezed my hand and within seconds both of us were a blubbering mess of tears. My heart swam with love.

Oh my God, Jordi. I forgot about Jordi.

I turned my worried gaze on Detective Huxton. "Is Jordi okay? Where is she?"

"Jordi is fine. Tyler called me and gave me a quick rundown on the situation. She came around and said she wouldn't be seen dead in an ambulance."—*Ha, typical Jordi*— "But she did agree to let Tyler drive her to the hospital. He called me just as I arrived. The doctor said she will have a few bruises but other than that, she's in the clear. Another very lucky escape."

I slapped my forehead and huffed a huge sigh out, letting the knot in my chest leave with it.

"Thank goodness."

"An ambulance is on the way. While we're waiting do you think you can extend on the abridged version of the events and tell me what happened?"

I nodded, glad to get the whole nightmare off my chest. "Turns out Stanley Bain is a witch and not a very nice one. His wife was accidently killed, and he was trying to bring her back to life with the resurrection spell. It consists of four rituals." I sucked in a deep breath ready to continue when the rumble of gravel scraping under speeding car tyres turned my gaze to the driveway.

Tyler's 4WD pulled to a grinding holt metres from where we sat. All four doors opened and the rush of feet and concerned gazes descending on us was akin to a water gushing down a road after a rainstorm. Three worried witches and Tyler made four.

Aunt Edie had tears in her eyes, and she threw her arms around me and squeezed. I could feel her racing heart against my chest. She pulled back and looked me over.

"Are you hurt? Is anything broken? I knew something was terribly wrong when my messages weren't getting through to you. It was as though my mind and my heart was cut off from yours completely. The worst feeling in my life."

I shook my head and smiled with as much love as I could muster. "I'm fine. A little tired, but otherwise okay."

"Thank goodness Tyler called when he did, I was going stir crazy out of my mind."

"Harriet and Jordi are the ones who copped it most. Jordi's okay, thanks to Tyler." I paused and looked at Tyler's frowning expression. I smiled and he softened and gave a brief nod. "Harriet has a cut on the side of her waist. We're just waiting for the ambulance now."

"I can take care of that," Aubrey said as she handed over her hat and bag to Olive. She side-stepped around Harriet's outstretched legs and looked at Detective Huxton who was crouched on the ground, his hand still pressed to Harriet's side. "Do you mind if I jump in there, Detective? I'll have that cut fixed before you can say crab apple cakes, and I promise there won't even be a scar."

"By all means." He stood and made room for Aubrey. Standing back, his gaze connected with Aunt Edie's and she tilted her head and nodded mouthing the words 'thank you'. He nodded back.

Harriet's widened gaze held strong as she focused on Aubrey. I held my breath watching enthralled by Aubrey's calm demeanour.

"You're a healer, too?"

She nodded and smiled at Harriet. "I'm a lot of things, Evelyn, including a healer."

She removed the jacket and held her hands above the open gash. Harriet sucked in a sharp breath and squeezed my hand as though bracing for potential pain.

"This won't hurt a bit, but it might tingle a little."

Aubrey's fingers fluttered and a cascade of white light drizzled from her palms and hovered above Harriet's side. My jaw dropped and I wasn't alone. The gash began to mend itself centimetre by centimetre. It's not like magic is new to me, but I'd never actually seen a healer at work before. It was truly magnificent.

Harriet closed her eyes and her whole body breathed in one enormous breath of air. And with the air came a renewed beginning. She opened her eyes and smiled at Aubrey, tears of gratitude glistening her eyes. "That…was…amazing. I don't know how I can ever thank you."

"Pfft," she said, brushing her hands together as though she were clearing them of breadcrumbs. "What good is being a healer if I can't use my powers for those who need it, hey?"

Detective Huxton cleared his throat. "Evelyn was in the middle of explaining what happened as you arrived. Do you think we could pick up where we left off?" he asked.

He looked straight at me.

Olive took a step in and squeezed Aubrey's hat in her hand. "Yes, would you? Did he kill Camille?"

I nodded. Olive clutched her stomach and the pain in her eyes tore my heart out. "Stanley Bain is a witch and not one I'd have on my Christmas card list. His wife was accidently killed, and he was trying to bring her back to life with the resurrection spell. It consists of four rituals."

Aubrey's monotone voice rattled off the Rituals one by one. "Rise of the Crescent Moon,

Beckoning of the Harvest, Celebration of the Goddess of life and—"

"The Final Awakening," Aunt Edie said, her gaze locked with Aubrey's.

What the...? If you knew about them, why don't I know about such rituals?

Before I had a chance to ask her for real, I heard Aunt Edie's soulful voice in the back of my mind.

'Because those type of rituals are outlawed, forbidden to be practiced. The dead return changed by the afterlife. They are not the same people and it can have dire consequences.'

But...

'Evelyn, love, I had hoped such rituals would stay buried and you wouldn't have to ever deal with them. Now I see I was wrong.'

Harriet grunted. "Evelyn, if you and Aunt Edie are done chatting to each other, maybe you could finish telling the story."

Heat filled my cheeks when I turned and saw everyone staring at me. "Of course." I glanced at Aunt Edie with an expression that clearly said, this conversation is not over. "Camille worked out Stanley was the one who killed Cynthia."

Tyler held up his hand and I paused. "Who is Cynthia?" he asked.

"Cynthia is, or was Camille's sister. She was a high priestess and he needed her blood for the second ritual. Camille was in Saltwater Cove following the trail of Cynthia's killer. She worked out it was Stanley and confronted him. They had an argument outside The Four Brothers and Camille issued him an ultimatum: turn himself in or she would do it for him. He lied and said he would."

"Is that the argument Harriet witnessed?" Aunt Edie asked.

I nodded. "Turns out Vivienne was just a convenient scapegoat. Wrong place, wrong time." I looked at Harriet and smiled. "The fourth ritual combines the heart of a new witch."

Harriet raised her hand about ten inches. "That would be my heart he was hoping to use, but I'm quite partial to it, thank you very much."

Her comical tone went a long way to easing my racing pulse. "The final ritual combines the heart of a new witch with the blood of a high priestess." The familiar high-pitch whirr of a siren in the far distance signalled the ambulance wasn't far from reaching us.

"What will happen to Stanley?" Harriet asked Detective Huxton.

"Don't you worry about him. He will get exactly what's coming to him," Huxton said, shaking his head. "All I want you to do is worry about feeling better."

"Exactly." Aubrey said, in a renewed bubbly light tone. "And when Detective Huxton is through with him, rest assured he will be dealt with by the witch community."

The booming siren roared up the street drowning the sweet birds that had been singing their mid-morning tunes. Detective Huxton looked in their approaching direction and then back to Harriet. "I promise, he won't get away with murder and attempted murder."

"I'm just glad everyone is okay," Tyler said with an exaggerated sigh.

His focus zeroed in on me and I gifted him a confirming smile.

"I guess this would have to take the cake for the most eventful Halloween Saltwater Cove has seen in years."

I cringed and remembered how much Aunt Edie was looking forward to this Halloween.

"I'm sorry to have spoilt your favourite holiday, Aunt Edie."

"Spoilt? Good God child," she snapped, her forehead creasing. "You haven't spoilt anything. You caught a murderer and freed Vivienne all in the space of one morning. In fact, I would say this is a day of celebration, don't you?"

There were smiles and nods all round. Aunt Edie stopped and folded her arms across her chest and glared directly at Detective Huxton. "Vivienne is free now, isn't she, Micah? I mean now the real murderer has been apprehended?"

The ambulance cut the siren as they pulled up the driveway. Detective Huxton stepped aside.

"Once the paralysation spell wears off, I'll interview Stanley. But as far as I can see by the statements made here by Evelyn and Harriet, it's safe to say Stanley Bain set up Vivienne to take the fall for Camille's murder so yes, she is a free woman."

The heaviness weighing down my heart over the past few days vanished and I floated like a bird soaring through the sky for the first time. "That is good news."

"It certainly is," Olive said. She stood with Aubrey, both ladies gleaming from ear to ear. "You're a brave and clever witch, Evelyn, and I expect once Harriet masters her powers, she will be just as exceptional."

An expression of jubilation spread across Harriet's face. "You really think so?" Harriet asked as the medics tended to her injuries.

Olive nodded. "Oh, I have no doubt."

"Okay," Aunt Edie clapped her hands together. "It's time to let these gentleman whisk Harriet away to the hospital to make sure nothing is broken. If my calculations are right, there is still around six hours before the annual Halloween celebrations at The Melting Pot. We have a lot to celebrate and I see no reason why it shouldn't go ahead as planned as long as Harriet and Jordi are well enough."

"Count me in," Harriet said as they strapped her to the gurney. "No hospital is going to keep me from your cooking."

I squeezed Harriet's hand one last time. "Tyler and I will meet you at the hospital once we drop Aubrey, Olive and Aunt Edie back at to The Melting Pot." She nodded. Tyler edged up beside me and I watched them wheel her toward the back of the ambulance.

"A celebration sounds like a wonderful idea. Olive and I couldn't think of a better way to spend Halloween than with our new friends," Aubrey said.

Aunt Edie turned to Detective Huxton. "What about you, Micah? Will I see you there?"

I held my breath and chanced a sly glance in the detective's direction. Aunt Edie deserves to be happy, after all she's put up with me since I was eleven and that can't have been easy. I smiled and bit my bottom lip. I know she still has feelings for the man. Maybe they just need a push in the right direction.

"I'm sure Detective Huxton would love to come, wouldn't you?" I said before he could answer. His gaze stuck on Aunt Edie. "I mean if it weren't for you arriving when you did and sending the police in to apprehend Stanley, he may have come after us. You deserve to celebrate just as much as any of us."

Was that overkill? Okay, I'll shut up now.

"I have full intention on attending," he said, offering a cheeky grin in Aunt Edie's direction. "As long as everything pans out with Stanley's arrest, I will be there with bells on."

A rosy blush filled Aunt Edie's cheeks. I wanted to jump up and high five Tyler when I saw the electric connection between the two of them. I'm sure I wasn't the only one who noticed it.

"We will let you get back to it then." Aunt Edie cleared her throat and turned to Tyler. "Okay, young man time to get this show on the road."

CHAPTER TWENTY-ONE

"**H**arriet, no," I said, placing my hand on her shoulder as she tried to get up off her chair and head to the dance floor. This year, Aunt Edie insisted we move some tables and make room for a dance floor inside. She was adamant this year's Halloween dinner was going to be a celebration of the highest order. She even opened the outdoor entertaining area for additional partygoers.

Harriet folded her arms and pouted, sticking her bottom lip out. "Not fair. How come I can't dance? Aubrey and Olive look like they are having the best time."

I glanced at the makeshift dance floor and it took me a moment to find Aubrey and Olive laughing while they did the Macarena with Vivienne. It was packed with every type of Halloween character or costume ever created. Aubrey and Olive were decked out in full witch wear and blended in quite well as if they'd lived in Saltwater Cove their entire lives. An infusion of warmth filled my chest. They did look like they were having the time of their lives. I scanned the rest of the crowd of people gathered to celebrate and it was clear the word of today's events had spread along the town gossip vine. They turned out in droves to help celebrate Vivienne's release and Stanley's incarceration.

"It might have something to do with the Doctor's orders forbidding you to exert yourself or do any strenuous activities for the next few days," Tyler said. He took his Zombie coat off and draped it over the back of his chair.

Harriet pressed her lips together and sneered in his direction. An eruption of giggles struggled to stay locked inside my belly. It burst through and I met a wide-eyed and jaw dropping glare from Harriet. "I'm sorry, but you do look so cute when you pout like that."

My gaze slipped past Harriet to the man standing in the dark back corner dressed as Dracula and a shiver ran up my spine squashing my jovial vibe instantly. He stared in my direction as though looking straight at me, all suspicious like. There were so many Draculas here tonight it was hard to tell one from another.

"Everything okay, Evie girl?" Tyler asked, his zombie brow creased in concern.

I looked his way and smiled. "Better than ever. I'm glad you're back from overseas and my other two besties are safe and well. What more could a witch ask for?" I returned my gaze to the corner and the man was gone.

Where are you? More to the point, who are you?

The main door opened and Detective Huxton shuffled through the door. Dressed in a fresh suit he stood out among the witches, warlocks, Draculas and plethora of other Halloween characters. His gaze searched for Aunt Edie, I expect. The memory of the key was burning a hole in my back pocket and spurred me into action.

I shot up from the chair and gathered some of the empty dishes. "I better go and see how Eli and Aunt Edie are faring. It's been a pretty busy evening and I think my break should have been over about fifteen minutes ago. Catch you later." I turned to walk away and paused looking over my shoulder. "Oh, and Tyler?"

"Yes?"

"I'll hold you personally responsible if I see Harriet, or Jordi for that matter up on the dance floor. Do I make myself clear?"

He smirked at Harriet. "Yes, ma'am."

344

Smiling to myself, I headed in the direction of Detective Huxton, cutting him off on his way to the counter. "Detective Huxton, so glad you could make it. Aunt Edie will be happy to see you."

I swear he blushed at the mention of Aunt Edie's name. He cleared his throat.

"Yes, I had hoped to be here sooner, but the Stanley interrogation and paperwork took a little longer than expected."

"Oh. He is still going to be charged with Camille's murder, isn't he?" My stomach knotted. I turned and put the dishes on the bench behind me in the middle of a pretend smoking cauldron and a big stack of glowing pumpkins.

"Already done, and the attempted murder of Harriet. It just took a little longer to get the confession out of him than I expected." He looked around, I presumed for Aunt Edie.

"There was one aspect of Stanley's story that has been bugging me all afternoon." I'd got his full attention with that comment. He ushered me to the side out of earshot of any passing partygoers. His gaze intently drilled me as if I were one of his suspects being interrogated.

"I'm all ears."

"Stanley had an ironclad alibi for the time of the murder. I mean he wasn't even in Saltwater Cove, he was at the banking symposium in Dawnbury Heights. A bunch of witnesses saw him." I hesitated and swallowed the anxious lump in my throat. "He did it, but how?"

"That was one of our stumbling blocks and it took a hell of a long time for him to crack, but he finally did."

"And?" I said, butterflies impatiently thrashing against the walls of my belly.

"And…it seems he used his charismatic charms to woo a bank manager from interstate and they spent the night together in his room."

Ew, someone actually spent the night with that man? Now I was utterly sick to my stomach.

I cringed. "That is just gross."

He huffed and grinned but continued. "When we got around to discussing his alibi there were just too many holes in his story and with a little push he finally confessed. Yes, he met the woman and they spent the night together in his room, but he put a sleeping spell on her. According to her, they were together the whole night. It allowed him to slip out unnoticed. He hired a car under a pseudonym, drove back to Saltwater Cove, killed Camille and returned before the woman woke."

I shook my head. "Wow, I would not have picked it."

He smiled and took a step to the right and I quickly followed suit blocking his way. A frown creased his brow. "Was there something else?"

"Um, yes." I pulled the old key out of my pocket and tapped it against my palm. "I know you're a Leodain and I was hoping you might be able to tell me something about this key?"

I held it up and his gaze fell on the antique object. "Why? Does it have something to do with the case?"

I shrugged. "I'm not sure, maybe. I was hoping you might give it a go and see if you can learn something about its past. It might hold some vital information."

"I think it's a very good idea," he said, taking his coat off and folding it over his arm. "Since we have the murderer in jail behind spell blocking bars, I think it's safe to say we can rest up tonight and do some celebrating like everyone else. How about you pop into the station sometime next week and I'll see what I can do?"

He was right. Of course. I smiled and shoved the key back into my pocket. As Halloween's go, this has been one I am glad is coming to an end. Vivienne's stellar reputation has been restored, my best friends are safe, and Aunt Edie gets the chance to celebrate her favourite holiday with all the bells and whistles.

"Sure, I can do that."

"Do what?" Aunt Edie's voice rang out in my ear from behind me.

I gasped and jumped, turning to see a big smile on her face and her wand in her hand.

"Um…get Detective Huxton a drink. Yes, that's what I was going to do. What's with the wand?"

She winked and picked up my hand and squeezed. A soft glow filled her eyes and she gave me a peck on the cheek. If my heart were any fuller of love for this woman, it would overflow a million times over. "I love you, Aunt Edie."

"I love you too, Evelyn Brianna Grayson." She placed her arm around my shoulder, and we walked over to the main entrance and surveyed The Melting Pot. From cheering Halloween characters on the dance floor strutting their stuff to jovial laughter flooding from the tables. Love was in abundance everywhere I looked.

"I couldn't think of any place I'd rather be living and working than with you right here at The Melting Pot. You have exceeded all my expectations, Evelyn. As a witch and as my niece. Your mother and father would be so proud of you. You've shown you're ready to move ahead with your witch training. Your courage and wisdom are a credit to you, and I will forever be thankful you came into my life."

My gut clenched and chest tightened at her outpouring of love. Soft tingles covered my arms and I knew if she didn't stop with all the love talk, I'd end up a blubbering mess and then my cleverly designed witch makeup would resemble Tyler's zombie face. "Okay Aunt Edie, enough with the emotional stuff. I get it and I too am blessed to be here with you."

I threw my arms around her neck and we hugged it out. I pulled back and wiped my damp cheeks with my sleeve. "I do hope all your favourite holidays are not going to go down the same adventurous path?"

"Oh, I don't know. Christmas is not far away followed closely by New Year." She paused and giggled. "You never know what trouble they could bring with them. Not everyone makes the nice list, you know."

I stared at her speechless, my jaw dropped.

She pulled me close in a hug and held her wand up high.

"I'm only teasing, besides only good things happen at Christmas. Now are you ready to show these people a magical Halloween spectacular to rock their britches?"

I gifted her a smile that overflowed with love. "You bet I am. Let's rock this place."

Thank you for reading **Pumpkin Pies & Potions.** If you enjoyed this story, I would really appreciate it if you would consider leaving a review of this book, no matter how short, at the retailer site where you bought your copy or on sites like Amazon or Goodreads.

YOU are the key to this book's success and the success of **The Melting Pot Café Cozy Mystery Series.** I read every review and they really do make a huge difference.

You can sign up for my newsletter here:
https://www.pollyholmesmysteries.com/

Keep up to date on Polly's book releases, signings and events on her website:
https://www.pollyholmesmysteries.com

Follow her on her Facebook page:
https://www.facebook.com/plharrisauthor/

Check out all the latest news in her Facebook group:
https://www.facebook.com/groups/217817788798223

ABOUT THE AUTHOR

Polly Holmes is the cheeky, sassy alter ego of P.L. Harris. When she's not writing her next romantic suspense novel as P.L. Harris, she is planning the next murder in one of Polly's cozy mysteries.

According to Polly, the best part about writing a cozy mystery is researching. Finding the best way to hook the reader, a great way to murder someone, a plethora of suspects and of course a good dose of sweet treats thrown in for good measure.

Polly lives not far from the beach in the northern suburbs of Perth, Western Australia with her Bishion Frise, Bella. When she's not writing you can find her sipping coffee in her favourite cafe, watching reruns of Murder, She Wrote or Psych, or taking long walks along the beach soaking up the fresh salty air.

You can visit *Polly Holmes* at her website: www.pollyholmesmysteries.com

Book 2 Coming Soon

Read on for an excerpt of book 2.

CHAPTER ONE

"Evelyn Grayson, stop right there." Prudence snapped as she tore the guest list from my hands. "My New Year's Eve party will be the event of the year. If you'll pay attention, I'll explain it one more time?" She huffed and shoved her hands on her hips and shook her head. With her lips pursed, she looked like she was sucking a sour lemon. "It's like we're back in school all over again and you're the new girl in town who can't follow simplest of instructions."

I bit my tongue hard to stop the rebuttal ready to burst free. For the life of me, I cannot work out why Aunt Edie allowed Prudence McAvoy to hold her New Year's Eve party at *The Melting Pot*. It's not like we're friends.

Before today, I had the best life. You see, I'm a witch, a graduate witch to be exact, and a good one. Next year, I'll be twenty-four and then only one more year until I get my full witch qualification. I'm lucky enough to share my life with the coolest Aunt in the world who also happens to be a master witch. Saltwater Cove is home, at least it is after my parents died in a freak accident when I was eleven and Aunt Edie took me in.

You can never really prepare yourself for losing a parent, let alone two, but I had Aunt Edie to see me through the horrifying nightmares. Prudence and I were in the same situation, both of us lost our parents at a young age.

You'd think it would bring our lost souls closer together, wouldn't you? Wrong.

Aunt Edie taught me to see the good in everyone. I know deep down, Prudence McAvoy is a good person. Deep, deep, deeeeeeep down. It was the best and worst time of my life. I got to move in with the coolest most amazing aunt in the world who helped me come to terms with losing my parents and being a witch, and the worst…Prudence McAvoy.

She was the girl in the school everyone wanted to either be, hate or kill. I was in the latter category, hypothetically of course. Human spawn of one of the richest families in Saltwater Cove and direct descendants of the town founders, Christian and Elsebeth McAvoy. Without any powers to her name, she was a whole different kind of witch. A bitchy witch. A giggle rose from my belly and I cleared my throat focusing my mind back on the yapping woman in front of me.

"Evelyn you are so…so…are you even listening to me? You do realise, the party is less than twenty-four hours away." she said, her cheeks as red as a capsicum.

I gritted my teeth together and forced a smile. She was a paying customer after all. "Of course. I am listening, Prudence."

How could I not when you have such a loud whinny voice?

She glared daggers right through me. If she were a witch, that spiteful glare would have incinerated me into minute particles of dust quicker than you can say graduate witch. She huffed and folded her arms across her chest, her pink and silver pointy acrylic nails tapped away on her elbow keeping perfect timing with her foot. She flicked her blonde shimmering locks over her shoulder and waited.

Her pompous, 'greater than thou' attitude grated on my nerves, like fingernails down a chalkboard. Simmering knots rolled around in my belly and I was an inch from telling Prudence exactly where she can put her precious guest list. No sooner had the thought entered my mind, I sensed the soothing loving soul of my Aunt Edie nearby. She eased her arm around my shoulder, pulled me tight to her torso and smiled down at me. Although, it looked more like a grimace than a smile.

"Everything going okay with the final arrangements, ladies?"

Prudence's forehead creased and her lips pouted like a spoilt brat unsatisfied with their birthday presents. Prudence had proven time and time again she was a master manipulator. When it comes to getting her own way, Prudence takes the gold medal. "I don't know if this is going to work, Mrs Peyton. Evelyn can't seem to follow simple instructions even though I have explained it to her a dozen times."

"Me?" My body temperature rose to boiling point and I swear, if Aunt Edie hadn't been standing next to me, Prudence would be a smelly toad right about now. "I am up on all the changes you've made so far. I even have some ideas on how to make the theme a real hit including all the wait staff wearing matching gold glitter masks and vests to compliment the party theme."

Aunt Edie squeezed me close again and plastered on a professional smile. "That's wonderful. It's going to be the best New Year's Eve masquerade party Saltwater Cove has ever seen."

Prudence nodded and beamed like a ray of sunshine at Aunt Edie's pandering words. "I know. I do throw the best parties." She turned her focus solely on Aunt Edie. "I hope it's okay with you, Mrs Peyton, but I invited a few more people. With your master cooking skills, I'm sure you can whip up some more yummy treats. It's only another twenty or so."

"Twenty or so?" I blurted. According to Prudence, rich blood flowing through your veins meant you could get whatever you want, whenever you want, and for the most part it worked. Not now, not if I can help it. "That is rather a lot of extra guests, Prudence. I'm not sure we'll be able to accommodate the additional numbers with such short notice."

Aunt Edie's calming voice echoed inside my head. It amazed me how she had the ability to talk to me through her thoughts, or that I could even answer her.

'It's all right, Evelyn. We'll manage, no need to make it into something it's not.'

But Aunt Edie, she's doing this deliberately.

'I know, and the best way to deal with it is not let her know she has got to you, just smile.'

I cleared my throat and turned the corners of my lips up into a huge smile. "On second thoughts, I'm sure we'll be able to sort something. Although, we may have to hire additional staff for the event."

Like my best friend, Jordi. I know there's no love lost between you two, but banning her from the party guest list was a bit over the top. But you never said she couldn't join the staff list.

Prudence waved a dismissive hand in front of my face and huffed. "Not a problem. Bill me and I'll take care of it. Now, I really must be off and pick up my dress and shoes." Prudence flicked her golden locks and spun on her heel. She took one step straight into the oncoming path of Miss Saffron, my Chausie familiar cat as she catapulted off her hind legs, landing in Prudence's arms instead of mine.

"Aww," she yelled, her face screwed up tight like she'd just eaten a bunch of sour grapes. "Get this thing away from me." She stretched her arms out and held Miss Saffron away from her as if she had the plague. She gasped and her head tilted back followed by an almighty high-pitched sneeze bursting from her nostrils almost exploding my eardrums.

Holy cow. We're lucky it didn't shatter the windows. "Bless you," I said, easing Miss Saffron into my arms. She snuggled into the crook of my neck, her golden oval shaped eyes glowed with mischief and I bit my bottom lip to keep from commenting. If I didn't know better, I'd say she did that on purpose.

Prudence huffed and grunted as she brushed cat hair from her face and clothes. She glared straight at me and took a step forward. "Mrs Peyton, I am highly allergic to cats so there will be no cats allowed at the party tomorrow night."

Aunt Edie nodded. "Of course, Miss Saffron will stay next door in the house the whole evening. You have my word."

Blonde curly locks bounced around Prudence's shoulders as she flounced away toward the exit. Her backside swaying in time with each step. Jordi stood in the doorway blocking her exit and my stomach dropped through the floor. I glanced at Aunt Edie and whispered, "This can't be good. I better save Prudence before she says something she'll regret."

Miss Saffron bounded from my arms and I high-tailed it toward the door, arriving just in time to wedge myself in the middle of a brewing war. "Jordi, what a great surprise. Prudence was just leaving," I said, weaving my arm through Jordi's and dragging her to the side.

She turned her hazel eyes my way and unfurled my arm from hers. "I'm happy for her, but I came here to see you."

"Good, because I wouldn't waste my breath on you," Prudence bit back, prancing past Jordi as she left.

Before I moved to Saltwater Cove, Prudence and Jordi had tolerated each other. For some unknown reason, Prudence decided to make my first few weeks at school a living hell. I guess she didn't like me crashing her popularity party. If it wasn't for Jordi dishing out several doses of her own medicine, I don't think I would have made it through normal school let alone witch school. Jordi has been paying for it ever since.

"What is it with that woman?" Jordi said, heading toward the kitchen area of The Melting Pot. "What did I ever do to her except maybe put her in her place once or twice. Nothing she didn't deserve. If I didn't do it someone else was sure to." She flopped down on a chair in the corner and smiled. "Afternoon, Aunt Edie."

Aunt Edie's honey-brown eyes glowed with warmth. "Afternoon, Jordi. How are you, love?"

"Good." Jordi smiled. Aunt Edie always treated my two best friends, Harriet and Jodi as part of the family. As if they were my sisters. "Do you need any help with anything?"

I can think of one thing that you could do to help us out.

"Actually, I have a favour to ask," I said, a thrill of electricity filled my chest. "Well, not so much a favour as an idea and you know my ideas are the best. Are you in?"

Jordi raised her eyebrows and glared at me suspiciously. "I'm not sure I like the sound of that statement."

"Hear me out. This is the first New Year all four of us have been in Saltwater Cove in years. You, me, Harriet and Tyler, and I really want to spend it with my best friends and bring in the New Year together."

"But aren't you and Harriet working at *'Her Majesty'* Miss Prudence's New Year Eve masquerade party here at The Melting Pot?"

I nodded. "Yes, and Prudence just informed us there will be an additional twenty guests. We'll need some extra help. I was kind of hoping you and Tyler might throw caution to the wind and help us out. That way we'll all be together to see in the New Year."

Jordi's top lip curled into a sneer and I could see she was holding her tongue in front of Aunt Edie. She stepped in closer and said under her breath, "I'd rather shift into an Andean Condor and feed of her dead carcass."

Gasping, I pulled back at the depth of disdain coating Jordi's words. "You don't mean that?" An awkward moment of darkened silence passed between us.

Did she?

Jordi paused and bit the inside of her lip. "No, of course I don't mean it. I was trying to make a point," she said, poking her tongue out and play punching me in the shoulder.

"Aww," I muttered, rubbing the shot of pain her fist left. "Come on, it'll be fun. I'm sure Eli will be there. Aunt Edie gave him the night off." Jordi's eyebrows shot up and I knew I'd piqued her interest.

Eli Pruitt was Saltwater Cove's newest bachelor. Tall, tanned and a body made for pure pleasure. That is, if you're looking for that type of man. I for one, am not. Between his busking and working part-time at The Melting Pot he managed to slot into life in Saltwater Cove as if he'd lived here all his life. With a voice to die for, and a body to match, his popularity among the single females has hit an all-time high.

She sighed and flicked her raven black silky hair over her shoulder. "I suppose I could suck it up for one night. I mean it would be great to have the four of us back together again especially on New Year's Eve."

Warmth spread throughout my chest. "Perfect."

Jordi's hand shot up, curbing my enthusiasm. "On one condition." I stood frozen, waiting. "You get Tyler to agree as well."

Piece of cake. "Deal," I said, grinning.

Lightning Source UK Ltd.
Milton Keynes UK
UKHW010828301020
372506UK00001B/43